NEVER CRY MERCY

JACK NOBLE BOOK TEN

L.T. RYAN

LIQUID MIND MEDIA

THE JACK NOBLE SERIES

Receive a free copy of The Recruit by visiting http://ltryan.com/newsletter.

1

LOST.

No other way I'd rather have it.

I'd been driving for close to four weeks. Easy to do when there's no destination.

I left Florida and continued north. Every mile of distance between me and Mia was a good thing for her and my brother and his family. I was fortunate he was willing to take her in, and that they could disappear for a few weeks. As far as I knew, they were still out of the country.

Every state line I crossed meant another buried memory. Ohio was good to me for a couple days. The rolling hills of Iowa lulled me into a state of serenity for a little while. Next, I headed southwest and stopped off in Colorado for half a week. Montana took the second half, and I holed up in the mountains, soothing my soul. Unfortunately, the feeling never lasts.

And it was that restless sense of uneasiness that drove me south again. The Jeep I'd traded for started having problems before I'd reached Oklahoma. I pushed on anyway. No way I planned on stopping in Kansas. The old Wrangler finally quit on me along a dusty highway in the Texas panhandle, not too far from New Mexico.

The engine choked, spit smoke, then groaned through seven gritted teeth. None of the instrument gauges worked, but it didn't take a mechanic to figure out the Jeep was dead. I knew she was on her last leg a couple hundred miles ago. I figured I could get to Albuquerque at least.

I was wrong.

An eighteen-wheeler cruised past, honking, kicking up a fresh layer of dirt and grime that settled on top of me, turning the lines of sweat on my forearms a shade of dark brown. It looked like the aftermath of a flash flood that had raged through the desert. I watched the trailer, waiting for brake lights that never lit up.

I craned my head to look in the direction I'd come from. Had to be at least thirty miles to Boise City. Only a couple miles to the last little outpost I'd passed through. But there was nothing there. Just a small town with fewer than a hundred people, if that.

So I shifted my attention to the west again. The eighteen-wheeler had raced out of sight. In its wake, New Mexico lay a few miles down the road. Maybe a town, too. All I needed was a mechanic, or a car lot. Could find another Jeep.

I stood there on the blacktop, staring at the shimmering road ahead and contemplating my next move. The heat hit me from every which way. The asphalt, the sky, riding the wind.

Live with the misery you already know, or stake out on an uncertain future. Everyone faced the dilemma at one point in their lives. Most more than once. I'd stared down that barrel a thousand times. No matter which decision I made, the outcome was routinely the same.

But I often fared better when I plowed ahead rather than traced my steps backward.

So I slipped the keys into my pocket, grabbed my bag, and set off toward New Mexico.

THE PICKUP LOOKED like it had weathered its share of storms. Pockmarks lined the hood. The front and rear were different colors. It slowed, came to a stop half on the highway, half on the shoulder. I wasn't sure if it would last much longer than the Jeep, but after thirty minutes in the sun and heat, I'd take any ride I could get.

The old guy's eyes looked like large brown orbs trapped behind thick glass walls. The frames of his glasses were bent, held together with paperclips and tape. The lines in his forehead were so deeply etched, they told the stories of five lifetimes. He wiped away a layer of sweat with his forefinger and flicked it out the open window. Drops hit the side mirror and slid down a jagged path.

"Seems to be the problem, son?"

I shrugged and looked back at the Jeep. "Engine blew."

With a nod, he said, "From around these parts?"

"No, sir."

"Well, that's probably a good thing, but mostly a bad one."

"Why's that?"

"Hop in," he said, ignoring my question.

The old truck vibrated as though we were driving down railroad tracks. Diesel fumes filled the cabin. The old guy lit a cigarette, took a single drag, then held it between two fingers set atop the steering wheel. I was surprised the sudden burst of flame hadn't created an explosion. The shaking truck kept the ash low as the cigarette burned down. We passed a couple cars on the desolate highway. The old guy managed a nod and slight raise of his hand at each. The motorists replied in kind, their gazes sweeping past him and settling on me.

Who's the stranger, they likely wondered.

"Up ahead." He aimed the cherry of his smoke down the road.

I broke my stare off from the flat, brown landscape and spotted the town. The road turned into a canyon bottom, running between a line of two- and three-story buildings on what I assumed was Main Street, or some other common street name. Everything shimmered, appearing to send every last bit of the Texas heat back into the atmosphere.

We slowed to a crawl. The old guy glanced over at me a few times. I wasn't sure if he wanted to tell me something, or was reluctant to bring me into town. What if I was trouble? He'd be the one responsible. No one wanted that.

He pulled over onto the shoulder and shifted into neutral. The diesel engine grumbled low. The old guy folded his weathered hands in his lap.

After a minute of silence, he said, "This is my cousin's shop we're heading to. I'd like to tell you he'll treat you fair, but I'd be lying. He knows you're pretty much screwed out here."

"I can always buy something used."

"Where?"

"No lots here?"

"Nope."

"Up the road then."

"How're you gonna get there?"

"Call a cab. Maybe try that Uber thing."

"Uba...what?" He shook his head. "See, this is why I'm hesitant to bring you into town."

"I'm just saying there's options."

He shook off my suggestions. "We're gonna go in and talk to my cousin. Then I'm bringing you back to my house."

"Sure about that?" I said. "You only just met me."

He chuckled. "Don't worry, son. You ain't my type." He fingered another cigarette, turning the butt brown with dirt, but returned it to the pack. "My wife and I have a spare room at the house. You'll stay there until your car is fixed. It's better than anything else you'll find in this dusty old town."

"That's generous, but you don't need to do that."

He held up a hand to silence me. "Listen, things aren't so great these days, and we can use all the karma we can get."

There was no point in arguing. I agreed to meet his cousin then go back to his house. A shower and a good night's sleep wouldn't hurt. I could start fresh in the morning. Bound to be a trucker coming through who'd give me a lift to Albuquerque. At least there I could pick up a halfway-decent clunker that might last a few months.

A couple minutes later we pulled into an oil-stained parking lot. Water filled a pothole, reflecting a greasy rainbow. On one side of the lot were two antique gas pumps that probably hadn't been in use since the sixties, judging by the price per gallon of thirty-three cents. On the other side a tow truck about the same age sat empty. Probably dead, too. A few other late model cars were parked nearby.

A younger, heavier, less handsome version of the old guy emerged from a shaded car bay. He wiped his face with a grease-covered rag, brushing his wiry grey-and-brown hair out of his eyes. The two men nodded at each other, then both looked at me. A familiar sensation passed through me. I had the feeling I was being set up.

The old guy hopped down, crossed the lot. He and his cousin stood a few feet apart. No handshake. Only the nod they shared when we pulled up. I stood back and watched the encounter as the two spoke for a few minutes. The old guy waved me over.

"Keys?" his cousin asked.

I fished them out of my pocket.

"No surprises?" he asked.

"None."

"Name?"

"Jack."

"Just Jack?"

"Just Jack."

"Sounds good." He turned and moved slowly to the tow truck. Guess I was wrong about it. "If it's the engine, it'll probably be a week."

"A week?" I said.

"Gotta get parts, friend." There was nothing friendly about his tone. He climbed into the truck and fired up the diesel engine. The fumes clung to me as the smoke cloud washed past.

"Ready, Jack?" the old guy asked.

"Sure, why not."

"Hey," he said after we were seated in the truck. "You wanna know my name?"

"Nope."

2

THE OLD GUY NAVIGATED THROUGH PILES OF RUBBLE STACKED in the rear parking lot, which dumped us into a narrow alley. We were blanketed by weathered wood, and decades-old brick on both sides. The buildings looked worse back here. Whatever effort the townsfolk had put into maintaining them over the years clearly stopped after the front facade. Half the structures looked as though they were moments away from collapsing.

A few blocks later, he turned right onto a fairly busy street, by small town standards at least. A couple old men were sitting outside a barber shop. A young woman pushed a stroller on the wide sidewalk, the wheels mushing down the weeds and grass that grew through the cracks. There were other folks out walking, standing around, loitering. Couldn't be many jobs available in a place like this. Wasn't like it was close to anything. They had to be in retail, school, or farming. The rest were out of work, I presumed.

"Good steak in there," the old guy said, pointing at a square, faded-green building with a sign that read BAR. "But keep to yourself. You don't want to draw the attention of some of the locals in these parts."

I nodded, said nothing. I avoided attention as best as possible. It typically managed to find me, though. I knew that would be part of the problem with being trapped in this town. It was also the reason I had no intention of staying around past tonight. I'd head down to the bar, have a steak, a couple beers, grab a decent night's sleep, and find some way out of there the following morning.

A minute or so later the old guy slowed the truck to a crawl. The tires crunched against the curb. The whole thing groaned as he punched the emergency brake a couple seconds too early.

I followed him up to the weathered house. The grass was a month overdue for a mowing. The whitewashed wood siding looked as though someone had taken heavy-grit sandpaper to it. It sagged in places. Hung off in others. Cinder blocks stood where porch steps had once been. The screen door sang a hollow song as he pulled it open, longing for a forty-year-old memory.

He stopped there and forced his shoulder against the main door. Pushed several times before it opened with a crack.

After entering, he stepped aside, gestured for me to step into the kitchen. They say the longer you're with someone, the more you grow to look like each other. It was true in this house. A slim older lady who could've been his twin stood with her back to the stove. Flames rose up around the bottom of a small pot. Water rumbled as it boiled. The woman scowled at me, but managed a smile and slight nod.

"Jack," the old guy said, "this is my wife Ingrid."

She crossed the room with a grace that belied her age. I imagined at one point she had been a dancer, perhaps ballet or maybe ballroom. Although, if she'd grown up in this town, chances of that were slim. I grabbed her extended hand and gave it a gentle shake. Any more might have broken her delicate fingers.

"Herbie didn't give you too much trouble, did he?" Her smile widened, seemed genuine.

"No, ma'am," I said. "Whatever you're cooking over there, he earned it."

"Jack's car broke down a few miles from town," Herbie said. "He's gonna stay with us while my cousin is fixing it."

The two exchanged a long glance before Ingrid cut off the burner, then turned toward the hallway. The look spoke volumes about her feelings toward the cousin. Or perhaps my being there.

"I'll get the guest room ready," she said.

I reached into my pocket and pulled out a wad of cash. "Don't worry. I'll pay you for your trouble."

"I wouldn't think of it," Herbie said, pushing my hand away. But Ingrid stopped at the bannister, looked toward us, and nodded.

I shoved the money back in my pocket for the moment. They both knew they needed it. I'd slip it to Ingrid later. Herbie, like many men, let pride get in the way of help. Hell, I was reluctant to accept their assistance. I wanted a decent night's sleep was all.

A few silent minutes passed. Herbie and I exchanged a couple glances. Ingrid returned and lifted the weight off the room. She led me upstairs and showed me where I'd sleep. It was basic, with a bed, dresser and nightstand. Window facing the west. Nothing stood out. Which was how I wanted it.

"Can I make you a sandwich, or a cup of coffee?"

"No thanks, ma'am. I think I'm gonna lie down for a few."

A couple minutes turned into two hours. I woke to fading sunlight knifing through a slit between the curtains. I lay there for a few moments. Heard the raised voices of the old couple as they went back and forth. Their words were muffled, but their tone sharp. I stepped out of bed as the argument subsided, made my way downstairs, and found them in the kitchen. He was seated at the table and she was standing in the same spot where I'd first met her. They avoided looking at each other, and me.

"If you folks don't mind, I think I'm gonna go check out that steak dinner you recommended, Herbie."

He nodded without shifting his gaze from the same spot on the floor it had been focused on since I entered the kitchen.

Ingrid held out her hand. Said, "I think that's a fine idea. Just stay out of trouble. There's some unsavory kinda folks that hang out in that bar."

And I figured she'd say that about most bars, too.

I smiled, nodded, yanked the door open and made my way into the cooler evening air. The smell of burning charcoal lingered. The smoke rose over a neighboring fence. The voices and laughter of kids and adults rose and fell in stark contrast to the tension behind me.

I thought about Ingrid's comment about the bar's patrons. Herbie had shared a similar sentiment with me. Now, it could've been that these old folks were part of the old guard in the community. The last few who believed in and lived certain values. Held specific beliefs. And anyone who thought or acted otherwise was an unsavory type of person. No point in reading too much into it. I'd get a feel for the place within five seconds of entering anyway.

I found myself on Main Street, which had slowed down compared to earlier. There were a few people out, and a couple vehicles passed, but the feeling was subdued now.

That'd change.

The car that stopped next to me had slowed a few moments prior, staying a little behind, following me. I hadn't bothered to turn around and see who it was. And I didn't stop walking when two sets of boots hit the ground, and a guy said, "Who the hell are you?"

3

"Hey, asshole." Loose asphalt crunched under his boots. "I'm talking to you."

I heard the faint chatter of a police scanner. Here I thought some locals were trying to screw with me. Turned out to be worse.

Local law enforcement.

"Stop where you are," the guy said. "Put your hands in the air and turn around slowly."

I considered refusing his request, but I already had a bed for the night, and it sure as hell was more comfortable than a cot in a jail cell. I lifted my hands about shoulder-high, and turned to see two men staring at me, hands on their holstered pistols. They looked like carbon copies of each other, separated by twenty years or so of age. Blond or light brown hair. Long, narrow noses. Similar round-rimmed glasses. Lips so thin it looked as though they didn't have any. I couldn't read their name tags, but had no doubt they matched. This was a father-and-son outing, no doubt.

"Who are you and what are you doing in Texline?" the older guy asked.

"Nobody," I said. "And I'm just passing through."

"Got ID?" His gaze followed my hand as I reached for my wallet. "Easy, fella."

They approached as I retrieved the fake ID. It was one I'd never used before. An identity created without anyone in the government's knowledge.

"Jack Smith," the older cop said, "of New York City." He paused deliberately between each word.

The identity was as basic as I could make it. A name with thousands of matches. Several hundred in New York alone. Once anyone determined that the address was bunk, they'd waste days trying to figure out which Jack Smith they were after. And if they narrowed down too far, I'd simply say that I go by Jack instead of John.

"I'm gonna ask you again," he said. "What the hell are you doing in my town?"

"I'm gonna tell you again," I said. "I'm just passing through. My Jeep broke down. Some old guy offered to help, put me up while his cousin's shop fixes it."

The two officers shared a glance, nodded. Maybe they check out the garage from time to time. Saw my Jeep. Asked Herbie's cousin a couple questions. The older guy handed back my ID.

"Keep to yourself, Mr. Smith, and you'll do all right here." He started back to the cruiser, stopped, turned toward me. "Believe me, you don't want to go mixing with the locals around here. They see a city boy like you, and start thinking they can take advantage, if you know what I mean."

"I believe I do. And I don't want any trouble while I'm here. Gonna do my couple days, then be on my way out."

I'd made it half a block before the car doors finally closed. The engine revved. Headlights swept past me, steady at first, then cutting to the left and disappearing. The rumble of the V-8 faded as they drove in the opposite direction.

I continued on, heading into the wind. I passed two dozen or so shops and nondescript buildings before reaching my destination.

The bar's faded neon sign buzzed like a drunken house fly, flickering off every few seconds. Through the window I saw that a couple tables were occupied. An empty bar top stretched the length of the establishment. A wave of hot air saturated with beers and burgers washed over me as I pulled the heavy door open. The patrons at both tables repositioned to see who'd entered. The middle-aged couple at the nearest table glossed over me with little interest and went back to their conversation. Two large biker-looking guys didn't. Their gazes followed me as I crossed the room. The one with his back to me turned to his friend, who nodded.

I anticipated a confrontation, but instead the two focused their attention on their burgers.

I took a seat at the end of the bar where there was nothing to block me from an escape. The mirror along the wall left me with a view of the bar. Beer taps partially shielded me from that same view.

The swinging door at the other end of the bar burst open. An older guy with a bald head and a thick salt and pepper beard came out from the kitchen and made his way toward me. Through narrowed eyes, he sized me up. Perhaps he determined I was a threat, because he stopped six feet away and asked me what I wanted. I ordered a pint of Revolver stout, and a ribeye cooked rare. He nodded, poured my beer, and then disappeared into the kitchen again.

The room felt still. No chatter. No clanking of silverware against a plate, or the soft thud of a mug hitting a table. Just the light whirr of the ceiling fans.

I kept the reflection of the biker guys in my peripheral, antici-pating that one or both would come over at some point. The guy facing my direction glanced over a couple times, his hand covering his mouth in a veiled attempt to hide the fact he was talking about me. They remained seated, though, and I considered them a limited threat.

For now.

The kitchen door swung open. The big guy emerged with my steak. He slowed halfway, inhaled the scent of seared meat, then set the plate in front of me. It was a healthy cut, heavily marbled, sitting in a pool of juices.

"Need some A1?" he said.

"You seasoned it, right?"

"Come on, you gonna insult me like that? This ain't Oklahoma, man. 'Course I seasoned it. My own rub. Best damn recipe in Texas."

I cut into the steak and sliced off a piece of half-meat, half-fat. Held it in front of my mouth. "Then why'd you ask if I wanted sauce?"

He chuckled, said, "'Cause you look like a city boy." He turned toward to the kitchen. "Just shout if you need anything."

I didn't think I would. I had a beer, a steak, and a quiet place to eat.

The only problem was the other patrons had plans to disrupt the serenity.

4

CRYSTAL RIVER, FLORIDA, 1988

Jack Noble stood on the front porch watching the sun descend into the trees. The air was thick with humidity. A sheen of sweat coated his brow. Behind him, his brother Sean and sister Molly laughed at a joke made at his expense. They had been born two years apart. Molly in '72, Sean in '74, and Jack in '76. Because of this, all jokes were made at his expense, and there was little he could do about it.

"Just 'cause mom and dad ain't around don't mean you two can pick on me," Jack said.

"Like hell it doesn't." Sean got up and threw a jab in Jack's direction. Jack feigned left and countered with a right uppercut that caught Sean in the gut. The older Noble boy didn't care for that and three seconds later had Jack pinned against the railing.

"All right, you two," Molly said. "I will send you to your rooms."

"Then what?" Sean said. "Gonna call Mike and have him come over?"

The boys followed the comment with kissing sounds. At twelve years old, Jack had only had a girlfriend in the most basic sense of the word, and a real kiss was something he hadn't experienced yet. Nor did he care to. According to Sean, that would change soon.

Molly disappeared for a few moments. The boys fell silent, both focused on the setting sun and the kaleidoscope of rays that filtered through the branches and leaves. It was a scene they'd watched hundreds, if not thousands of times. The home had been the only one they'd ever known. It was their sanctuary, a place where no harm had ever befallen the family. Not that they were free from grief and the negativity of the world. Those things occurred outside the walls and beyond the property lines. And pretty much away from Crystal River, Florida. Their father dealt with the world so they didn't have to.

"Life, Monopoly, or Clue?" Molly said. "Jack, you pick."

"Monopoly," Jack said.

"You're not gonna cry again when I bankrupt you, are you?" Sean said.

"Bite me," Jack said.

The older siblings laughed as Molly set up the game board and distributed the cash.

"What're we doing tomorrow?" Jack asked.

"Fishing," Sean said. "Should be a good day. Dad said we can take the boat out as long as we stick to the canals."

"I'll go," Molly said.

"For real?" Jack said. It had been a couple years since their sister had joined for a day of angling. Pretty much since she started dating Mike her freshman year of high school.

"Yeah, why not? Gotta find out what my little bros are really up to, and I know your inner most secrets come out while fishing."

"Whatever," Sean said. "Not gonna find out anything about me."

"I already know, Seanny-boy," she said with a wink. "I already know."

"You don't know shit," he said.

Jack and Molly shared a smile.

"You little asshole," Sean said. "What did you tell her?"

Jack shrugged, passed GO on the board and said, "Pay me my two hundred dollars."

A banging echoed through the house and out to the back porch. The three stopped, looked around, waited.

BANG-BANG-BANG.

"Who do you suppose that is?" Jack asked.

"Probably Aunt Jackie coming to check on us," Molly said.

"Would she knock?" Sean said.

Molly shrugged. "I'll go check."

5

THE TWO BIKER-LOOKING GUYS ROSE AND CROSSED THE ROOM. The shorter of the two was about my height, but had at least fifty pounds on me. Fat, mostly. The other guy was three or four inches taller, lean like a flag pole, with long, rangy arms. From the front, neither appeared to be armed. But the mirror only told half the story.

I cut into the steak and shoved another bite into my mouth, washing it down with a gulp of the stout. The head foamed up when I set the glass down on the bar.

One of the guys cleared his throat.

I swiveled the barstool a hundred and eighty degrees.

The pair stood about four feet away, tattooed arms crossed over their chests, heads cocked, hardened looks on their faces, like a couple of wrestlers doing a promo shoot before a cage match. If that was the best they could do to intimidate me, it would be an easy night for me.

"Help you?" I said.

"We were wondering the same thing," the flagpole-looking guy said.

"I'm doing all right on my own." I kicked the floor and spun back toward the bar. Flagpole reached out, grabbed my shoulder with his bony fingers. My momentum stopped. I swung back toward them.

They stood in the same positions, the skinny one a little closer than before. Neither spoke.

"I'm just passing through," I said. "Don't want any trouble. Don't need it, frankly. But if trouble comes looking for me, I'm ready."

My words must've delivered a shot of adrenaline to the heavy guy because his breath quickened and his face darkened. He prepared to attack. But it wasn't him that did.

The skinny guy darted forward, moving faster than I figured he could. He grabbed my collar with one hand as he cocked the other back. He held his fist there. Big mistake. He should've struck when he had the chance. Now all I needed was for him to swing and throw himself off balance.

The kitchen door banged and swung open again. Both men diverted their gazes down the bar to the other end of the room.

"Linus," a woman said. "Get your damn hand off him. Now, I mean it. Both of you, get back to your table."

The skinny guy, Linus, let go, brushing my shoulder off before retreating back a few steps and ultimately returning to his seat. His heavy partner had already found his way to their table. My gaze bounced between the pair, waiting to see if either decided to defy the woman.

And who was this woman? She commanded the two men, who easily combined for five hundred pounds, like they were her children. They cowered off to their corner without a word in return.

I turned to face her, expecting to see someone who matched my old partner Bear in stature, and possibly looks.

But she didn't.

She looked like someone I'd known years before. A woman who'd been in my life for a brief period of time, but left one hell of an impact. A crater I hadn't managed to crawl all the way out of.

She wasn't an exact replica, though. The face, eyes, shape and size of her body, they were as I remembered. But the hair was wrong. Too short. Too trendy. Too blonde.

The woman stood with the edge of the door pressed into her back. Smoke from the grill wafted through. Her stare was fixed on me. Her lips remained parted, like she'd become stuck mid-breath. Had she stopped breathing?

She made her way down the bar, eyes narrowed, head angled. A dozen memories flooded my mind as I recalled the intricate web of secrets that drew us together the first time.

She stopped in front of me. Brushed her short hair back.

There was no doubt of her identity as I stared into her eyes.

"Reese," I said under my breath.

I'd met Reese McSweeny several years ago when a job Frank Skinner had brought to me turned upside-down in every way imaginable. Reese was an NYPD homicide detective, but her story ran far deeper than that of a cop. A foster brother turned SOG operative. A husband turned terrorist supporter. In the end, all forces merged into one final showdown, and she was forced into witness protection. I'd often wondered what had become of her. Never imagined she'd end up working in a dive bar in the middle of nowhere.

She leaned in close to me. Her mouth was inches away. The mixture of grill smoke and her body lotion made my mouth water and my face burn with desire.

"Jack," she whispered. "Don't call me that. Everyone here knows me as Billie."

"Billie, huh? They give you a last name?"

She started to answer, but her eyes shifted to her right, toward

Linus and his partner. "We can't talk like this right now. They'll get suspicious. Can you stay for a while?"

"I got all night."

And maybe tomorrow, too. It was a good thing I had a place to stay and no car to get me out of town.

Her hand brushed against mine. "We'll talk when this place empties out."

As she walked away, Linus called out, "The hell, Billie? You know this guy?"

"Shut the hell up, Linus."

The kitchen door swung shut behind her. The bar fell silent. I didn't have to check the mirror to know that Linus and his buddy were staring me down. Perhaps knowing something was close to going down, the bald guy emerged from the kitchen and, with a slight nod at me, took a seat at the other end of the bar. He made no move to conceal his holstered pistol.

I watched the two men in the mirror. The heavy guy leaned across and said something to Linus. All I could see was the back of his head. The skinny man nodded at his partner. Linus dropped a wad of crumpled cash on the table, then both men rose and headed toward the door. They stopped behind me, a few feet further back than before. One of them was pretty ripe, their body odor overwhelming any other smell in the place.

How had I missed that before?

Must've been the steak. Now that my cut had chilled, it wasn't giving off the same aroma.

These weren't ordinary guys. They perceived me as a threat, and felt they had to take a stand before I made a move. That told me they were involved in something, and that they wanted no part of me getting involved.

Drugs? A theft ring? Herding people across the border?

Could be anything, although the choice of location for their operations left a lot to be desired. One thing it did offer was a sense of anonymity. Not in the town, of course. Hell, this was the kind of place where everybody knew everybody. I'm sure, in a way, they felt safer because of that. They were the town badasses. No one would mess with them. More importantly, no one would talk. And so in the grander picture, no one outside the small town would know who they were.

"That'll be all," the bald guy called out. He'd shifted on the stool, letting his right hand hang loosely over the butt of his pistol. The other arm had disappeared behind his large body. I figured he had a sap or crowbar or a pipe dangling from that hand. Just give him a reason, assholes.

Linus threw up his hands mockingly and stormed out of the bar with his partner right behind him. I knew that wouldn't be the last time I encountered them.

6

It took two hours for the bar to clear out. A few more locals came in, either solo or in pairs. Didn't matter. They all knew each other. They had a couple beers, a burger, and then went on their way. Nobody paid much attention to the stranger at the bar. These weren't the kind of folks who would care. I threatened neither them nor their operations in town.

Reese bounced between the kitchen, bar, and the floor. She did her best to ignore me. I did the same. No point drawing any more attention to ourselves. Still, there were several moments where our eyes met and lingered a couple seconds too long.

After the last guest had left, the bald guy walked over to me. "I'm heading out. You gonna be OK if those guys show up?"

I nodded. "They won't be a problem."

"They might not be, but you don't want to move up the chain past them. Things get messy at that level." He stared out the window for a few seconds, scratched his beard. "You can ask Billie to fill in the details if you want to know more. I need to keep my damn mouth shut."

I tried not to dwell too much on what he said. The two guys weren't a problem. But whoever they worked for might be. My best course of action was avoiding all of them. Talk to Reese to get a feel for what the threat level was in town. Hang around with her a couple days. Move on.

Perfect plan. Or at least I could convince myself it was.

The bald guy cut the barroom lights on his way out, immersing the area into one large shadow. It made it easier to see what was happening on the street outside. Which wasn't much. The area appeared deserted. A blinking light cast a yellow wash over the street and sidewalk every five seconds.

"People are going to ask how you know me."

I hadn't heard Reese exit the kitchen. She fumbled underneath the bar and retrieved two bottles. Handed one to me.

"The big guy ask?" I said.

"He knows I have a past." She took a long pull from the bottle, swallowed hard, exhaled against the carbonation burn. "And that I don't like to talk about it. He probably assumed you're someone I knew before I came here. None of his business. He's the kind that figures the less he knows, the better."

"He got a background?"

She nodded, said nothing. Didn't have to. I could tell by his demeanor he'd traveled on the outskirts of the paths I lived on.

"I've thought about you over the years," I said. "I don't normally do that. Once someone exits my life, they're gone."

She focused on the bottle cap she flipped between her fingers. "I didn't exit, Jack. I was forced out."

"I always wondered, you know, where we stood. We never got to talk about this. How much of it was an act?"

She lined our bottles up between us. A smile lingered on her lips as she contemplated the question.

"You don't have to answer that," I said.

"I can't answer that," she said. "I'm no longer that woman.

This...experience...has changed me. I don't know if it's for the better, either."

"You'll always be that woman." I reached out. Her hand felt cold beneath mine. "No place or job or forced life can change who you are."

"You think that, but reality paints quite a different picture." She pulled her hand to her chest, covered it with the other. "You don't know me anymore, Jack. And Detective Reese McSweeney might as well be dead. I mean, that's how I think of her. I'm Billie Weddle now. Got it?"

I said nothing. So many years had passed; we were both different people. Christ, I'd been set up by just about everyone I had faith and trust in, on some level. Everything in my world had been yanked out from under my feet. Why else was I traveling alone across the country?

My time with Reese had been brief, but intense. In many ways. Perhaps that's why the feeling lingered, and now rose so close to the surface.

"So, what are you doing here?" she asked after a few silent minutes.

"Passing through."

"Really?" Her gaze shifted to the door for a second. "You weren't sent here for *some* reason?"

I took a moment to imagine what life was like for her now. Stuck here in this one spot, always checking over her shoulder, startled by shadows. Never able to let her guard down because the moment she did, some asshole like me would show up and attempt to take her life.

"No reason," I said. "I'm not working. I don't work for anyone anymore. I really was just passing through. Damn Jeep died on me."

"Was?"

"I planned on leaving in the morning, but I'm thinking I might extend the trip a few extra days. Seems this little town does have a couple sights I'd like to see."

She smiled, leaned forward, reached for her beer.

"So what's the story with those biker guys?" I asked.

Reese's smile faded, and her eyebrows drew tight, while her lips thinned and the skin on her face tightened. "Couple of locals is all."

"Locals, huh? They sure seemed scared of you."

She looked toward the street, then back at me with an intense gaze. "They know I won't take any of their crap."

"Why does it feel like you're leaving an awful lot out of this story?"

"Look, Jack. The less you know, the better. This isn't your average small town. There are things going on here. And someone who is just passing through has no need to make what happens in Texline their business. Understand?"

"Maybe I should go in the morning." I slid my empty bottle across the bar to her.

"Maybe you should." She tossed it into the trash without looking. Perfect shot. The bottle shattered against the others.

Her eyes and the look on her face gave nothing away. She hadn't lost the ability to stonewall someone. I was a suspect she was preparing to interrogate. Didn't matter if she knew without a doubt that I was innocent, she'd break me into giving a confession or get every last bit of information out of me she could.

"Easy, detective," I said.

She rolled her eyes and took a step back while crossing her arms over her chest. "Look, I didn't ask you to show up here. You did that on your own. I'd love for you to stay a few days. Get reacquainted and all that. But you need to leave it at that. Don't get involved with this town and what's going on. If you do, you might not make it out."

"No worries there, Reese. My days of getting involved are over."

"Billie," she said. "You need to start calling me Billie. Anyone overhears you using my old name, it could cause problems. All it takes is one asshole to ask a question or make a remark to the wrong person here."

"OK, then, Billie, you don't have to worry about me causing a problem. As long as they stay out of my way, I'm out of theirs. I'm done solving other people's problems. Getting involved and watching everyone and everything that means anything to me die. I'm finished with the life. I'm just gonna drive around until the smoke clears, get my daughter, and settle down on the coast, or an island."

"Daughter?"

I nodded, smiled, pulled a wrinkled picture from my pocket and handed it to her.

"She's beautiful," she said, tracing the image of the girl. "What's her name?"

"Mia."

"Where is she?"

"Best I don't say. Never know what might happen."

She lifted an eyebrow and shrugged. "I'm sure her mother's taking good care of her."

"Only if she's watching over her from a cloud."

"Oh." Reese seemed taken aback. "Sorry, I didn't know."

"How could you? It happened recently. We had reconnected."

Reese drew her right cheek in and nibbled on it.

"Wasn't like that," I said. "We tried, it just wasn't there anymore. So we stayed friends, and I became active in their lives. Huge mistake. I know that's how they found her. I'm the reason she's dead, and Mia is in hiding."

The conversation turned to Reese's daily life, then died off. We each drank another beer, then headed out together into the cool, cloudy night. Reese was prepared and donned a Yankees sweatshirt.

"Can take the girl outta New York," she said with a wink.

"Horrible team," I said.

She rolled her eyes, then locked the door.

We got off Main Street and walked a few blocks in the dark.

"Got a place to stay?" she asked.

"A few blocks away," I said. "An old couple took me in. Herbie found me stranded on the road."

Reese smiled. "You met Ingrid and Herbie? They were the first ones to welcome me here. Got me the job at the bar. Herbie's cousin owns it."

"Besides the shop and the bar, what else does his cousin own?"

She laughed. "Different cousin. Besides, it's a small town, Jack. You have that kind of overlap in a place like this. Hell, I think his family built most of it anyway."

We stopped at the side entrance of the house. The clouds had parted, and the moon shone bright, glinting off Reese's eyes. I reached for her, took her hand in mine. She went along for a moment, and then pulled away.

"Not out here, Jack," she said. "Look, I'll be by in the morning."

"You OK out here alone?"

She pulled back, frowning and raising her fists like a boxer. "You think I can't take care of myself anymore."

I threw my hands up and apologized.

"If it makes you feel any better," she said, turning away from me and extending her arm straight out, "look in that direction and wait for a light to blink on three times in about five minutes. That'll be my sign for you to know I'm home safe."

So I stood on the worn stoop, watching Reese fade into the darkness. A few minutes later a light switched on, then off, and repeated twice more.

"Goodnight, McSweeney."

7

THE NEXT DAY STARTED TWO HOURS EARLIER THAN I HAD expected. A tinge of orange coated the lower horizon. I made my way downstairs, found Ingrid at work in the kitchen with her back to me. She'd started a pot of coffee moments earlier. The first few drips splashed on the bottom of the pot as I entered. Soon after the brew's aroma saturated the room. The old fluorescent tube light cast a yellowish gloom over the room. There were at least two dozen dead cockroaches littering the fixture.

I travelled across the kitchen silently, intent on getting through the door before Ingrid noticed me. But as my hand hit the knob, she told me there was no way she was letting me out of the house without a cup of coffee and a decent breakfast.

I didn't have to stop, but hell, the woman had offered to put me up for a few days. Least I could do was let her offer me some of her home cooking. So I took a seat at the table and waited while she fixed me a plate of bacon, eggs, and hash browns. I broke the yokes first, then soaked everything in it. Of all the breakfasts I'd had, this one ranked top ten, easily.

The meal turned out to be a quiet affair. We didn't speak until I put my fork down. Ingrid sat across from me, sipping her coffee and nibbling on a slice of bacon. She smiled every so often, and grabbed my mug when it closed in on empty.

I rinsed my plate and mug, and left them in the sink where a couple other dishes were piled.

"Will you be back for dinner?" she asked.

"Don't worry about me, ma'am," I said, exiting the house.

The air outside smelled sweet. Honeysuckle, maybe. The sky was a few shades lighter now. Seconds after shutting the door, a choir of birds broke the silence. I explored streets and alleys for the next ninety minutes until I'd gone almost full circle and found myself approaching the window I'd seen light up three times last night. It was on the upper level of a two story garage. One of the doors was raised, revealing a restored, black, early '70s Dodge Challenger.

I spotted Reese off to the side with a pair of shears in one hand, a hose in the other. She had on a blue checkered shirt and a pair of cut-off jean shorts that covered very little beyond her ass. She dropped the hose and started attacking a wily bush.

"Nice car," I said.

She spun, shears extended, ready to lunge. The first four buttons of her shirt were undone. She slid her hand under it, covered her heart, patted it, then wiped her brow.

"Jesus, Jack. I could've killed you."

"Too much distance. There's ten feet between us. You'd never reach me."

"Willing to place money on that statement? Hundred bucks says I wipe that smug grin off your face."

I sized her up. Her arms and legs were lean with muscle. Built for endurance, but displaying a hint of power. It was deceptive, that's for sure. She'd stayed in great shape. Hell, might've been in better shape than when I knew her. A detective's life wasn't always easy on the waistline.

"I think I'll pass. This time, at least."

She smiled, dropped the shears and walked up to me, stopping close enough that I could smell her body lotion. "What brings you all the way out here?"

I jutted my chin toward the garage. "The car, obviously. Care to take me for a ride?"

She glanced over her shoulder as she wiped her hands on a red handkerchief. "It might be a bit much for you."

"You're probably right. Where'd you find it?"

"I rescued it from a barn that was one heavy gust of wind away from falling over. A little old lady sold it to me for $500."

"Sounds like you took advantage of her."

Reese shook her head. Her gaze lifted and drifted past me. "It was her son's pride and joy. He'd saved all through high school to get that car. He planned on restoring it. Showing it, maybe. A month after he bought it, he joined the Army. Planned on sending money home to help his momma. He was Special Forces. Went off for a mission one day. Didn't make it back. She'd held onto it all those years, but with her life winding down, she decided to part ways. Said it wasn't about the money, she just wanted someone who'd finish what her son couldn't."

I said nothing while Reese paused and took a deep breath. The woman's story had made an impression on her.

On me, too.

"Anyway, I've spent the past four years restoring it. Still a bit left to do." She backhanded my stomach, caught me off guard. "I'm gonna change, and then we'll take that ride."

I found a weathered rocking chair off to the side of the garage. It was ugly, but sturdy. I ran my hand along the seat and back, making sure there wouldn't be any surprise slivers of wood. I carried the chair to the driveway, sat facing the sun. The morning heat cut through the gentle breeze, hinting at what was to come later in the day after the humidity set in.

"If you knew the critters that lived on that thing, you wouldn't be sitting in it."

Reese descended the staircase with a smile.

"I've sat in worse," I said. "Hell, think about some of the folks that have sat on that barstool I used last night."

She snorted, covered her face for a moment. Her smile held for a few seconds longer, then faded as she gazed down the street. I turned to take in the view and saw a familiar sight. The sun's reflection off the cruiser windshield made it difficult to tell if there were one or two officers seated inside. I doubted the father-son duo from the previous night shift were up and at 'em on the street before seven in the morning.

Seemed I was about to make a new friend.

"This something to be worried about?" I asked.

"Probably not," Reese said. "But you never know with these small-town cops."

The cruiser passed through the shade of a large oak tree. The glare dissipated, and through the windshield I spotted an older gentleman. Looked to be in his late fifties or early sixties. He pulled the vehicle to a stop twenty feet away. The engine whirred a notch or two higher as it idled. The man slid his sunglasses up on top of his silver hair as he stepped out of the car. He stood as tall as me. Similar build, but worn down by age. His face was lean, angled and cut, with a slight sagging under his chin.

"Mornin', Billie," he said with his gaze trained on me.

"Vernon," she said. "How's things?"

The man walked with a noticeable limp on his right side, though it didn't slow him down. He strolled past me, looking me up and down. Even when we were shoulder to shoulder, he kept me in his sights. I turned as he passed, saw his hand go to his pistol. His palm rested there, fingers relaxed. He was ready to draw.

"Heard you had a bit of trouble up at the bar last night," Vernon said, turning his head enough to the side to catch a glimpse of me in his peripheral.

Reese shrugged off his suggestion.

"No different than any other night. You know how those morons get sometimes. Have to show the world they're the badasses of the town."

"I'm aware of that, indeed. But what I was told had more to do with a stranger. In fact, a couple of my guys ran into a stranger late yesterday afternoon, and turns out he fit the description of the guy at the bar."

Reese squared up to the man, straightening, and pulling her shoulders back.

"I had no problems with a stranger last night."

"Well, that's what I'm curious about. See, the account I got from the bar was that you knew this guy pretty well. So, yeah, the description of a stranger might not do much for you. And so I got to thinking, and I said to myself, there's no way Billie would bring some hothead into my town. She wouldn't dare invite someone who would be starting trouble in my town."

"I'm not here to cause trouble," I said. "I'm Billie's cousin. Name's Jack Smith. Your guys shoulda been able to tell you that. They checked my ID."

He took a deep breath, absorbing what I'd said, then ignored me. "Billie, didn't you say you didn't have no family?"

"No immediate family," she said. "I haven't talked to my aunt in over twenty years. It was only through persistence that Jack managed to find me."

Vernon stood quiet and motionless for several seconds. Was he thinking of his next move? Another line of questioning? Playing a game to see if one of us would blink first?

Reese's gaze remained fixed on the man. She hardly blinked. Finally, he swung his hand around the back of his neck and scratched at the small tufts of grey hair that trailed down beneath his shirt. He turned, glaring at me as he walked past.

"Just keep your head down, Mr. Smith. This may seem like a quaint little town, but there are a lot of places around here where a city guy like you could get into big trouble."

8

After Vernon left, Reese figured it was best that we hold off on taking a ride. His unannounced visit had left her a little uneasy. She wasn't visibly shaken, and didn't delve too deeply into what bothered her. I imagined the last thing she wanted was for anyone to start digging for information on her. She told me they'd done it when she'd arrived in town, and they'd come close enough to uncovering her identity that she had considered running, outright leaving the witness protection program.

Over the years they'd continued to treat her like an outsider, but with an interesting twist. Vernon had picked up on Reese's detective skills. She wove a story and attributed it to spending time as an MP in the Army. A lie, but one constructed as part of her background by the FBI. There were even files stating that Roberta "Billie" Weddle had served for eight years following high school.

That was about all the Feds got right. Sticking her in a little town where she stood out was about as dumb a mistake as they could make. Naturally I assumed they'd done almost everything else wrong, too.

Reese gave me directions to a drugstore where I could pick up a burner phone to use while in town. I reluctantly purchased the dumbest device they had after going several weeks without a cell. The break had been nice, but I knew it wouldn't last forever. And at some point I'd have to think about finding Sean. I couldn't leave Mia with him forever.

From the drugstore I headed to Herbie's cousin's garage to check on the Jeep. Turned out to be a waste of a visit. The place was closed, not a soul in sight. I wiped some dirt off a window and peered inside. The floor was stained black with oil and grime. Tools were spread out everywhere. There were a couple of uneven stacks of tires in one corner. Looked like they would topple over if one of the doors slammed too hard. The place had four lifts, all in use. The Jeep was hoisted up on one of them. At least the job was in progress.

"What the hell are you doing here, man?"

I pulled my face back from the window and saw the reflection of two tall men. They appeared to be at least ten feet back, so I took a few seconds before turning. Once facing them, I realized they were the guys Reese had put in their place at the bar.

"Apparently I'm asshole shopping," I said. "And it's my lucky day since you two are the biggest I've seen in a while."

They stood staring at each other for a few seconds, presumably unsure whether they'd been insulted or complimented. Then the heavy guy charged at me. If he were a few feet away, he might've had a chance. But at ten feet, and at his reduced rate of speed, I had plenty of time to react and redirect his energy. And he'd built up a lot of it.

The guy grunted and leaned forward, head down, arms back, ready to pile drive me.

I stepped to the side, deflecting his upper arm with one hand while using the other against the back of his head to keep him moving forward. I thought he would slam into the bay door like a torpedo, maybe punch out a section of it. Instead, he tripped over his own feet and went down forehead-first into the asphalt. He yelled out as his skin grated against the rough surface.

I didn't stand around and watch him wallow on the ground.

The skinny guy made his approach. He looked even taller out in the open. He remained calm and cautious, coming at me from the side with his hands raised defensively.

I positioned myself so both men remained visible. The big guy hadn't managed to get to his knees yet. He pushed himself up, but his wobbly arms collapsed under his weight, sending him down and smacking his cheek against the ground.

"You're in for a world of hate, my man," the skinny guy said.

"Linus, right?" I asked, recalling his name.

He said nothing, tucking his arm behind his back.

"I told you both I didn't want any trouble. Yet here you are." I countered his steps, working myself into the open. "Are you both that stupid, or did someone send you out to follow me?"

Linus flung his arm around. A bowie knife glinted in the sunlight. His calm demeanor dissipated, and he charged me the way his heavy friend had.

Was it something I'd said?

He'd seen how I reacted to his friend. If he'd had any training, Linus would anticipate I'd react the same to his advance. So I changed things up, faked a move to the right, re-centered, and took him head on. He bit on the fake. I had set him up like a flat-footed linebacker. By the time Linus reached me, he was twisted at the waist in a way that prevented his long arm from reaching me. His weak attempt at slashing me with the knife was met with a boot to his solar plexus.

Linus went down hard on his hands and knees. The dislodged knife clanked against the asphalt and slid toward me. I kicked it, sending it tumbling through the lot and coming to rest in a patch of grass about thirty feet away. He scrambled to get to his feet. I drove my boot into the man's side, sending him sprawling.

The two guys lay a few feet from each other, Linus on his side, and his heavy friend on his back now. The heavy guy used his hand to shield his eyes from the sun. Streams of blood traveled down his face, falling to the side.

"So are you two just plain stupid?" I said. "Or stupid enough to follow someone's directions?"

Linus mumbled something, but it made no sense. Hard to talk without any oxygen in your lungs.

By this point a small crowd had gathered on the other side of the street. It wouldn't be long before Vernon or one of his men showed up. Then it'd be townie versus drifter. Didn't take much of a law enforcement background to see how that'd turn out.

"You two should think about getting out of here before I finish you off."

Linus opened his mouth to speak, said nothing. His gaze shifted down the street. The low rumble of a diesel engine rose above the murmur of the crowd. I took a few steps back and followed the man's gaze. An older GMC dually coasted into the parking lot and rolled to a stop not too far from us. The only person in the truck was the guy driving it. He looked to be about sixty, trim and in decent shape.

I looked past the truck, across the street. The crowd dispersed, some casting glances back toward the older guy as they walked away.

The man stood behind the open driver's door for ten or fifteen seconds, keeping his hands out of sight, and his gaze on me. There was nowhere close for me to take cover. A narrow alley that cut between the shop and the next building, then traveled behind them, stood about thirty feet behind me. I could cover the ground quickly, but not fast enough to prevent the guy from taking a shot at me.

Would he hit? I had no idea of his skill level, and I wasn't going to take a chance with my life to prove he couldn't.

The truck door slammed shut. The man took his time rounding the front of the vehicle. When he emerged, his hands were empty. But that meant nothing. A weapon was easy enough to conceal. He took his time approaching me, casting quick, disgusted glances at the two men on the ground, but not losing sight of his focus.

"You two all right?" he called out.

Both men strained to respond.

The guy stopped halfway between me and the truck. Forced a smile. Held his hands out to the side.

"I must be looking at the stranger."

"Depends on who you ask."

"Well, I ain't never seen you in town. These guys hadn't before last night." He took a rounded path toward them in order to keep me in his sights. The heavy guy managed to get up unassisted. The older man knelt next to Linus for a few seconds, whispered something to him. Then he and the heavy guy helped Linus to his feet.

I'd backed up toward the street, not that it offered much in the way of protection or security. Still, it was better than being hemmed in against the garage should another group of men show up.

The older guy walked toward me. "Mind telling me what happened here, stranger?"

"Why don't you ask them?"

He took two more steps, stopped, looked back. I didn't have to see his face to know the look he gave them. Linus and the heavy guy glanced away, ashamed at having been beaten by one man. The older guy turned toward me again.

"Not sure how long you're planning on being in town," he said, "but I recommend you do your time quickly and quietly."

"Problem is, trouble seems to find me no matter what I do. So maybe you should tell your guys to back off. Especially if they value their teeth."

The older man stuck his hand out, index finger pointed toward the sky as though he were warning me. "Don't let me run into you again, stranger."

9

CRYSTAL RIVER, FLORIDA, 1988

JACK FIDGETED WITH HIS STACKS OF MONOPOLY CASH WHILE keeping his attention focused on the corridor that led to the front door. Uneasiness, like the humidity, enveloped him. Only this feeling penetrated his gut. He glanced at Sean, saw that his brother was calmly watching the sun sink below the horizon.

Nothing to worry about, he thought.

He'd always been an anxious child. Sports and activity in general helped alleviate the uneasy feelings he carried around. But this didn't feel right, someone knocking at the door while his parents were away. It sent a wave of negative emotion through him. He sensed something was going to happen, but wasn't sure what.

"Relax," Sean said, seemingly picking up on his little brother's anxiety. "It's just someone checking in on us. You know how mom is. Hell, you get your nervousness from her."

The lock clicked, the handle turned, the latch gave with another clicking sound. The door creaked on those old hinges that their dad always said he'd grease, but never did. It had almost become a game between his parents, a way for their father to give their mother a little extra angst.

Jack's chest tightened. He forced himself to pull a breath in through his nostrils, trying not to make it too obvious. It bothered him when Sean picked up on his anxiety, and it only made his attacks worse. But his lungs burned from a lack of air, and Jack gulped in a breath, drawing a glance from his brother.

"Take it easy, Jack." The words were meant to comfort, but Jack saw concern in Sean's eyes now. Panic was imminent and there was little Jack could do but ride it out.

And then he felt Sammy brush against his legs, her tail slapping the chair. The Australian Shepherd glanced up at him, appearing to grin. Jack reached down and grabbed a fistful of her mane. His hand glided down her back. She was always there when his attacks happened. He figured she had a way of sensing it.

"Hello?" Molly's voice floated through the house. A moment passed. "Oh, hi. Yeah, I think I do."

"See." Sean leaned over and tapped Jack's chest. "Nothing to worry about."

Jack drew in a deep breath for the first time in what felt like hours, but in reality had only been seconds.

Nothing to worry about. Just someone we know, or someone selling something. Nothing to worry about.

He noticed a hint of cologne lingering after Sean pulled away. When did that start? Jack returned his attention to his Monopoly money, sorting through the stacks of ones, fives, tens, and hundreds. This time he'd win. He knew it.

"Not a chance," Sean said.

"Quit reading my mind," Jack said.

Sean only laughed. He always knew what Jack was thinking. Pissed him off to no end.

"What's taking so long?" Sean craned his neck to sneak a view down the hall. His smile faded, and in a moment, his demeanor went from calm and relaxed, to being ready to run or fight.

It happened so fast that Jack couldn't tell if Sean reacted first or if he heard Molly scream at them.

"Boys, run!"

Her words echoed throughout the hallway, out to the porch, and into the darkening yard.

10

I LEFT THE SCENE BEFORE LINUS AND HIS PARTNER COULD regroup and attempt to make amends with their boss. Or whatever he was. The only obvious conclusion I could draw was he had some power over them. In what capacity, I had no idea. It made sense given Reese's warning that the town was not what it seemed.

Whatever was going on, I wanted no part of it. It went against my new philosophy of letting everyone else screw up without my intervention. Hell, I'd done a good job of keeping my head down until those two idiots tried to take me out. And why? Because they'd been undressed in front of me by Reese the night before? Then why the hell did they respond to her that way? How was she scarier than me?

A lot of time had passed since my first encounter with Reese. I knew then that she had been placed in witness protection. Was she still in the program? By all accounts, the program isn't the best thing to be a part of. Perhaps she'd left it behind, started a new life out here. The bar could be a front. Maybe there was more to Reese than I knew. She put them in their place because she knew I was the kind of guy who could cause problems for all of them. Better to let me do my time in town than to let me uncover whatever it was they were all involved in.

Speculation. All of it.

And it was worth discussing with Reese later.

I navigated the town's street-grid layout and found my way back to the house. The smell of bacon in the kitchen hadn't faded. I called out to the couple, but no one responded. There was a note on the fridge telling me they'd gone out for the day and to help myself to anything I wanted. I cobbled together a sandwich and sat down at the table, replaying the encounter with the men at the garage.

My gut told me that the two dopes hadn't attacked on their own accord. Someone put the word out that they wanted me shaken up. And who better to do so than the town thugs? Only they hadn't accounted for my skills and background. Neither had whoever ordered them to attack.

It made sense, especially taking into consideration the moment the older gentleman showed up. It felt almost as though the ordeal had been planned to the minute. By the time the older guy had arrived, I would have been beaten pretty badly, but not dead. At least, if things had gone their way. Perhaps that's why he came across more defensive than his stature, and the townsfolk's reactions, indicated.

He wasn't prepared for the scene he found.

Wasn't prepared for me to be able to handle myself.

There was something about the guy that stood out. He exuded confidence. It was obvious in the way he held himself. He clearly was used to respect from everyone. He was the man who ran the show. And he didn't account for me being a thorn in his plans because he wasn't used to anyone being a thorn in his plans. If he was willing to beat down a stranger for no reason other than to shake me up, what would he do now that we'd become acquaintances?

He reminded me of someone, too. Someone I could and couldn't place. In those couple minutes, that old guy was a mashup of practically every military officer I'd encountered. Not necessarily his words, but his presence. The feeling was more intimate than that, though. He could've been an actual person from my past. Maybe some higher-up I pissed off on my path through the Marines, or during my early years with the Feds.

I tucked the thought away to let my subconscious work on it.

What had he done to his guys after their failure to detain me? I figured the beating they took was punishment enough, but if this guy had the background I figured, he considered what I did as only the beginning.

I finished my sandwich, washed up, and headed toward the back door. As I grabbed the knob, I heard faint crying.

"Ingrid?"

11

She sat on the old dark-green recliner, her knees pulled up to her chest. Her eyes and cheeks and nose were red. I hovered in the doorway a few moments, waiting for her to look up. She only sobbed heavier when she saw me standing there.

"What is it?" I said. "Herbie OK?"

She nodded and waved me off, a rumpled tissue dangling from her fingers.

"He's fine, Jack. It's nothing to do with him."

I hesitated a few moments, deciding whether to press or not. I was only passing through the town. It was almost as if I had to remind myself of the fact. I had no reason to get involved with anyone or in any situation.

Did that apply to Reese? Tougher question to answer.

"What's going on?" I asked.

"It's just..." She stared up at the plaster ceiling for a moment. The ridges of the swirl pattern stood out in the light coming through the window. "Things here aren't what they seem."

"So everyone says." I crossed the room, dropped to a knee so we were eye level, placed my hands on the recliner's arms. "What's not what it seems?"

She lowered her head and her gaze. "I really can't say."

"That's the theme of the day."

"I'm just concerned." She covered her eyes with the tissue for a moment. "For my family. For the people of this town. Heck, for the town itself. It isn't what it once was, and I fear it'll never be the same again. The young ones, they'd do right to just leave this place, with the state it's in now. Nothing for them here anyway. Definitely not like there was forty years ago. The jobs are all gone. Drugs have taken over."

I thought of Linus and his heavy counterpart, and the older man who'd shown up after I'd taken care of the morons. Were they all a part of the drug trade in Texline? Were the cops involved, too?

Ingrid's eyes welled with tears again as her breath quickened and her face flushed.

"You shouldn't be here, Jack. I don't know why Herbie brought you to our house in the first place. We don't need the extra attention from those men."

Perhaps she thought I'd consider packing my bag right then and leaving.

"Ingrid, what extra attention? What men? Has someone threatened you?" I shifted to lock eyes with her. "Look, you might be afraid of them, but I'm not. They think I'm some city boy with no ability to take care of myself, and that couldn't be further from the truth. You say things here aren't what they seem. Neither am I. If someone is threatening you, tell me. I'll handle it."

Ingrid said nothing.

"All right, it's obvious that my being here is causing you folks some problems." I let go of the recliner and stood. "I'm gonna get out of your—"

"No, don't even think about it." She blew her nose as she rose in front of me, then tucked the tissue into a dress pocket. "All this started long before you arrived. And it'll continue long after you're gone. We offered you our home, and you are welcome here as long as you need. Besides, our problems have nothing to do with you being here."

"You just said I shouldn't be here."

She looked away as her eyes misted over again. Then her posture changed. Shoulders pulled back, chest puffed out. She looked defiant. Ingrid and Herbie operated differently than most. They had a moral code, and their word was their bond. Unbreakable. They'd offered me help, and they'd ride out the storm no matter how bad the conditions worsened. The attention I brought be damned. Even if it meant their homes or their lives.

That was a cross I didn't want on my shoulders.

"Thanks for your hospitality, Ingrid. I promise not to be a burden the rest of my stay."

I didn't intend for it to last more than a couple of hours longer.

Ingrid forced a smile, but said nothing.

I turned away, headed through the kitchen, and out the back door. I decided to go see Reese again, ask if there was anywhere else I could stay. Maybe somewhere I could hole up and lay low for a couple days, either in town or close by. I'd made up my mind. I had to get out of their house.

No sooner did I hit the sidewalk than Vernon's cruiser rounded the corner. He flipped the strobe light on for a cycle, then slowed the vehicle to a crawl. The driver's side window inched down, whining along the track. A thick layer of dirt coated the outer weather stripping. Vernon propped his elbow on the ledge, let his hand fall to the side, his fingertips grazing the door.

"Jack."

"Vernon."

His gaze cut right past me, falling on the house.

"Might want to get that window looked at," I said. "I'd hate for it to get stuck during one of those sudden Texas hailstorms."

Vernon nodded. "Appreciate the concern."

I stood there for a moment, waiting for him to interrogate me. But he didn't say anything. His gaze swept left to right, stopping on me sometimes, moving right over me others.

"What do you want?"

He shrugged. Offered no reply.

"Have I done something?"

"Other than show up, cause a scene in a bar, beat up two of our townsfolk, and get Billie all in a tizzy?"

I shrugged back. Offered him no reply.

He opened the door, stepped out, stopped a few feet from me. "Hey, look, Jack. I got nothing against you. Those two assholes are always starting trouble. I know they started it with you in the bar, and again in the parking lot. Folks stood up and said so. Most of the time they don't. You get what I'm saying?"

"No," I said. "Why's that? Why'd they speak up this time?"

Vernon's lips parted. He drew in a deep breath and held it for a second, then whistled as he exhaled. "Well, that's complicated. Coming from a big city, you probably don't much understand small town politics. Especially in a place like this, a state like this. Hell, don't most of y'all think of Texas as another country anyway?"

I didn't bother to tell him I grew up in a small town. And he was the one who brought up the locals gossiping. Now he tried to talk circles around it.

"Vernon, why won't the townsfolk here talk whenever those idiots do something? Does it have something to do with that older guy who showed up in the truck?"

He glanced away. His silence spoke volumes.

"Who is he?" I asked.

"If I could get you a rental car here by tomorrow morning,

would you leave? I'm talking paid up so you can get to Albuquerque, where you can figure out your next step."

"Be happy to. But you didn't answer my question."

He fidgeted with his holster for a second while staring at the ground. He caught my stare out of the corner of his eye. Last thing he wanted was to give anything away through body language.

Too late.

"I'll find you in the morning after I have that car here. We'll get you out of town."

"What about my Jeep?"

Vernon chuckled. "That's not getting fixed. You ain't figured that out yet?"

12

VERNON CHARGED DOWN THE STREET AS THOUGH HE WERE chasing a getaway car. Presumably there wasn't much opportunity for that kind of action in Texline, so why not drive like a madman on the back roads of town?

After the dust settled, I walked off in the same direction.

He'd said so little, yet so much. It was all indecipherable, though. Like everything else I'd heard since arriving. I came to the conclusion that Vernon and his guys weren't in charge. Of everyone I'd met, and everything I'd seen, all signs pointed to the older guy in the GMC truck. Or perhaps his boss, if he had one.

"Don't overthink it, Jack," I muttered to myself. I had a ride out the next morning. Why not take it?

Looking up, I saw the reason why I'd decline the rental car. Reese stood in front of a window, phone up to her ear. Her other arm crossed her breasts and was tucked under the opposite elbow. Didn't appear she saw me as I walked up to the garage.

She answered the door wearing a white tank top and gym shorts. No makeup. She didn't need it. I caught a whiff of her natural scent and had to fight off the urge to reach out and pull her close.

"Back so soon?" A slight smile twisted her left cheek.

"Was hoping maybe you could help me out with an omelet."

"Keep dreaming, Noble."

"Hey, let's take it easy on the Noble thing."

"Then how about you stop calling me Reese."

I glanced around the doorway, up the staircase. Reese placed a hand on my chest, not pushing me away, but keeping me from leaning in any further.

"I've already checked," she said. "It's not bugged."

"You sure?"

"Positive." She gestured for me to follow her up the stairs, which I did willingly. "And if I was wrong, they would have closed in on me long ago."

We reached the top floor and I checked out the apartment. It smelled fresh. Reese had adopted a minimalist approach to decorating. A couple low profile chairs and a couch. No clutter or magazines laying around. Open shelving on either side of the kitchen sink had white dinnerware stacked neatly. A plate of pastries sat on the counter. I grabbed one and took a bite. Raspberry jelly flooded my mouth. It was too sweet.

"Ran into your buddy again," I said.

"Oh yeah?" She snatched the pastry out of my hand and brought it up to her mouth. "Which one?"

"Vernon."

She wiped sugar glaze from the corner of her lips. Swallowed. "What'd he want?"

"Made me an offer."

"What kind?"

I popped the last piece of pastry into my mouth. "Told me he'd have a car for me tomorrow morning to get out of town."

"You sure that was an offer and not a directive?"

"I've got a choice, whether he likes it or not."

She nodded, but crossed her arms. Couldn't tell if she was leery of Vernon's offer, or mad that I finished the danish. "Are you inclined to accept the car?"

"Depends, I guess. You know anywhere I can stay for a couple days?"

"Things bad between you and Ingrid and Herbie?"

"Things are bad for them because of me."

"How so?"

"They won't say. But I found Ingrid crying earlier. Practically in the same breath she told me to get out and to remain at the house. You know how the older generation can be. She made me a promise and refuses to break it no matter what personal discomfort it might cause her and Herbie."

"That's true," Reese said. "Dying breed. Not many around here like that these days. Not even in their generation."

"You gotta level with me, Reese. What the hell is going on here?"

She dodged the question. "You can stay here if you want. Couch is pretty comfortable."

I glanced toward her bedroom.

"Don't even think about it," she said. "I don't wanna open that wound if you're not gonna stick around here to clean up the blood."

I stepped forward, placed my hand on the counter. We were inches from each other. "You could come with me."

"Where?"

"Somewhere."

"You don't even know where you're heading next, Jack. Why would I give up the protection I get from the program to follow you off into the sunset?"

"I can protect you better than anyone in the FBI."

She shook her head. "I know the trail of bodies you leave

behind. Lots of collateral damage. You don't have many friends for a reason."

She'd body checked me into jagged glass.

"I'm sorry, Jack. That came out wrong." She slipped to the side, pulled a stool out and sat, leaning over the island counter. "What I mean is that you and I face the same problems. You know if I leave here and my identity is revealed, I could have a terrorist cell on me in an instant. Sure, the program landed me someplace where things are shady, but at least I'm not stuck in the middle of a bunch of suicidal homemade-bomb-vest-wearing assholes. I can take care of myself here. Elsewhere, without the proper vetting of the area? I don't know how long I'd make it."

I understood her point. And I decided that moment wasn't the time to press my agenda.

"So the couch," I said.

"The couch," she said. "You'll get a good night's rest on it."

I sprawled out on it, feet perched atop one arm, head resting against the other. "It'll do."

"I'll pull out some sheets for you to use."

"Nah." I rose. "I'll be fine like this."

"You got your stuff with you?"

"Gonna head back to the house and grab it in a few. Want to make sure Ingrid's had time to calm down. Not sure how she'll take the news that I'm not sticking around."

"She's survived everything else in her life. I'm sure she'll be OK."

"I'm sure you're right."

The conversation died after that. Reese put on a pot of coffee. After two cups, I headed out.

"Be careful out there," she said.

I stopped at the bottom of the stairs and looked back. The light silhouetted her frame. I couldn't help but stare.

"What?" she said.

I shook off the feelings rising for her.

"Reese, is there anyone in this town I can trust?"

"Besides me?"

"Besides you."

"Nope."

13

I took a roundabout way back to the old couple's house, veering off on side streets and alleys. Some connected, others didn't. Didn't matter. I didn't feel like rushing it. I had no idea how Ingrid would take the news, or if she'd let me leave, even though we both knew it was best I did. They weren't safe with me there. She'd illustrated that point.

Heat rose off the blacktop, shimmering in front of me, distorting the surroundings, filling the area with the aroma of tar. Had to be the hottest day I'd faced in a couple months, at least. Definitely the most humid. My shirt clung to my back, damp with sweat. I'd always thought these parts were more arid than humid. Perhaps it was the time of year.

Behind me, dark clouds advanced from the west. Dark wasn't even the right word. They were black. Ominous. We were in for a rough one, it seemed. I wondered if the approaching storm was a harbinger of what was to come. Maybe the weather was why no one was out. The locals knew better than I that these storms could hit fast, dumping a ton of hail, littering the area with lightning strikes, and spurring multiple tornados. I made a mental note of houses with cellars in the event I found myself stuck in the thick of it.

The low rumble of a diesel engine rose from the south as I neared an intersection. In a town like this, there had to be at least a handful of heavy duty diesel trucks. But it sure sounded like the one I'd heard earlier. I took up position behind a large oak tree that had grown through the sidewalk, driving the concrete upward, splintering it into a hundred fragments. Some were missing. Likely taken by kids who tossed them at each other, or windows, or whatever.

The GMC slithered past, tires wavering in the haze. The older man drove. Linus was in the passenger seat. I presumed his larger friend was laid up at home after the beating he took. Was it coincidence they were in the area I was staying? Were they out looking for me? It wasn't like we were in New York City, where their presence meant they had me in their sights. The town was small. Smaller than small, actually. They might've been going from one house to the next and just happened to be passing by.

The thought did little to settle me down. I remained on edge, anticipating an attack.

I repositioned myself against the tree so they couldn't spot me in the rearview. Two blocks later, they turned left and rolled out of sight. The engine faded amid the rumble of distant thunder. I backtracked one street in the event they decided to come down the same road again in a minute or two.

A group of kids around ten years old, give or take, huddled around the sidewalk. Their hands moved wildly. They spoke in excited tones, higher pitched voices rising and falling, each vying to get a word in. Eyes darted back and forth to each other, to the ground. Glances were thrown over shoulders. When the first one spotted me, he frantically waved his arms in front of him to stop the others. Someone was coming, and they didn't want to ruin their secret. They all straightened, turned toward me, stared me down.

"Gentlemen," I said, stopping about ten feet shy of their position.

"Sir," a boy of Mexican descent said.

"What's going on?" I asked.

"Nothing," the boy said.

They'd formed a wall of sorts. I took a couple steps forward, rose up on my toes to get a glimpse over them. A couple puffed up their chests, almost challenging me.

"Sure doesn't look like nothing," I said.

"It's nothing, old man," a blond-haired kid said. He looked to be the oldest of the group.

"Old man?" I stepped toward him. He met me half way. Top of his head didn't even come up to my chin. "Look, kid, if you guys did something, it's better you tell me than for the police to find out."

The blond kid laughed. "You think the police can do anything in this town?"

I shrugged. "They do in every other town I've ever been in."

"Yeah," the kid said. "Well you don't know shit about what goes on here."

"Why don't you tell me what kind of shit goes on here then?"

One of the boys reached out and grabbed the blond-haired kid by the shoulder. "Hey, man, that's enough. You know Darrow doesn't like anyone talking."

"Who's Darryl?" I asked.

"Not Darryl," the blond kid said. "Darrow."

"He drive a big truck, four wheels in the back?"

The kid nodded.

"C'mon, man," one of the boys said. "We need to get out of here."

All but the blond-haired kid turned and ran. They broke off in two different directions. The kid took a few steps back, eyeing me, almost like I'd insulted him personally, and he planned on doing something about it. The others called to him. Before running off, he spit toward me. The glob of saliva landed about halfway between where we stood.

"Better watch your back, old man," he said. "Darrow don't like people asking questions."

I watched the group until they were out of sight. Their voices gave way to laughter. Things never mattered for long when you're ten.

I walked over to where they had huddled when I first spotted them. Looked down at the ground. Didn't see anything. I squatted and traced the indented patterns in the grass. Something had definitely matted the ground. Could've been one of their shoes. Or a glove. Or a stack of playboys. Get a group of pre-teen boys together and who the hell knew. Whatever it had been, they'd been sharp enough to scoop it up and conceal it without me noticing.

I searched the immediate area for a few minutes before giving up and resuming my trek to the old couple's house. The black clouds were close to overcoming the sun, which resided right over my head. Wasn't long until the storm would arrive.

Perhaps in more ways than one, I thought as I spotted the old couple's kitchen screen door broken and resting on a single hinge.

14

CRYSTAL RIVER, FLORIDA, 1988

JACK WHIPPED HIS HEAD AROUND TO SEE WHO WAS AT THE door. He felt himself ripped out of his chair as he located his sister. Beyond her were only shadows. He forced himself to look again at the sounds of her struggling and pushing against the door. An arm penetrated the gap. She was losing ground.

"Molly," he yelled.

"Go," she yelled back.

"Let go of me, Sean," Jack said.

Sean's grip intensified as he dragged Jack away from the house. "Molly's in trouble."

"I know," Sean said. "I'll take care of it, but first I have to make sure you're safe."

Jack struggled with his brother. "I can take care of myself."

"Dammit, Jack. Listen to me." He grabbed Jack's shirt with both fists and drew him in close. They stood in the middle of the yard. "I don't know what's going on, but if something happens to you, Dad will have my ass for breakfast, lunch and dinner. I know you're a tough dude, but let me handle this. You're not ready."

Jack sulked back. Even though there were only two years between the boys, the physical difference was great. Sean had six inches and forty pounds on Jack. His brother was practically a man in stature. Hell, he was bigger than a lot of men at six-foot-two. The only solace Jack took from it was that in roughly two years, he'd be about the same size.

The brothers stood in the backyard, glancing around, listening. It was hard to hear anything over the cicadas buzzing. Then thick beams of white light hit the darkened trees.

"They're coming." Sean looked around, then shoved Jack toward the porch. "Get under there. Stay quiet. I'll be back for you in a minute."

Jack dove on the ground and squeezed underneath the porch through an opening only he could fit through anymore. Halfway in he had to shimmy his hips side to side to get past. He closed his eyes and allowed his other senses to take over. After a few seconds he heard voices.

"Where'd she go?" a man said.

Molly.

She'd made it out, got away from the men.

"I don't know, but we better find her." Different voice, but Jack couldn't place it either. "She saw our faces. It won't take long to track us down if she makes it to the cops."

Were they local? Wanted by the police? They didn't sound like they were from around Crystal River.

"She called out for the boys to run," the other guy said. "Any idea how many kids were in there?"

"No clue. But we didn't see them, so I doubt they saw us. She's our priority now. We'll take care of any others when we find them. We better hurry finding her, though. If those boys ran, it won't be long until the cops show up."

The planks above Jack creaked as the men passed. Flashlight beams knifed through the thin slits between the decking, illuminating his hands, head, the area in front of him. He searched the ground around him until he came up with a rock for each hand. The jagged edges dug into his fingers and palms. Would it do any good against a grown man? He supposed so, as long as he could work up a decent swing. That wouldn't happen where he was hiding. But it wasn't like the men could make it underneath the porch.

Their bullets could, though.

And that thought had Jack crawling back toward the house. The further from the opening, the less likely they'd spot him, if they looked under there at all.

"Look," one of the men said a few moments later. "There, in the woods."

Their heavy footsteps drowned out the ambient noises of the humid Florida evening. Jack waited a moment, started to move, then felt the vibrations of more men running across the porch.

The hell? How many are there?

He couldn't stay under there all night. Not while his brother was out trying to protect his sister. And not while Molly was out there being hunted. Hell with that. There were weapons inside, and he knew where to find them.

15

MY FIRST INSTINCT WAS TO RUN INTO THE HOUSE. TRAINING and experience took over. This was a case where I knew not to trust my gut. If someone wanted to draw me into an ambush, this was the perfect way.

Herbie had been out of the house. Ingrid was supposed to follow. I figured after our conversation, she had left. No point hanging around alone. It made perfect sense that the older guy would use Linus or another of his guys to set a trap like this. Bring a couple fresh bodies along. Lure me in by making me believe something happened to the old couple. If they'd been watching the house, they knew Herbie and Ingrid were gone.

I dashed between two houses, hopped a fence. A dog barked from inside. If anyone heard him, they ignored the racket. For the moment, at least. I crossed a freshly mowed yard and found a spot where I could peer through a crack between two fence boards. The wind had picked up. Grass clippings blew into my face. The busted screen door swayed, banging into the heavy wooden door. I waited as the sunlight dimmed and the gusts increased. The first patter of rain hit, followed not long after by the banging of pea-sized hail.

No one came out of the house. The hedges didn't move unnaturally due to someone hiding there and growing impatient. If this was a set-up, the men behind it were more disciplined than I pegged them for.

I decided to make my move toward the residence. There might be an attack, but the conditions were in my favor. I went up and over the fence in a single movement. I felt a jolt shoot up my right leg. The ground where I'd landed was uneven, and I'd rolled my ankle. I grimaced against the flash of pain. Last thing I needed was an injury that limited my mobility.

Three steps into my dash across the street and I thought I was going down. I hopped across the rest of the way on one foot, keeping my focus straight ahead so I wouldn't throw off my balance. The hail thickened and pelted everything in sight. It ricocheted off my head. Each piece felt like a tiny hammer against my skull. I took cover at the side of the house, protected somewhat by the overhanging roof. The chunks of ice still hit, but with a much reduced frequency.

Using the house to support my weight, I tested my ankle. The pain had subsided. I completed a couple test steps with a slight limp.

At the screen door, I stopped and scanned the area. It felt almost calm amid the driving rain and hail, lightning strikes and thunder, and heavy wind.

The screen door banged against my back as I reached for the kitchen door handle. I eased the door open and slipped inside. Water dripped off me, splattering the floor. A puddle grew at my feet. It felt like I had entered another dimension, the air was so still. The sounds of hail hitting the tin roof echoed throughout the kitchen. I waited there, gaze loosely fixed on the next room, listening for any movement.

I grabbed a chef's knife from the block, then moved into the living room. The recliner was toppled over. The television lay flat on the floor. The coffee table had been smashed in the middle. Magazines and newspapers littered the floor. No bodies, though. And no blood.

I climbed the stairs. Approached the first landing cautiously. Left arm ready to defend. Right prepared to attack with the knife. I steadied myself, took a deep breath, and whipped around to the next set of stairs.

The bottom half of a leg protruded from the top floor, hanging over the first couple steps, toes pointed down. I could tell by the brown leather shoe it was Herbie. Once eye level with the floor, I saw the rest of his body, lying face-down in a pool of his own blood. I stepped over his lifeless body and continued straight down the hallway. At the end of the corridor, the door to their bedroom stood open a couple inches. A bloody handprint started about halfway up and slithered to the floor in a thick, meandering red line.

I pushed the door open with my foot. It swung without resistance. The body I expected positioned behind it wasn't there. It didn't take long to find her, though.

Ingrid lay stretched out on the bed, resting on a pillow. Looked like she was sleeping. A single bullet hole in her forehead told a different story. I figured the blood on the door was Herbie's. Ingrid had been there, knelt at his body. Perhaps she caught him as he fell. She tried to flee to her room as the assailant pursued, and tripped at the door.

I lifted her body forward. The bullet had gone through, but there was no indication she'd been shot in bed. A small pool of blood had saturated the pillow, but the splatter I would expect to see did not coat the wall. She hadn't been killed in the bed. In fact, it looked as though she'd been cleaned off before being placed there. I scanned the room, found the spot where she was murdered near the window. She'd tripped and fell past the door. Bloody handprints littered the carpet. She had managed to get to her knees, then feet, and perhaps went for the window to escape or call for help. The assailant gained her attention and opened fire when she turned around.

Or when they forced her to turn around.

But why not leave her there on the floor where her lifeless body collapsed?

I didn't have to think about it too long. The killer knew her. Which meant they knew Herbie, too. At least in passing. But the way the bodies had been left indicated they had a connection with Ingrid. So much so that they felt compelled to lay her to rest gently, going so far as to remove the blood and brains that had surely coated her face.

"Ingrid," I whispered. "I'm so sorry. You tried to tell me. I heard you, but I didn't listen to what you were saying."

16

I SEARCHED THE HOUSE FOR CLUES AND ANYONE HIDING OUT. Found neither. Several thoughts raced through my mind. Who did it, and why? What were the final moments like for Ingrid and Herbie? Had anyone heard? But the idea that brought on a cold sweat was the possibility that someone had remained outside, where I couldn't see them. They could've waited for me to arrive and then called the cops.

They would've been here by now. The town wasn't that big. The station was a couple minutes away. Hell, even if they were on a call, they'd have dumped it and come to get me. Murder takes precedence.

I debated whether to leave then, or call the cops myself. Not sure how they'd react, I called Reese instead.

"Billie," she answered.

"It's me."

"What's going on?"

"I need you to come over."

"Where?"

"You know where."

"Have you seen the weather?"

"Ree—," I paused, corrected myself in case anyone snooped on her calls. "Billie, listen to me. Forget the weather and get over here."

"You think I'm taking my car out in this?"

"I don't have time for this." I split the blinds and checked outside. Rain poured heavy. The street remained deserted. "Find a way to get over here as soon as you can."

There was a break in the storm a few moments after hanging up. Reese showed up not too long after. She came in through the backdoor dressed in sweats, her hair matted from the rain during her short jog from her car to the door. I was standing in the kitchen, backed up against the fridge.

"The hell, Jack?" Her gaze swept past me and froze on the living room. Her furrowed brows lifted. Mouth dropped open. Angry eyes grew concerned.

I turned, headed into the room. "Follow me."

"Dear God," she said, stepping through the threshold from the kitchen to the living room.

"It gets worse." I climbed six steps, stopped on the landing, looked back at her. "It's bad, Reese. Probably as bad as anything you saw in the city."

"I can handle it."

"You sure?" It was one thing to strip away human emotion when you were looking at just another homicide. Sure, there'd be some that would stand out more than others. But when it came to people you knew, it was almost impossible to ignore it.

She nodded, pushed past me. At the first step she hesitated and whispered Herbie's name. I followed her up, trying to see everything for the first time again. Perhaps I missed something due to the shock and surprise of the situation.

There were no bloody footprints on the carpet. No torn

clothing left behind, at least not anything clearly visible. No casings. They probably wore gloves.

Reese stopped in front of the bedroom door, reached out and let her hand hover in front of Ingrid's bloody print. I remained behind, near Herbie's body. The detective in her had to process what she was seeing without my interference. First, she had to get past what she knew she was bound to see.

She pushed the door open, took a step inside, froze. Her head turned to where I could see her profile. Tears streamed down her cheek. Her gaze was fixed on Ingrid's lifeless body.

I broke my plan to stay behind and joined her in the bedroom.

"She was murdered over there." I aimed a finger toward the window. "I figure she was with Herbie when he was murdered, judging by that bloody handprint on the outside of the door. Or she managed to get upstairs shortly afterward, while the killer was still there. She ran to the room, stumbled and hit the door, crawled along the floor there where there's blood stains, then tried to get to the window to escape or call for help."

Reese glanced back at the bed. "She was shot in the front."

"Right," I said. "She faced her executioner. She looked into the son of a bitch's eyes, probably pleading by name for him to let her live."

"But he didn't," she said. "He took her life, and then put her to bed."

I nodded, said nothing.

"They knew her." Reese looked at up me, tears still welling in her eyes. The detective was losing the battle with her emotional side. "I mean, everyone in this town knows each other, but this person knew her well enough to want her corpse to rest comfortably. In some way, they loved her. They didn't show Herbie that same consideration."

I continued nodding.

"Christ," she said.

"That's right," I said.

"We have to call Vernon." She already had her cell out. The screen flashed on.

I knew it had to be done, and it was probably best that I be there both when the call was made and when the cops showed up. No doubt I would be on the suspect list, given that I'd been staying at the house and no one in the town knew who the hell I was. With the exception of Reese. Vernon already made it clear how much weight that held.

She paused before pressing the send button, looking at me for direction.

"Go ahead," I said. "We need them out here to start working this. The damn storm's gonna make it impossible to get anything from outside."

Reese placed the call. It was quick and professional, with the exception of her having to repeat the main reason for Vernon to get out there as fast as his cruiser could carry him. The shock affected them all.

"You didn't see anything?" she asked.

"I saw lots of stuff," I said. "Doesn't mean I know anything about why this happened or who did it."

"Tell me everything that happened on your way here from my place."

"You interrogating me?" I said.

"No," she said. "But Vernon is likely going to. And I want to hear your answers to make sure you don't incriminate yourself."

"I'm pretty good in the interview room."

"I know. I've interviewed you before. But these people down here, they do things differently. They make it work in their favor, not yours."

"I can handle it."

"Jack, just play along." She grazed my chest with her fingers. "What did you see?"

"I saw that same GMC truck from the garage. I saw the same older guy driving it, and Flagpole Linus sitting in the front seat. Then I backed up a block to avoid them, and came across a group of kids. Ten- and eleven-year-olds, I guess. They were messing with something on the ground. Didn't want me seeing it. One of them got up in my face, and then they ran off with the evidence."

"That could be related." Her cop-brain was working overtime.

"You think a group of pre-teen boys came in here, trashed the living room, killed Herbie, then executed Ingrid? And then, instead of running home or off somewhere to hide, they stand around in plain sight making a fuss over who knows what. And when questioned by an adult, a large one that they'd never seen before, they stand up to me. That makes sense to you?"

"Well, no, not when you put it like that." She ran her hands through her hair. Her shoulders hiked up tight a couple inches as she paced toward the bed and back. "But, I don't know, maybe they saw something?"

"Maybe, but what? I mean, they didn't seem like they witnessed a murder. You and I've both been there. It affects you. Imagine how a kid would take it? Christ, I know I didn't handle it well when Molly was murdered. I wasn't much older than those kids I ran into."

She nodded slightly as she processed it. Then she looked up from the floor. "You know what I want to know?"

"What?"

"Why didn't we hear anything? You should be able to hear a gunshot, let alone two shots, from anywhere in town."

"You know a suppressor would cut down on that."

"Would it?"

"Sure as hell it would, Reese. It's not going to silence the shot like in the movies, but it'd quiet it down to nothing more than a penny clanging into a tin jar. You're not gonna hear that outside."

"Who here would have access to that?"

"Anyone and everyone here could get one. Christ, they could probably make one if they had the right materials. No different than back in New York. If the desire is great enough, there's nothing going to stop them from getting what they want."

Reese walked to the door, stepping wide over the blood stains on the carpet. "There's lots of desire in this town. Too much, perhaps."

17

VERNON'S CRUISER PULLED UP OUTSIDE THE HOUSE THE SAME time we made it back to the kitchen. Staying upstairs any longer would have been a recipe for incrimination. Especially if the killer had been as meticulous as I believed.

Red and blue lights bounced off the walls. Vernon cut the siren, but left the strobe going. He barged through the backdoor. His face was pale. His hands shook. It took a few seconds for him to ask what had happened, and even then, he stammered through the simple question. No doubt homicide was not a skill he'd grown into.

Reese asked me to give the rundown since I'd been the one to make the discovery. I proceeded cautiously, avoiding saying anything that I thought might incriminate myself. I felt my report was textbook. Reese nodded her agreement when I finished.

"You got some investigative experience?" Vernon said.

"A bit," I said, trying to play it off. I didn't want to give him anything to dig with. "Military."

He nodded, glanced over at Reese. "Good enough, I guess."

Through the window I spotted another cruiser. It pulled up alongside Vernon's, blocking the road. Two officers I hadn't seen before stepped out. They looked to be in their mid-thirties. Vernon gave them a quick rundown. Grabbed one to go upstairs with him, and told the other to remain with Reese and me.

"Don't you two go nowhere, OK?" Vernon said.

Reese answered for both of us. "We'll be right here if you need us."

Ten minutes passed. I followed the sound of their footsteps through the investigation. They were in the bedroom now. An unmarked patrol car arrived, driven by an officer in plain clothes. He walked into the house, ignoring me and nodding at Reese. She offered a half-hearted smile in return. A silent ambulance pulled up right after.

"They're gonna move the bodies," I said. "The hell are they doing?"

"They don't have much experience at this," Reese said.

"We have to stop them. Forensics needs a chance to work this."

She laughed. "What forensics?"

"Damned if I know. The highway patrol, then. Something. Somebody has to process the scene before they butcher it."

"We're in a world trapped fifty years in the past, Jack."

"Then I'm going up to stop them."

She grabbed my arm. "Stay here. You'll just make it worse if you go up there. Let them do what they need to do. Not like all that other stuff is gonna make a bit of difference here."

My cheeks and ears burned. But like she said, there was little that could be done. I sensed that Reese wanted to get away from the house, but that wasn't the reason she held me back. I'd only make things worse for myself. After all, I had no doubt that soon I'd be the number one suspect. That's why we changed our story slightly and told Vernon that she came to the house with me after I told her how upset Ingrid had been. Reese wanted to talk to the woman, make sure she was OK, and that nothing serious was going on. It was nearly foolproof, so long as they didn't find those kids. Outside of them, it had been deserted with the storm pressing down.

Vernon came down the stairs, stopping in the threshold between the kitchen and living room. He leaned against the wall, his face pale, brow sweaty. Perhaps he was about to pass out. He brushed silver strands of hair away from his forehead. His hand continued around the back of his head.

"You OK, Vernon?" Reese said.

His head bobbed up and down twice, and then he exited the house. A cool gust of wind blew in. Thunder rumbled in the distance.

"Ingrid was his mother's best friend," Reese said.

"Christ," I said.

"His mom passed away fifteen years ago, but Vernon made it a point to check in on Ingrid and Herbie every few months, at least. If they needed anything, or had trouble with anyone, he took care of it."

"So he cared for her."

Reese nodded.

"Did he care about Herbie?"

"Jack." If she could've exhaled fire, I'm sure she would have roasted me right there. "What are you saying? He did this? You honestly think that? He's a cop for Christ's sake."

The ties ran deep. Didn't matter how long she'd been off the force. Didn't matter we were in a small town in Texas. Vernon was a cop. In Reese's mind, he deserved every last benefit of the doubt.

"You know that doesn't mean a damn thing," I said.

Our hushed conversation drew stares from the remaining officers. They knew enough to consider us possible suspects until we were cleared, so they moved closer in an attempt to listen.

"We can't talk about this now." She glared at the plain clothes officer. "Just keep quiet until we're out of here."

Vernon came over and stood back a few feet from us. He said nothing, stared up at the ceiling. Outside, low, dark clouds raced past. I wondered if the storm had more in store for us. How would that affect the investigation?

"Billie," Vernon said, "is it OK if your cousin stays with you for the time being?"

She nodded.

"Good," he said. "Won't be able to stay here anymore, and I'd prefer if he were somewhere I can find him when I'm ready to talk."

"I'm standing right here," I said. "You can talk to me now."

Vernon shot a cross look in my direction. "I'll come get you when the time is right. Don't go nowhere. And I mean nowhere. You only leave that apartment with Billie. In fact, I want you by her side and only her side for the next forty-eight hours."

"How do you know she won't leave?" I said.

"Because you won't let her," he said.

"And how do you know that?"

"I can tell you're the kind of guy that doesn't want an innocent woman getting slapped with an accomplice tag. You'll do everything in your power to keep her from doing something stupid." He moved in front of me. I could smell today's lunch on his breath. Chili dog and a beer, maybe two. "Besides, why run unless you have something to hide?"

"Because sometimes it doesn't matter if you did it or not," I said. "If someone wants an outcome bad enough, nothing is going to stop them from reaching for it."

Vernon nodded slowly. "Get out of here so we can finish up what we have to do. I'll be in touch soon."

Reese grabbed my arm and pulled me toward the door. The screen door banged against the side of the house. We stepped out and took the most direct route to her place. The clouds thickened behind us. Streaks of lightening raced across the sky. The next storm was minutes from hitting.

A few blocks into the drive, Reese spoke up. "Jack, you should get out of here. I've never seen Vernon like that. The way he stared at you, it was like he could see you with the gun that killed them."

"You know if I go they'll arrest you. You'll be guilty by association."

"They won't. It's not me they want."

"We already gave them a story that we went to the house together. They're either gonna figure I was trying to hide my tracks after killing them, or that you helped me kill them and we were stupid enough to admit to both being at the scene together."

"I'll tell them that you slipped out in the middle of the night. You can take my car, get someplace you can hop on a bus or train and disappear again. They'll be trying to follow a bullshit identity. It's just gonna lead them to a dead end, right?"

She had allowed her feelings and passion to cloud her judgement. Her words stared logic in the face and laughed at it. For whatever misguided reason, she believed Vernon wouldn't come down on her. How could I get her to understand?

"Reese, what's the first thing you would do if you were afraid of someone fleeing?"

"Put a car on them."

"Look back."

She glanced over her shoulder. "What? I don't see anything."

"Look further."

"Dammit," she said after spotting the plain clothes in the unmarked car inching along a perpendicular street two blocks back.

"I'm not going anywhere," I said. "They've got nothing on me. I've survived being tortured. There's no way these guys are gonna coerce me into a false confession. Let's ride this out and try to piece it together ourselves."

"OK. I have little faith they're gonna get it right anyway. We'll see what they do, then go from there, I guess."

She cut through an alley so narrow we wouldn't have made it if someone had set a trash can out there. We emerged a few houses down from her place. It cut about a minute off the drive.

It didn't matter, though. The plain clothes was already parked out front.

18

CRYSTAL RIVER, FLORIDA, 1988

JACK CRAWLED TOWARD THE OPENING. THE LIGHT HAD FADED, but through the hole he could see the final speck of sunlight. He paused a few feet away, closed his eyes and listened. He realized during the first few silent seconds that his anxiety and panic were gone. No matter how hard he thought about it, they didn't return. It was a welcome development for the young man.

Over the years, his father had taught him to think tactically. Whether during chess matches, or their self-defense lessons, Jack had learned to plan several steps ahead, and anticipate the movements of others.

Outside, the strangers called to one another. A series of code words were used to check in. Jack picked out the distinct voices and tallied it up to at least five men. He'd counted three coming across the porch. So that left two. They had probably come around the side of the house, clearing the area. They'd leave at least a man or two out front.

Seven total. Maybe more.

That was a lot for him and his brother to take on. But they

didn't have to face them all at once. The guys may have size and training on their side, but they didn't know the land like Sean and Jack. The woods were their territory. Even in the dark they could maneuver without thought. And night fell fast.

"All right, sweet cakes," a man said. "We know you're in there. Just come out and nothing will happen to you or your brothers."

How did he know she had brothers? She'd yelled out *boys, run*, but that didn't necessarily mean *brothers*. Had they been scoping out the house for some time? After all, the men showed up the night that Jack's parents were away. Why? To rob them? That would make sense, except for the fact that several of the men were outside now, where Sean, Jack and Molly were. If they wanted to rob the place, it would've made sense to let the kids run and then ransack the house. They weren't there to steal. They were hunting.

"There you are," another man said. "Just settle in right there."

Jack crossed the final few feet to the opening, remaining just inside. He scanned the yard. The sky hidden behind the foliage was a deep red, almost purple in some spots. The trees looked like black statues, the tops swaying in the breeze. Fireflies danced among the leaves. He saw outlines along the edge of the woods. Men, he presumed. But where was Molly?

"Just do as I say and nothing's gonna happen," the guy said.

Jack couldn't figure out where the man was. None were gesturing. They all appeared to be standing ready to attack.

"God damn bitch!" the guy yelled.

Molly screamed. It wasn't pain or fear. It was something primal. She had attacked in an attempt to protect her life. Gunshots followed. Jack felt his heart in his throat. His stomach wasn't far behind. Panic filled him as he feared the worst for his sister. But this was different than anything he'd ever experienced. The feeling drove him to action.

"Dammit," the guy said. "She made it deeper in the woods."

Flashlight beams cut into the trees, but didn't make it far into the tangled weave of branches and leaves. Molly knew the woods as well as Jack and Sean. Hell, she'd shown them secret spots they never managed to find on their own.

"All right," the guy said. "You two stay here. The rest, come with me. Let's find this bitch."

With the men's attention focused on Molly and the woods, Jack knew it was time to make his escape from under the porch. He turned over, reached up and grabbed a beam, then pulled himself out from underneath. As he sat up, he heard a creaking sound. The guy stood five feet away, glancing over his shoulder into the house.

19

REALITY SET IN WHEN WE WERE ALONE. THE DETECTIVE IN Reese took a back seat, and she broke down. My shirt grew damp with her tears as I held her tight. After the initial wave, she told me she needed a little time alone. She went to her bedroom and locked the door behind her.

Through the blinds I studied the front and rear areas outside the apartment. The unmarked car was parked in plain view out front, at the end of the driveway. The lone plain clothes officer. It wouldn't stay that way long. He was lending a hand, and would be relieved at some point. Hell, I didn't know if he was a member of the town's department, or a highway patrol officer that lived close. I decided to keep a close watch on the guy. He wasn't planning on being here. I figured he had less staying power for the job than if he were on duty. If I was going to make a move, it'd be about the time he zoned out.

On the other side of the apartment was a simple maze of fence and clothesline that led from the garage, past the house, and through a neighbor's yard. I could manage it without being spotted if I climbed out the back window. Something to consider if things took a turn for the worse. Of course, Vernon might anticipate that, and would have an officer waiting on the next street over.

I stepped out front for a breath of fresh air. The storm had passed, and a cool breeze cleared the sky of the dark clouds. The slight gusts left the area smelling fresh. The sun hovered in the western sky. It felt warm, but the heat and humidity had gone with the storm.

The cop stepped out of the car, leaned back against the rear door. He adjusted his shirt, showing me his pistol. His palm rested on top.

"Easy there, fella," I said. "Just getting some air."

He said nothing, remaining still, his gaze fixed on me. The guy lived by the book. Definitely a state trooper. He'd be easy to get past, if necessary.

I picked up on the low rumble of a diesel engine. No doubt the truck from earlier. It drove past the closest intersection. The older man's arm rested on the window frame. The passenger seat was empty. I glanced back, wondering if he had dropped Linus or someone else off a few blocks away. Perhaps they were approaching, holding off on their attack until the guy gave them the signal to make a move.

The engine faded, then grew louder, getting closer. I saw the truck again, this time headed toward me. I wanted to run in and tell Reese to ready herself, but then I'd provide them the opportunity to reposition without my seeing.

The GMC stopped at the end of the street, idling. I heard the door open, then close. He never exited, though. He remained there, stared at me for a few moments. Then he drove off.

The officer never looked back. His only responsibility was to keep tabs on me. Hell with everything else. Didn't matter there was a murder investigation going on. A chill slithered down my spine as I realized they'd already determined their number one suspect.

"You see nothing wrong with that?" I said.

"With what?" he said.

"That creeper stopping down there and staring at me."

"Didn't see anything," he said. "How can there be something wrong when there was nothing for me to see?"

"The hell is wrong with you people? Got no damn clue how to operate a homicide investigation."

I walked back to the apartment. Behind me, the officer returned to his vehicle. The door slammed and the engine revved. But the car didn't move. I figured it wouldn't, either.

When I reached the top of the stairs, I found Reese standing in the kitchen. She had her back to me and was wearing considerably less clothing than the last time I'd seen her. Just a pair of tiny gym shorts and a cut off t-shirt. She stood in front of the coffee maker as a fresh pot brewed. The aroma of the dark roast and anticipation of caffeine had me feeling more alert already. Or maybe it was her clothes.

"Hope you don't mind," she said.

"The coffee," I said, "or the outfit?"

Her subtle smile distracted me from the situation. From everything, really. And, at the same time, she reminded me of every problem I'd faced in the past seven years. She'd entered my life around the same time that the Old Man, Feng, had. She had been involved when I nearly lost my life to a terrorist and her bastard ex-husband. She wasn't at fault, of course. Our paths, destinies perhaps, were intertwined. Was it random coincidence we'd found each other again in a tiny Texan town?

"What's going on outside?" She turned to face me and leaned back against the counter with her thumbs hooked in the waistband of her shorts.

"One of Texas's finest is positioned at the end of the driveway. I feel safe now, I guess."

"They're doing their job, Jack." She didn't try hard to disguise the fact she was lying. "You know how it is."

I didn't respond. Wasn't much to say that we both didn't already know.

The final rush of coffee raged through the machine like a class IV rapid. Reese poured two mugs and brought them to the table, then sat down, facing me. I leaned forward, inhaled the aromatic steam. It tinged the inside of my nostrils. The first sip went to work, relaxing my nerves. Taking me to a place where I wasn't so damned on edge. Hell, I'd been ready to take out a branch that was tapping on the window.

Reese dropped a sugar cube and a splash of cream in her mug. I took mine black, like usual. No point in messing with perfection. We drank in silence, though our gazes rarely left each other's. She traced an alternating pattern on her upper chest. I did my best not to follow her finger as it dropped lower.

She was first to break the silence. "So, what now?"

"For me?"

"You, me, us?"

"I expect someone will be by to escort me, and possibly you, too, to the station for some questioning."

"Probably a good idea we have our stories straight then. There's no way they'll allow us to be in the same room once they take you."

We had cobbled the story together on the fly. There was no harm in going over it a few more times. If one of us slipped up it would just invite another hour or two of interrogation, and a possible change from person of interest to suspect.

"You think they have reason to suspect me?" I asked. "I mean, I know they want to make me a suspect. It's too damn easy. But based on what you know, is there a reason to?"

She shrugged. Said nothing.

"Put on your detective hat, McSweeney. Would you suspect me?"

"Yes." There was no hesitation. No inflection in her voice. She said it straight and simple. "And in this town, that would be a very bad thing, Jack."

We spent the rest of the day inside. Another round of storms passed through, knocking out the power. It stayed down, even after the storm passed. I found myself drifting off on the couch, watching the last traces of the sunset.

20

I LEAPT FROM THE COUCH, ARMS UP, READY TO STRIKE THE source of the noise. All I struck, though, was the low-rise coffee table with my shin. I went down hard, twisting so I landed on my side. Cool air from the floor vent washed over my bare torso, chilling the sweat that coated my skin.

A loud rap at the door startled me again. I hopped up, turned toward the source of the noise. Where did Reese keep her hand-gun? Even if I knew, it wouldn't matter in the pitch black.

A flood of light penetrated the room. Reese stepped through the doorway, wearing a blue robe, cinched tight at the waist. She led with one arm out. The other was behind her back. She called me off as I jumped ahead of her to go downstairs.

"My house," she said. "I'll get it."

I shuffled back into the shadows. Figured it'd be better to remain out of sight, should Linus and one of his cronies be at the door. They'd clear the stairs and be sent sprawling.

The door creaked open. Reese didn't gasp or scream or call out for my help.

"Vernon?" she said. "You have any idea what time it is?"

"Of course I do, Billie." He cleared his throat. "And I'm sure you know why I'm here at this hour."

I moved to the top of the staircase so I had her in view. It'd also make things easier when Vernon came in for me. I was in plain sight. No chance of an *accident*.

The robe slipped off her left shoulder as she shrugged. "Oh, I don't know, Vern. Maybe you're out secretly recruiting for a new cult, and want to talk to me about it?"

I chuckled at her sarcastic remark. The man at the door didn't.

"Dammit, Billie. This'll be a lot easier if you two just come with me."

"Are we under arrest?" she asked.

"Of course not." There was a cough. "At least, not yet."

"Vernon," Reese said. "Be straight with me here. Is Jack in serious trouble?"

"I don't suspect you," he said. "But we need to spend some time with you and your cousin. And I mean together. We're not gonna go and split you up right yet. Just want to ask you both some questions. Review some details of the crime scene, and what you might remember. Things like that."

"Things like that," she repeated. "All right. You guys wait here. We'll be out in a minute."

The door made it ninety percent of the way shut, but bounced back before latching. A younger officer forced his way in. Reese blocked him from taking the stairs.

"I know you've got weapons in there," Vernon said. "Best if we keep an eye on you."

She pushed back against both of them. "None of you perverts are watching me get changed."

I chuckled again. The men at the door didn't.

Again.

"Just do what you gotta do, Billie." Vernon stepped through the doorway, positioned himself next to the younger officer inside, and then aimed a finger at me. "When Miles gets up there, you're to throw a shirt and some pants on and come outside with me."

I stood there until the young guy got up top. He didn't blink as I dressed. We then headed down and waited at the base of the stairs for a few minutes. The clouds had rolled out, leaving behind a freckled night sky, revealing every star visible to the human eye right then. The thought crossed my mind that it might be the last time I had a full view of the sky without bars obstructing it.

Or a casket and six feet of dirt.

I considered running. But with two cops standing there, one was bound to get a shot off.

Reese joined us downstairs, and Vernon led us to his car. I half expected him to cuff me, but he didn't. Reese slid across the back-seat. I sat next to her. Vernon assumed the driver's seat with the young guy up front next to him.

I detected the rumble of that damn diesel engine in the moments before Vernon fired the ignition. The dark street gave no hints as to the location of the pickup, or if it were nearby at all. I was on full alert. Adrenaline was pumping. It could've been my mind messing with me.

"What is it?" Reese leaned toward me. Her hair brushed against my cheek. Short, quick breaths blew hot against my neck.

Why hadn't I brought up the thing with Darrow? How the boy had used his name, and him showing up in his truck earlier that day. As much as I needed to find out what Reese knew about the guy, now wasn't the time.

I shook my head. "Nothing."

"What're you two talking about?" Vernon asked.

Neither of us responded. I caught his gaze in the mirror. His eyes looked like coal in the dark.

"All right," he muttered. "Let's take a drive."

It was freezing in the car. They'd left it running with the AC on full blast while inside the house. Reese pushed her arm and leg into mine as she squeezed in closer.

The cruiser rolled forward with another car close behind. Its headlights cast shadows inside our vehicle. After a few turns, we were separated from each other. Or they'd fallen behind. Easy to do with the number of turns it took to navigate town. But we hadn't turned recently. It only took another minute for me to recognize that the route we were on would lead us out of town. I glanced at Reese, whose puzzled look confirmed what I feared.

A few moments later, she said, "Vernon? Where are you taking us?"

Vernon remained silent. His young ward glanced at him for a second. There was fear in his eyes. They were breaking protocol, and in turn, the law. Reese took the opportunity to pounce on the kid.

"Miles," she said. "What's going on here?"

"Uh," he said. "I'm not sure, ma'am."

"Miles," Vernon said. "Shut up, OK? Don't speak unless I tell you what to say. Got it?"

Miles nodded and turned toward his window. Whatever happened now definitely wouldn't be by the book.

21

Reese spent five minutes asking questions she never received answers to. Vernon gave up telling her to remain quiet. Once she finally stopped pestering him, we spent the next ten minutes in silence.

We rolled out of town to the east, and then turned off the highway to the south on a one lane paved road. From there I lost track of where we were after a series of turns that led us to a rutted dirt road. The cruiser plowed along, bouncing and scraping and sending me and Reese careening into the door and each other.

"It's a funny thing, Jack," Vernon said, breaking the silence. "You show up to our peaceful little town just a couple days ago, raise hell with a couple locals, and sure as shit now I got a double homicide on my hands." He revved the engine, breaking free from the dried mud tracks we'd been following. "Doesn't that seem like an odd coincidence to you?"

I cleared my throat of the dust and grime that had accumulated during the drive. "Well—"

"Shut up," he said. "I don't want to hear a goddamn word out of you right now."

I hadn't heard anger from him like that before. Not even at the old couple's house after they'd been murdered. The knot in my stomach grew as doubts rose that either of us would make it back to town alive.

"Vernon," Reese said.

"You either, Billie." He brought the vehicle to a stop, kept a tight grip on the steering wheel as he twisted around to look at us. "Jesus Christ, Billie. You come at me with this story about this guy being your cousin. I mean, how many times had we talked, Hon? Huh? Dozens? Hundreds? Christ, at least that many with me perched on a bar stool drinking a beer. And on many of those occasions, when I asked you about your past, you said you had no family. No ties. Not a goddamned soul on earth."

Reese glanced down for a second. That was the worst gesture she could make at that moment, and she knew it. She should've remained defiant, even if she said nothing. Instead, she gave away her position.

Vernon continued. "I specifically asked you if you had any aunts, uncles, or cousins. You remember your response?"

Reese said nothing.

"You said no, Billie. No. 'No, Vernon, I don't have any family at all.' So, was that a lie? Did you think that would stop me from digging too deep, looking up people from your past?"

She remained silent, her gaze now fixed on the rearview.

"I'm torn," Vernon said. "On the one hand, I want to believe you. I want to take your word that this Jack Smith guy sitting here really is your cousin. But then I wonder, how does he end up in town with a busted up Jeep, staying at Ingrid and Herbie's house, instead of yours? What sense does that make?"

I had an answer ready, but didn't bother with responding. Vernon's anger had led him to another world, and there was no pulling him out of it.

"And you, Jack," he said. "I gotta tell you, it'd be real easy to pin this on you. I mean, I think there's more than enough circumstantial evidence that this would be a slam dunk case. You don't strike me as a fella that can get decent legal representation, either. The DA would eat you alive in this case. The jury—" he paused to laugh "—hell, they'll be ready to fry you after the opening statements."

"So what're we doing out here, then?" I said.

He glared at me. "Because out here I can say whatever I want, and you can answer however you want, and not a single word of it is going to be recorded."

"What about slow Miles here?" I said.

"He'll do whatever I tell him," Vernon said

"And what about your dashboard cam?" Reese said.

Vernon's lips parted and formed a half-snarl, half-smile. "That's why we're getting away from the car."

A few minutes later we stood fifty or so feet behind the cruiser. Miles had been instructed to wait inside and only come out if Vernon called out for help. If it came to that, Miles had permission to shoot us without hesitation. I doubted he had the capacity to do so, though. Still, I didn't want to chance making a break for it yet. It wouldn't take long for the others to figure out what had happened. We'd be caught within a couple hundred miles, at most. Vernon was hot right now. Once he settled down, and was willing to listen to logic, I felt I could reason with him.

"All right," Vernon said. "Just the three of us. Who wants to go first?"

Neither Reese nor I spoke.

"Aw, come on now. This is your chance to come clean. Speak now and I'll keep in mind that you cooperated. Say nothing, and I find out that you've been lying, well that's not gonna look good in front a jury of your peers."

I wasn't inclined to say anything. We'd given him a background story that he'd have a hell of a time disproving. If the FBI had done their job right, any search of Billie's past would return an endless maze that dies a couple years before her arrival in town. And unless my old contact Brandon had sold me out sometime in the past couple months, there was no way Vernon could uncover anything using my alias. Jack Smith of Fourth Avenue, Brooklyn, New York led a boring life. Every search for his family history would result in dead ends.

"Already told you, Vernon," Reese said. "I can't help it if you refuse to believe anything I have to say."

He looked down at the ground, nodding. "So, how come he ends up here with a dead Jeep and stays at someone else's house?"

Reese held his gaze but did not respond.

"Such a simple question, and yet you can't give me an answer. Not even a lie."

"You know how the Geotz's were," she said.

"I wasn't even sure Billie was here," I said. "I was able to determine that she ended up in a small town in this area of Texas. If she were here, I'd find her. And I did. Pretty damn quickly, too."

"So you just get in your car—"

"Jeep."

"Excuse me, your Jeep." Vernon paused and shook his head. "And you drive all the way down to Texas figuring that if Billie was here, you'd somehow find her."

I nodded and kept my mouth shut. Had he run the registration on the Jeep? If not, would he? I contemplated accounting for that now, but decided against it.

"Ok," he said. "Plausible, I suppose. I guess I just have one more question."

"What's that?" I said.

"Not for you." He took a step to the side and squared up with McSweeney. "Who the hell is Reese?"

22

CRYSTAL RIVER, FLORIDA, 1988

JACK MOVED AS QUICKLY AND SILENTLY AS HE COULD, BUT IT didn't matter. The guy whipped his head around and in an instant he was on top of the boy. Jack's leg caught the edge of the porch, and an unwieldy nail dug into his thigh, tearing his shorts and the flesh beneath. He gritted his teeth and kept from yelling out.

The man had little trouble with Jack. He positioned himself behind the boy, placing him in an arm bar. His other hand wrapped around Jack's mouth. His fingers smelled like cheese puffs and whiskey. So did his breath.

"Just keep quiet, OK?"

The stink burned in Jack's nostrils.

The guy stepped back, dragging Jack into the house. He let go of the boy's mouth to shut the door. He mumbled something about the others in the woods. Jack managed to turn his head enough to get a look at the guy in the light. His beard had flecks of silver in it. His eyes were dark both in color and rage. They were opened wide, flicking side to side as if the man were on the lookout for someone, or something.

Son of a bitch is crazy.

Jack tried to bite the man's hand when he returned it to his mouth, but the guy's grip was so tight that Jack couldn't spread his teeth far enough apart. At some point he'd relax the grip, or adjust the arm bar. That would be the time for Jack to make his move. And he was ready. The panic that crept up at times was still nowhere to be seen. The situation wouldn't allow it. He heard the words of his father echoing in his head.

Stay calm. Stay alert. Stay in tune with your body and surroundings.

It didn't matter if they were hunting, fishing, or sparring. The mantra his father repeated throughout his life had now taken hold of Jack. And he knew he'd need it as the guy dragged him through the house and up the stairs, finally stopping in front of a bedroom door.

The guy couldn't have picked a worse room to enter.

It was Jack's room.

23

Her mouth dropped open as Vernon repeated the question. Her identity had been compromised. Had I been careless? Had he heard me call her by her name? Had someone else? Was her apartment bugged after all?

"I'm not sure what you mean," she said.

"Oh, you're not," he said. "Pretty simple question, right? Who is Reese? Either you know, in which case you tell me, or you don't. And in that event, I'd expect you to say something like, 'I don't know.'"

"It was her nickname as a kid," I said. "You know, like the candy. She couldn't get enough of it, so we called her Reeses, which shortened to Reese."

She nodded. "Jack's the only person left that calls me that anymore. He must've let it slip at some point, I guess."

"Yeah," I said. "I guess."

The look of contempt on Vernon's face deepened. He spit to the side, then turned and walked to the cruiser, motioning for us to follow a few steps into his journey. His limp grew more pronounced as he neared the car, almost as if he'd tried to conceal it earlier but finally gave up. The taillights cast a soft red glow on the ground, enough to make out obstacles. I stumbled over a large rock, but managed to get back in the vehicle without re-tweaking my ankle.

Where were we going next? Did they have a spot already planned further in the desert? Some place with pre-dug graves, just waiting for the right moment. Or maybe back to town so he could place me under arrest, and hit Reese with an accomplice charge.

Vernon dropped the transmission in gear and cut back across the field. After bouncing through the landscape, he found the rutted path again. We bounced and collided for a few minutes until Reese finally braced herself against me and we moved in unison for the most part. We were headed back to town. This time the drive felt like it took half as long.

We took the highway into town. Drove past the garage. I peered into the darkness, looking for the Jeep and wondering if it was still there. Maybe they'd already sent it off to the junkyard, figuring I'd be out of town by morning. The double homicide investigation changed all that.

A block further down I spotted that old GMC pickup parked on a side street. The cab appeared empty. Was the house it was parked in front of where Darrow lived? I made a mental note of the street and house, a white or light colored Cape Cod with hedges around the front.

We stopped in front of the police station. Miles hopped out, went in through the front door. Vernon took us around back. He parked in a spot near the rear entrance.

"Don't do anything stupid," he said, letting us out.

Reese led the way inside. Wasn't much to the station. From the back door, I could see clear to the front. There were two rows of chairs on one side of the room, a receiving desk on the other.

Cinder block walls separated us from where I assumed the cell block and interrogation room were located.

Vernon stood behind the receiving desk, shuffling papers and stacking them into a neat pile. He picked up a couple pens and put them in a cup already loaded with several others. Then he dusted the surface off with his sleeve, shaking his head with a look of disgust on his face. Once everything was in order, he unlocked a drawer under the desktop and pulled out a keyring.

"Follow me," he said, opening the only door along the cinder block wall.

We stepped into a fluorescent-lit room. Everything was coated in the same shade of dim-yellow. Two empty jail cells waited at the far end of the room. A cluttered desk with an old CRT monitor was placed in front of them. There was a small room to the right of the door we entered through. To the left were a coffee maker, microwave, and a small fridge, all up against the cinder block wall

Vernon spread his arms wide. "Welcome to our holding cells, interrogation room, and break area."

His demeanor had changed. Perhaps it had something to do with the three surveillance cameras mounted to the ceiling. No way to bypass those.

"Not too shabby, Vernon," I said. "I take it that's not your desk."

He shook his head and puckered his lips like he wanted to spit at the messy workstation. "I don't spend any time there, no." Then he shot a look at Miles, who immediately went to work cleaning off the desk.

"So what's the plan?" I asked.

Vernon started a pot of coffee and ignored my question. I waited a few moments, and then asked again.

"Why don't you let me worry about that," he said.

"You didn't wake us up in the middle of the night, then drag us out to the desert, then back here for nothing. Let's get to it. Get this shit over with."

"This shit," he said, "as you put it, has to do with the murder of two of our town's oldest, finest, and most-respected and beloved residents. They were among the original citizens who built this place from the dirt up. I'm telling you right now, we'll take as long as we need to get this figured out. So why don't you get nice and cozy and keep your damn mouth shut until I ask you a question."

"You think I don't realize what happened?" I said. "I found them, man. I saw that poor old woman shot through the head only a short time after I found her crying, afraid that something was going to happen to them. So why don't you quit dicking around, ask us what you gotta ask us, then get to searching for the bastards who did this."

Vernon lunged at me, put one hand on my throat and hit me in the stomach with the other. It might've been a small town, but he was still a cop. Even with the cameras in the room, I knew that striking back wasn't an option. They could spin it anyway they wanted. Hell, the system would have most likely malfunctioned at that moment. At least, according to them. And no one would second-guess them. For the next few seconds I countered his moves. Blocked his second punch, a wild haymaker aimed at my face. I broke his chokehold and arm barred him to prevent him from going after my neck again. Every move was defensive.

Miles jumped on Vernon's back and pulled him away. Reese placed herself between us to keep me from going after Vernon, and stopping him from lashing out again.

"Christ," she said. "The hell is wrong with you two?"

"I'm tired of being jerked around," I said. "I know you are, too. And look at this bastard. I say what he needs to hear and he jumps on me. Son of a bitch. You're lucky we're in here, Vernon, and not back in the middle of nowhere."

"We can easily go back, boy," he said.

"That's enough." Reese put her arm across my chest and pushed me back to the wall. She lowered her voice a few decibels.

"Jack, come on. You're only going to make it worse acting like this. Let them do their thing. Once they question us, they'll have to let us go. They have nothing on us."

"They're wasting time," I said. "You know it. We should all be out there looking for who did this."

"All of a sudden you're invested in this town?"

"I couldn't care less about this town. But I care that an old woman tried to tell me something was wrong and I missed it. Christ, I ignored it. I could've stopped this." I pulled away from her grasp and wrapped my hands around the back of my head.

She took a step back. Her eyes wavered left and right, then focused on mine. "How?"

24

I DIDN'T HAVE IT FIGURED OUT. NOT ENTIRELY, AT LEAST. Everything pointed to Darrow and his men. But it was all a secret. People told me to hang back, not get involved. In what, though? I could speculate all day, but with no firsthand knowledge as to what these guys were into, I couldn't find the link between them and the murder. They disliked me, which would have been a solid reason to take me out. Perhaps that's why they went to the house. Herbie and Ingrid got in the way. Collateral damage. That explanation was too easy, and I had a feeling the real reason was far more insidious. They were the intended targets. Herbie and Ingrid had built the town from the dirt up. Darrow and his men threatened the foundation of the place. They weren't going to take it any longer. Maybe that's why Herbie took a chance on a guy stranded on the side of the road. Perhaps he thought I could lend a hand. In the end, they paid for their convictions with their lives.

"Jack?" Reese said.

I looked past her at the two cops standing near the far wall. Vernon's beet-red face and heavy breathing told me he hadn't settled down yet. Miles shuffled foot-to-foot and fidgeted with his holster. Looked like a kid who couldn't hold his piss any longer.

"Jack?" She backhanded me across the chest.

"Not now," I said. "We'll talk about it when we're out of here." I leaned in closer, whispered, "And I need you to answer my questions one hundred percent truthfully. Got it?"

She nodded, said nothing.

"Vernon," I said. "I apologize. I got upset and lashed out. It won't happen again."

So long as the bastard didn't make another move against me.

Miles attempted to take on the role of peacemaker. He stepped forward, arms outstretched. "Hey, it's OK, man. As long as we can sit down and talk about this like—"

"Jesus, Miles," Vernon said. "Shut the hell up and go pour everyone a cup of coffee."

Vernon unlocked the interrogation room and directed us inside. I'd thought he'd split us up, attempt to find holes in our story. I'd assumed wrong. We talked for an hour, going over the details four or five times. Then he asked me to recount my last conversation with Ingrid, when I'd found her crying. I managed to do so almost word for word, emphasizing that she wanted me to leave, that she felt like she was in danger. And then how she insisted I stay. Figured she felt as though she owed it to me to keep her husband's promise.

"That's the kind of people they were." Vernon wiped the stained edge of his mug, took another sip. His gaze lifted up to the wall or ceiling behind me. He stared there for a minute, smiled. "She used to watch me when I was a little boy. Man, I thought she was the best thing ever back then. Hell, I thought that for a long time, matter of fact. Wasn't until I matured and found my wife that I really appreciated Ingrid, though. She was there for us, time after time, helping out with my little ones. Helping my wife through horrible bouts of postpartum depression. You see, my wife got it bad with kids two and three. I thought she wasn't going to make it at one point."

There was a brief pause when Miles stepped into the room.

"Ingrid gave so much to everyone she met," Vernon said. "Even the assholes in this town. See, that's why this makes no damn sense, and that's why it's so easy for all of us to point the finger at you, Jack, because no one has anything to gain by killing Ingrid and Herbie. I swear, the only logical explanation is that some psychopath did it so he could get off."

The room fell silent for several minutes while Vernon presumably meandered through his memories of Ingrid. His eyes went misty, and he looked down at the table. I understood how he felt. I'd been there myself. But, damn, to think the only possible conclusion was that I was a psychopath.

"All right." Vernon slapped the table. "Let's get back to it. Start from the beginning, when you broke down outside town."

I went over everything one more time, meeting Herbie, the bar, and the encounter with Linus and his large friend. I told him again about the fight at the garage, and the older man in the pickup truck. He confirmed that was Darrow. I paused there, waiting for Vernon to add something else about the guy. He didn't. I recounted Ingrid's last conversation with me, the clues I missed. And finally, I told him how we found the bodies. He seemed deflated when I'd finished. Perhaps he expected me to slip up somewhere, get some detail wrong, something he could pin on me.

"Anything else?" I asked.

Vernon shook his head. I figured he'd take us through another round, but there was no point. I knew it, and he realized it. He led us outside, behind the station.

"I take it you can make it back to Billie's from here?"

We were already walking and didn't respond.

"Jack," he said. "Don't leave town. We'll need to talk to you again soon."

25

"Who's Darrow?" I said. "What's his deal?"

Reese didn't lift her gaze from her cell phone. I craned my head. Looked like she had a crossword puzzle up.

I rolled the twist cap from the beer bottle in my palm, pressing the sharp points into my flesh. They left deep, dark indents in my palm. I tossed the cap over her phone. It bounced off the table and landed in her lap.

She took a deep breath, glanced up at me. "Where'd you hear that name?"

"Nowhere."

"Then why are you asking?"

"Because."

"That attitude is not going to get you far, Jack."

"Come on, Reese. If you know something, tell me."

"I thought I warned you to keep your head down. Now you're asking about Darrow. Tell me where you heard the name."

I took a long pull from the bottle, draining about a third of it.

The carbonation burned a touch going down. The hoppy bitterness drowned out the sensation.

"Well," I said. "I heard it from a kid."

"A kid?"

"Yeah, a kid."

"What kid?"

"On my way back to Ingrid and Herbie's, from here. When I found their bodies. Before I got there, there was that group of kids huddled around something on the ground. Little bastards wouldn't show me. When one started talking, another said, 'Darrow don't like no one talking,' or something like that. I got the boy to confirm Darrow drives the old dually I keep seeing."

"I'll start by saying that if you continue down this line of questioning outside this room you'll be opening up a can of skunk that you can't shove back in. The smell is going to envelope you. Probably me, too. We'll be screwed."

"And we'll stink. At least it'll be together."

She rolled her eyes at me.

"We'll be in the crapper because Darrow doesn't like anyone talking, right?"

She nodded. "Precisely."

"This guy scare you?"

"What guy?"

"Darrow."

She shrugged. "Not sure what you mean."

I rose and paced the perimeter of the apartment, moving books and the few knickknacks she had placed on shelves and window sills.

"What the hell are you doing?" she asked.

"Checking to see if the place is bugged," I said.

"You're not going to give this up, are you?"

"Have you known me to give up on anything?"

"For a while I thought you'd given up on me. Hell, took you long enough to find me."

"You think this was planned?" I opened a random book to a sketch of an elephant. It was decorated like it was going on parade in India.

She nodded. "From the moment I saw you in the bar, I knew you'd been searching non-stop for me."

"Happy accident, McSweeney."

"You only call me McSweeney when you're trying to hide your feelings." She swiped my beer and finished it. "Some kind of buffer that allows you to address me as one of the guys or something."

"Now you know everything about me, huh?"

"You're not that complicated, Noble."

"You're right about that."

"So are you saying you're not happy to have found me?"

"I was."

"But now?"

"This whole double homicide and possible murder-one indictment against me changes things a bit."

She rose and crossed the room, stopping inches in front of me. She smelled like heaven even after the ride out of town, standing in the desert, and sitting in the interrogation room. Her hand wrapped around mine. She placed her other on my chest, nails digging into the muscle.

"Let it go until the morning, Jack."

I followed her to her room, and managed to forget about everything that had happened, for a little while at least.

26

I LEFT MY WATCH ON THE PILLOW. IT WAS SOMETHING MY father had given me the first time I returned home as a Marine. I slipped out of the apartment. Reese would be pissed at me for leaving without waking her, but at least I was coming back. She might not forgive me for taking her keys and leaving in her car.

The street was deserted. The night watch had gone, and no replacement had come to take their place. Maybe we were off the hook with Vernon. Or perhaps he knew we wouldn't leave. Either way, when we parted yesterday he seemed resigned to the fact that our story was legit and he'd have to look elsewhere to find the killer. Anger had led him down the wrong path with me. He was thinking straight now, and would run a proper investigation.

Or call in folks who could if his department was incapable.

The old muscle car roared to life with a flick of the key, loud enough that I feared it would wake Reese. I imagined her flying down the stairs at that moment, bursting through the door and blocking my escape. I eased out of the garage onto the dirt and gravel. She was nowhere to be seen.

I drove toward Herbie's cousin's shop, but turned a couple blocks early onto a residential street.

The old GMC dually was parked in the same spot I'd seen it last night, in front of the unassuming Cape Cod. It was white, with blue trim and a stained front door. I drove past the house, turned, and parked a few houses down in a spot with nothing to obstruct my view.

Bacon saturated the steady breeze that blew in through the open driver's window. My mouth watered, stomach clenched and growled. I hadn't eaten. Hadn't had a cup of coffee. The latter would have been most helpful.

Five minutes passed with no action on the street. It was barely seven a.m. Not like the people here had to brave a lot of traffic to get to work. If their shift started at eight, they could leave five or ten 'til and make it on time. If they worked out of town, they were gone by six.

My cell phone buzzed. I diverted the call to voicemail. Only one person had the number, and I wasn't ready to talk to her.

The Cape Cod's front door swung open. Out strode a thin, pretty blonde woman, probably thirty to thirty-five years old. She left the door open and crossed the yard. A yellow lab with happy-butt disorder came out, tail wagging so hard his rear moved damn near a foot in either direction. I thought he was going to flip over. The blonde turned, bent over and petted the dog, then shooed him inside. A little boy, maybe six or seven, came out a few seconds later. He had a red book bag larger than him strapped to his back. He was going to have a hell of a problem with his back later in life. What did a kid need with that much stuff on a daily basis?

The boy followed the woman to their grey minivan. She held her arm out, aiming something at the vehicle. The side door creaked, then slid open on its own. Once the boy was secure in his seat, the woman ran back to the house. She leaned inside with both hands pressed against the door frame. Her hair fell to one side and hung down over a foot. She yelled something indecipherable, then jogged back to buckle in the little boy.

And then the blond-haired boy from the day before, the apparent leader of the eleven-year-olds, appeared. He dragged his book bag across the yard, leaving behind a trail of matted down grass. He stopped mid-way and pulled a cell phone from his pocket.

"Son of a bitch," I muttered, replaying his warning about Darrow in my head.

The front door remained open. A figure walked past. I tried to make out who it was, but I could only see shadows inside. Was it the older guy? Darrow? I doubted it. Why would the kid refer to his old man like that? Maybe the guy was his stepfather. Made sense, given the age difference between Darrow and the blonde woman.

"Come on, Roy," his mom yelled.

The kid swiped the screen of the phone, shoved it in his pocket, then picked up his bag with both hands. He ran across the yard and jumped into the front seat of the minivan. The vehicle rolled backward a few feet, and came to a jarring stop. I looked toward the house. A bare arm stuck out in the sunlight. The rest of the figure remained a shadow. The woman stuck her arm out and waved it, then continued away from the house.

Reese's car heated up over the next several minutes as the sun rose above the houses and trees. The wind had faded, leaving behind the lingering aroma of breakfast. I considered going up to the house. Knocking on the door. Breaking in. Whatever. Every fiber of my being, my instincts, all told me not to do it. It would make things a hell of a lot worse if I was found breaking and entering. Hell, even knocking on the door and having the guy open it would make a mess of things. Especially if he carried the clout I thought he did.

And if he was the kind of man I'd pegged him for, he'd notice things. Like an unusual vehicle parked on the street a few houses down from his. And with that thought, I decided it was time to move on.

I drove to the end of the street, hung a right and parked at the edge of the business district. As I cut the engine, the phone buzzed again. This time I answered.

"You got some damn nerve," Reese said.

"I know. I'm sorry," I said.

"Damn right you are," she said. "But not as sorry as you're going to be."

"I had to take care of something." The breeze picked back up, cooling the sheen of sweat on my forehead.

"What could you possibly have to take care of here?"

"Remember what I asked you last night?"

She paused. Her breathing rattled over the line.

"About that person, or name, or whatever?" I said.

"Jack, you need to leave that alone, OK? Whatever you're doing, stop. Come back here and I'll fill you in."

"OK, sounds good."

"I'm serious, Jack. Come back now."

"You got it."

"Dammit, Jack."

I hung up. She knew I wasn't coming back yet. And I wouldn't until I had an answer for all my troubles thus far.

I got out and took a walk down the road. Passed a few folks along the way. They studied me with curious eyes. One nodded. Another smiled. I responded in kind. Someone yelled from the other side of the road. I glanced over and saw two women arguing. I tried to figure out what their disagreement was about, but the low rumble of a diesel engine overtook their voices. I swung my head toward the source. Toward the truck. Linus stared down at me from the driver's seat. He smiled a bit too much for a guy I'd recently beaten the piss out of.

Then I felt why.

Someone drove a foot or shoulder or maybe a baseball bat into my lower back, sending me to my knees. A thud at the base of my skull drove me the rest of the way to the ground.

27

CRYSTAL RIVER, FLORIDA, 1988

"Now you and me are gonna have some fun." His hot, foul breath coated Jack's neck, making its way around his face. The same cheese puff and whiskey smell nearly gagged him. The man's grip relaxed. "Scream and I'll kill you."

Jack squirmed out of the hold, lunged forward, and spun around with his hands ready. His gaze honed in on the pistol aimed at his head.

"Scream, and I'll kill you," the guy repeated slowly. A smile broadened on his face. His top and bottom teeth were crooked and stained yellow. One of them was so black it must've been dead.

Stay calm. Stay alert. Stay in tune with your body and surroundings.

The words continued to echo in his father's voice, Sean's voice, Molly's voice. They competed with each other until they melted into one unified voice, shouting into Jack's consciousness. Jack had only used his father's lessons in practice and occasionally in the schoolyard when someone got out of line with him or someone who couldn't defend themselves. When he'd asked his father what he had been teaching him, his dad told him it was the only self-defense he'd ever need. That was good enough. He figured everything else was for show. The most important thing was to neutralize your opponent. And Jack did that well, even though he'd never faced a real-life opponent of this size.

"How you feeling right now?" the guy asked, smiling while he undid his belt with one hand.

Jack said nothing.

"Wondering what I'm gonna do to you, huh?" He licked his lips. Jack wasn't sure if the man wanted to torture him or rape him. Either way, the man wouldn't get what he wanted without a fight. "Well, don't worry too much. Ain't nothing I've never done before. I should have it down to a science by now."

In those moments while the man stood there, planning his next move, Jack itemized the potential weapons in his room. There were trophies from football, baseball, and soccer perched on shelves out of his reach. Three baseball bats, one metal, one wood and one aluminum, sat in his closet. Between his mattress and box spring was his knife, a piece his father gave him. Said it had belonged to an Air Force pilot who'd been a POW.

None were within reach.

The guy stood in the way.

"Let's get started."

28

My face pressed hard against the concrete sidewalk. It tore at my cheek. Dust filled my nostrils. Grit scratched my eyes. The guy smelled like he'd inhaled a dozen chili dogs a few minutes earlier.

He outweighed me by fifty pounds or more, and was experienced in jiu-jitsu or wrestling or something similar. He countered every move I made. I couldn't get to my hands or knees. The moment I planted my palm on the ground, my arm was knocked out from under me, sending me face first into the concrete again. Warm blood trickled down the side of my face. Pain radiated from the right side of my forehead. I felt another trickle pouring over my lips from my nose. The breeze stung the cuts and scratches.

I feigned defeat, letting my body go limp. My assailant lifted his weight off me as he went to pull my arms back.

Wrong move.

I pushed up with all the force I could muster and whipped my head back, then slung my right elbow around. Both collided with the guy. I'm not sure where I caught him, but it was enough to earn a couple grunts, and to force some of his weight off me. I pulled out from under him. Made it to my knees. Almost got to my feet. I clung to a store window in an attempt to pull myself up.

Car doors grated opened and slammed shut. Boots hit the ground. The sounds echoed between the row of buildings. Three men rushed toward me from both sides. I prepared for the onslaught. The first blow came from behind, catching me on the side just under the ribs. Another caught me on the jaw. A weathered leather cowboy boot connected with my gut. I had enough time to tighten my stomach, minimizing the damage. The next one I wasn't so lucky. It smacked dead center in the solar plexus. I coughed out any remaining air in my lungs and collapsed on my left side.

The assault continued for another minute, each man taking a turn. I never much enjoyed getting my ass kicked. Sure as hell wasn't going to start liking it today.

"He's had enough."

I couldn't see who said it, but my guess was Darrow.

"Back off boys," someone else said.

The beating stopped. The men formed a half circle around me, cutting off any escape unless I suddenly developed the ability to scale a brick wall in a matter of seconds.

I rolled onto my back. My arms and legs and stomach ached. Did I have a broken rib or two? Too soon to tell. My face felt as though a battering ram had smashed into it. Same for my chest. They yanked me off the ground, dragged me down the sidewalk. I glanced over and caught a glimpse of myself in the store window. A large gash spread across my forehead. One eye was swollen. Blood dripped off my face and stained my shirt. I looked like I was dressed for a zombie-themed costume party.

Practically felt like I was the real thing.

We stopped in front of the pickup truck. They twisted my arms behind my back and secured my wrists together with thick zip ties. The passenger doors opened and I was thrown onto the rear bench seat. Someone leaned on my legs as another man zip tied my ankles together. My mouth hurt too badly to open, much less think of a comment to make. Blood from my face spread and pooled on the seat.

Linus threw his arm over the front seat, twisted, and peered down at me.

"Mr. Badass himself," he said. "Not so tough now, huh?"

I said nothing.

"Wanna tell me what you were doing hanging out in front of my house watching my wife and boys?"

"That was your wife?" I mumbled, apparently cohesively.

"Hell yeah," he said.

"Is she your sister, too?"

Linus laughed, but only for a second. He rose up, swung, connected his left fist with my mouth. Blood coated the inside of my cheeks, my teeth, and tongue. I managed to part my lips and let it trickle out, adding to the collection on the seat.

The truck lurched into first gear and pulled away. I wasn't sure where they were taking me, but I had a good idea who'd be there. We hadn't gone far when the truck stopped abruptly. The tires chirped on the asphalt. The smell of rubber filled the cab. Linus opened his door, stepped out, then pulled mine open. I expected to be dragged out. Instead I got a fist to my stomach. Everything turned black as they pulled and cinched a bag over my head. What was next? Torture? I wouldn't put it past Darrow. Whatever criminal endeavor he was involved in, he surely took on the role of brutal overlord as opposed to savvy businessman.

A few seconds later, we were on the move again. I lost track of how many rights and lefts we took. I tried to keep up with the seconds and minutes as the drive lingered on, but I struggled to remain conscious. The pain in my head intensified. I felt more nauseous with each turn. A concussion had taken hold.

We stopped again. The transmission groaned as Linus put it in park, leaving the engine on to idle for a couple minutes. Some country song played on the radio. It was never my genre. Sounded older, though. Linus alternated between humming and whistling the tune in the wrong key. I thought about telling him to shut up, but decided I ought to pick and choose my battles a little more carefully the rest of the day. Plus, I wasn't sure I could talk.

The engine choked and sputtered and shut off. The low rumble slowly faded away in my ears. When it dissipated, all that was left was a vacuum of air, like we were in the middle of a void.

Linus's door opened. Boots hit the ground, crunched on rocks. My door swung opened. Someone racked the slide of a rifle.

"You hear that?" Linus said.

"Yeah," I uttered through the burlap sack.

"One wrong move, do one thing different than I say, and that bullet is going through your damn head. Got it?"

I sucked in a warm breath of stale air. Pain pulsed throughout my body. "Yeah, I got it. One question, though."

Linus laughed. "I thought you said you got it, man."

"I do. I just have a question."

"What?" He spat. It thudded against the ground.

"Got some whiskey?"

He laughed again. "Yeah, man, I got some whiskey inside."

"Inside where?"

He fumbled with the cord around the sack, then lifted it off my head. Sunlight knifed through my eyes and felt as though it cut into my brain. I recoiled against the sensation, drawing yet another laugh from the skinny man. Once I had adjusted, I stared outside at a whole lot of nothing. An expansive field stretched as far as I could see.

"Where are the others?" I asked.

"Don't you worry about that," he said. "Just so long as you understand I'm not the only one with eyes on you at this moment.

You might be able to get away with taking me down, but you won't make it far."

He backed up a few steps.

"Go on, man," he said. "Get out."

I felt like a damn worm, wriggling and turning, angling myself so I'd fall on my shoulder and not my head. All the effort I put into it didn't matter. As soon as I was close enough for gravity to take over, that son of a bitch grabbed hold of me and accelerated the process. I crashed on top of my head, and rolled through as clumsily as possible.

Linus laughed for a few seconds before kicking me over. He cut the ankle tie, then he reached down, grabbed my wrists and started dragging forward. For such a skinny guy, he was a helluva lot stronger than he looked. I scrambled to make my legs work. As soon as I managed to upright myself, Linus let go and dropped back, keeping a good six feet between us.

"You so much as look back at me again and I'm gonna give you another hole," he said.

I didn't believe him. If they were going to kill me, they'd have done so already. Someone wanted me here, and that someone wasn't going to allow me to die until after they met me. Still, there was no point in taking any more of a beating.

The only structure in sight was about a half-mile down the dirt path. The rest of the landscape was barren, save for some fencing and cattle off in the distance. Warm wind swept in from the west, carrying with it a fine layer of dirt and the smell of manure. I adjusted to both at around the halfway mark of our trek. The black curtains along the edge of my vision lifted as we walked. Good thing, too. I figured that meant the swelling in my brain was diminishing. Though my limbs and chest ached, nothing seemed to be broken. If anything, a rib or two, but that wouldn't stop me if I got the chance to take someone down.

We reached the unassuming weathered cabin. A twelve-by-eight covered porch offered some shade from the glaring sun. The structure trapped the wind. It circled my body, cooling my aching muscles.

"Wait here." Linus entered the house and shut the door behind him.

I glanced around. There was nowhere to hide. They'd have a clear view of me if I ran. And if Linus was a decent shot, I'd be dead. So I waited there, leaning against a post, letting the breeze work its magic.

The door opened. The voice that followed belonged to someone other than Linus. It was heavy, southern, mature.

"Let's get one thing straight here," he said. "You're probably not going to survive this, Mr. Noble."

29

How the hell did they know my name? Every inch of my body tensed at the possible implications. They had Reese. There was no doubt about it. They had her too, and had managed to get my name out of her. How badly had they tortured her for it? No matter how pissed she was about this morning, she wouldn't offer it up easily.

"I often wondered if I'd see you again," the man said.

I hadn't looked back at him, instead keeping my focus on the truck, shimmering in the heat a half-mile away. *See me again?* There was something about the guy. Maybe I'd known him in the past. "Aren't you the least bit curious?" he said. "Go on, Mr. Noble. Turn around."

I steeled myself for the worst and forced my body off the post and turned. Would he be holding a gun to Reese's head? Perhaps only a gun aimed at me? The latter I could handle. The former might send me over the edge.

I stared Darrow in the eye, offered no reaction to his presence.

"Don't recognize me?" His lips drew thin and stretched downward. His eyes narrowed. Had I disappointed him?

I said nothing.

"I guess it was a long time ago," he said. "You see, we have a
similar background, you and I."

"Were you one of the bastards involved in planning my
missions?"

He smiled. "No, I got out before that. But I know all about you
and what you've done for this country. The good...and the bad."
He gestured with his head to move inside.

I shuffled toward him, keeping eye contact until I had passed.
The room was dim, dusty, smelled like mold. The door clicked
shut behind me, sealing me off from the wind gusts. I strained to
see who else was in there while my eyes adjusted to the low level
of light. Linus leaned against the back wall. I didn't see Reese, or
anyone else. I turned to face Darrow.

"So who are you?" I said. "How do you know me?"

"You're the spitting image of your father at this age."

"You served with my old man?"

He nodded.

"How'd you turn out to be this big of an asshole?"

The man laughed. "Got the old man's sense of humor, too."

"I suppose."

He drew in a deep breath, crossed his arms, leaned back
against the wall. "Yeah, I served with him. Against him at
times, too."

"Got a name?"

He nodded.

"Gonna tell me? I mean, you were able to pick me out of a
lineup, but I have no idea who you are."

"Name's Darrow."

I narrowed my gaze. "Everyone in this town seems pretty
scared of you, Darrow. Why is that?"

He shrugged. "Got me. As you can see, I'm quite hospitable."

"Yeah, you're a regular Rockefeller as far as I can tell."

He smiled, winked. "That wit, Noble. Let me tell you, it's going to get you killed one day."

"Yeah? How soon?"

"Sooner than you think if you keep it up."

I called his bluff. "If you wanted me dead, I'd be dead already."

His smile faded. He said nothing.

"What am I doing out here?" I said.

"That's what I'm wondering," he said. "How the hell did Jack Noble end up in my little corner of Texas?"

"Chance and coincidence."

"I don't believe in either."

"Hate to disappoint you, but that's all it is."

He uncrossed his arms, took a couple steps toward me. "I tend to think there's a reason behind everything. And, as you might have guessed or become aware of, I've got a few things going for me here. All above water, I might add. So when someone who's worked in a clandestine agency known for breaking the rules shows up in my town, I get a little concerned. I start wondering which of my enemies might still want to take me down. I start connecting dots." He waved his hands in front of him, point to point. "It appears random at first, you know, but then an image starts to form. Now, I'm not quite finished yet, but I've got a few ideas of who and why."

He stared at me as if I should respond. I didn't.

"There's at least five people you have worked with or for that I butted heads with in the past. Now, two of them are deceased. Unfortunate for them, I suppose, but it does help me eliminate the possibilities. So, I'm curious, when's the last time you had contact with Frank Skinner?"

I said nothing. Things between Frank and I had been tenuous at best for most of the past decade. Hell, a few months ago I held a gun to his head, and had it not been for Mia's presence, I would have ended Frank's existence.

"From what I understand, you spent a good chunk of your career under the man, either directly or accepting contract work. I know you've recently engaged with him. Now, I never had too much of an issue with him, but as former leader of the now defunct SIS, he might have had some interest in things I've *seen* going on out here. And I'm concerned that he might think I'm involved. Lord knows I don't want the Feds coming out here for nothing."

"This is why you beat me and dragged me out to this cabin? You think I'm a spook out to take you down?"

"Never know who's watching, Noble. I can see for miles around out here. If someone's watching, we can easily abort." He tapped a trap door on the floor with his foot. I hadn't noticed it prior. I assumed it connected to an escape tunnel. "Now, why don't you answer my question? When's the last time you had contact with Frank Skinner?"

I decided to play along.

"Couple months ago," I said.

"Did he offer you a job? Specifically, did he ask you to come out here and investigate me?"

"Did you recognize me?" I asked.

"Not sure what you mean," he said.

"When you pulled up at the garage, after I'd kicked the shit out of those morons in the parking lot."

Darrow shook his head. "While you were busy watching me, I had someone across the street nab some close-ups of you. I forwarded those on to a friend still sympathetic to me. He ran your image through a number of databases, which, I might add, is not as easy as it sounds with a guy like you. Did you know your image matches up with somewhere around twenty-five different names?"

I knew, but didn't tell him.

"He thought he had you right away, but the name didn't match the ID you gave the cops."

The only way he would've known that was if the cops were in his back pocket. Didn't surprise me.

"So he kept going," Darrow said. "Another result, then another. It was obvious you were more than a mere passer-through, so my guy kept digging. He had to call in a huge favor, and I'm going to owe him pretty big when this is all over. Anyway, I'm sure you know where this is going."

"DB-22," I said. "A list of the government's top agents. Only a handful of people have access to that database. Your guy isn't one of them, but he's buddies with someone who is."

"I wouldn't call them buddies."

"Whatever," I said. I assumed Darrow's guy had something on the other man. It was enough for the man to risk his career and give me up.

"You ever wonder how many people out there would love to know your exact location, Noble?"

"Not something I like to dwell on, Darrow."

"I'd bet it's in the fifties, maybe sixties. I bet some of them would pay a good sum for a chance at your head."

"You're not giving me enough credit. I'm more of an asshole than you can imagine."

Darrow laughed. "So much like your old man. I swear. How is he these days?"

I said nothing.

"Anyway, back to Frank Skinner." He paced across the room. "Did he send you?"

"The last interaction I had with Frank was me sparing his life, and that was only because of witnesses. If it were up to me, he'd be dead. As far as I know, Frank doesn't give a damn about you and whatever it is you are or aren't doing down here. And since I last saw Frank, I haven't had contact with a single person in any agency, in this nation or any other, for that matter."

"So you just drifted your way here, is that right?" He leaned back against the wall, arms folded. His posture and the look on his face indicated he didn't believe me.

"That's right."

"And you just so happened upon a former NYPD detective that you once worked with."

I tried not to show surprise to the fact that he knew Reese's identity. Was that the reason she wouldn't go into it when I asked about Darrow? Had she come to an agreement with the man that she wouldn't speak so long as he never revealed her identity?

"That was a bonus to landing here. Only reason I didn't abandon the Jeep and hitchhike my way out of here." Playing dumb would have been a mistake and possibly brought more grief on Reese than she deserved.

"Perhaps you should have done just that." He stopped, cocked his head to the side. "You don't seem shocked that I know her secret?"

"You were able to figure out who I was. I have no doubt you can get information out of the FBI."

Darrow laughed. "Never liked those sons of bitches myself."

"Well, you'll hate Frank Skinner even more then."

"Yes, I heard about his promotion."

A few silent moments passed. Darrow's gaze flitted from me to Linus. He nodded slightly.

"So what now?" I said.

"I think I need to do a little more checking on you," he said. "I'm inclined to not believe your story, but I don't want to kill you for no reason. I'd hate to waste such talent. Hell, we could work this out over the next few days, and you might take me up on an offer to come work for me."

"Don't hold your breath."

His smile faded. "Right, I understand." He crossed the room, opened the door. "Linus is going to bring you back to town. Mr. Noble, please heed my advice. Don't go anywhere, and don't get too comfortable."

30

MY MUSCLES HAD STIFFENED DURING THE INTERROGATION, but overall I felt better. Wounds had stopped seeping. My head had cleared, and I no longer feared a concussion. At least not one that would keep me down for any number of days. Linus wasn't as tense on the walk back to the truck. Maybe he figured after my talk with Darrow I'd be more cooperative. Perhaps Darrow told him to go easy on me. Or the plan might be to get me halfway there, then kill me.

When we reached the truck, the hood went back on. My hands were zip-tied in front, which made the ride a little easier. Several minutes passed before the truck stopped again. Linus got out, opened my door, pulled the hood off and cut the zip ties.

I moved to the front seat.

"Nothing funny," he said. "We're being watched now. You won't get far. And frankly, I don't fancy my boys growing up without their daddy."

"Then why work for a guy like Darrow?"

"Don't know what you're talking about, man."

"I'm pretty sure I got a good read on the situation."

He shook his head. I prodded with a few more questions, but Linus had dug in and had no plans on giving me any intel.

"You stupid or something, man?" he said, staring at me out of the corner of his eye. "Let it go. Seriously, quit trying to figure out what Darrow's doing. Lay low for a couple days, and you'll likely be on your way."

"Likely, huh?"

He said nothing else. We entered town from the same direction I'd arrived the first time. The garage had its bay doors opened. A couple mechanics were working. The Jeep was nowhere to be found. I gave up on ever seeing it again. No big deal. Not a big loss.

"Shoulda turned there," I said after we passed the road that led to Reese's apartment.

Linus said nothing.

Another minute went by and we were still on Main Street.

"Where the hell are we going?"

Linus didn't answer.

I leaned toward the window and let the wind dry the sweat on my forehead. Then I settled back against the seat, closed my eyes for a few. I felt the truck slow. I looked up at the parking lot we were approaching.

And then I saw it.

"Son of a bitch," I said, going for the door handle.

"Don't do it!" Linus said. "They'll shoot you."

The side mirror on the passenger side had been busted out at some point. I stuck my head out the window and looked back. One cruiser followed close behind. The truck hit a dip about ten miles too fast, throwing me into the dash. My left arm absorbed the impact. Linus pulled to a stop. A car quickly moved to the front, and two others on either side. I think every cop in the town had come out. Some took cover behind open car doors, armed with rifles. Others waited in plain sight, Glocks drawn.

I looked back. The trail car had pulled up perpendicular behind us. I was boxed in.

Linus exited the truck, hands held up in plain sight.

"Thanks for bringing him in, Linus," Vernon said from somewhere to my left.

They had me trapped. I had two options.

Death or surrender.

31

CRYSTAL RIVER, FLORIDA, 1988

"WHEN I WAS IN COUNTRY, KID, LEMME TELL YOU," THE GUY started. "What I did, ain't no horror movie out there that compares. It wasn't just the VC. Hell naw, not just them. Them sons of bitches were boring. We were there to take care of them, so we did our jobs quickly and efficiently. The others," the guy broke into a maniacal fit of laughter, "well, let's just say they were for fun."

Jack inched back. He wanted to be close to the wall so when the man made his move, he'd collide with the wall as Jack leapt out of the way.

"The easiest were the whores. God, those delicious whores, man. Their pimps weren't nothing. We'd take a group of us, three or four, get a couple of them whores. Pimp would always want to come along. He'd be the first to go. Usually quick and relatively painless, unless they put up a fight. Then we'd drag it out, make the girls watch. Occasionally, if there appeared to be a family connection between pimp and whore, we'd let the guy live till the end. Made him watch it all."

Jack said nothing. He kept his gaze fixed loosely on the man, trying to remain in tune with his every movement. Follow the belly button, he remembered. The body has to go with it.

"We'd have our way with the whores, and then we'd punish them the way them sinners deserved." He smiled. "That bother you?"

Jack didn't respond. He thought about the man's words and the picture they painted. He was obviously former military. Were they all? Did that have something to do with why they were there? His dad had been a military man. Army. High ranking. He'd been in Viet Nam. Did these guys know of him? Perhaps know him directly?

"I asked you a question, boy." The guy lunged forward with speed that belied his physical stature.

Jack felt rooted in place. His brain sent a message to dodge right, but his body wouldn't or couldn't follow the directive. The man landed a backhand across Jack's face that sent him sprawling, colliding with his bed. A fog enveloped him, clouding his thoughts and judgment as he tried to decide what to do next.

Stay calm. Stay alert. Stay in tune with your body and surroundings.

32

VERNON STOOD A FEW FEET IN FRONT OF THE TRUCK, HANDS out, palms facing me. His pistol was tucked securely in its holster. Guess he figured with all the firepower surrounding him, it might be to his benefit to look unthreatening toward me.

"Out of the car, Jack," he said

Questions raced through my mind. I knew why they were there. Obviously they were there to arrest me for the murder. *But which me?* Jack Smith? Or had Darrow revealed my identity to Vernon?

The passenger door of the nearest cruiser swung open. A young woman I hadn't seen before took three quick steps back, pistol drawn and aimed center mass.

"Come on, Jack. Let's do this the easy way, OK?" Vernon said.

I placed my hands flat on the dash, but didn't move otherwise. My instincts said escape. But I had nowhere to go. No way out. I had one friend left in the town, and she wasn't there. Had they arrested Reese, too? Was she sitting in the back of one of their patrol cars? It wouldn't surprise me considering our story was that she had found the bodies with me. At the very least, they could charge her with being an accomplice.

Miles moved toward the door, tucking away his pistol. The female officer I'd spotted moments earlier backed him up. Two other officers stepped up past her. Miles pulled my door open, backed out of the way. The other two officers rushed the truck. I didn't react. One of the cops grabbed my right arm, forced it behind my back. The other waited while the first yanked me halfway out of the truck. Then they both jumped on me. We hit the ground with over six-hundred pounds of force. Two-thirds of it landed on top of me. They cuffed me, yanked me back up, slammed me into the side of a cruiser.

Vernon walked over, said, "Jack Smith, you are under arrest for the murders of Ingrid Goetz and Herbie Goetz." He proceeded to read me my rights.

I said nothing during or after.

We caravanned to the station. Blue lights bounced off every building. The car pulled up to the back where officers were waiting with the door open. We entered there, then went through the door in the cinder block wall. Stale coffee aroma filled the room. A half-filled mug sat on the desk in between two stacks of papers. I thought about making a smart ass remark, but decided against it. There was no hesitation on their part. Two officers stood on either side of me. Another opened the cell. They all took part in forcing me inside.

The room emptied. Only Vernon remained. He eyed me for a minute or so before cutting off half the overhead lights and leaving. The room sunk into a shade of piss-yellow. The echoes of footsteps faded, leaving only my breathing and the rattling of the desk fan as the only sounds in the room.

I reflected on what had happened that morning. How I had ended up here. I wondered why I wasn't dead. What kind of deal had they worked out? I thought about Vernon's long stare before he left the room. Was this his doing? Or had he been ordered?

Darrow didn't want me going anywhere, so he had Vernon arrest me. The two men were working together. Plain and simple. Perhaps it was a common occurrence. Or a permanent one. Either way, one or both of them knew the identity of the murderer. They had to. Why else arrest me with nothing more than circumstantial evidence? They did it because they knew how it all went down.

They knew the identity of the killer. The how and why. They knew every damn detail and could use that knowledge to successfully pin the murders on me.

Did Darrow think this was the way to get me to talk? And if I did, would they release me, or keep going with the phony charges? I knew a trial here would be a farce. Christ, if there was ever a time I needed to reach out to Frank, this might be it. The saliva in my mouth turned sour at the thought. And after our last encounter, I didn't know that he'd even answer my call for help.

Thinking it through, I knew jail would never be the option. Darrow knew who I was. He'd revealed enough for me to warrant calling in someone to investigate him. I surmised that the only reason I was still alive was that he was waiting on more details regarding my current situation. I had no doubt he planned on killing me. When, though? After a trial? Would he risk keeping me locked up that long? I figured he had the resources to keep watch over me as long as I was confined.

I lay back on the cot, ready to forget about it all. I needed to recover from the day's events. My arms, legs, side all hurt. At least the fog in my head had cleared. Who knows what I might have said had it not. The only positive I could take out of my current conditions was that the other cell was empty. They hadn't gone after Reese. Yet, at least. They would have arrested her first. Brought her along as a way to coerce me into going in easy.

Did she know about this? Had Vernon given her any advanced

warning? Or was she sitting at home, pissed off that I hadn't come back yet? They'd taken my cell phone in the parking lot, and hadn't offered me a call before locking me up. I doubted I'd get one any time soon, either. Vernon seemed content to let me sit. Perhaps that's what he'd been told to do.

I let all thoughts go for a few minutes and stared up at a massive water stain on the ceiling. Almost half of it was yellow from smoke and water. The paint on the walls peeled back in spots. The drywall cracked in others. The longer I lay there, the more the smell of mold overpowered stale coffee. It wouldn't be my home forever. Eventually they'd take me off to a real prison.

Neither option appealed to me.

I wondered what it would take to appease Darrow. Would making up a fake involvement with Frank Skinner work? If I said Frank sent me down to investigate what was going on here, would that be enough for Darrow? Or would he want more? Specifics, I suppose. And I had none. No one would tell me a damn thing about the guy. For all I know, he could be manufacturing meth and became overzealous anytime someone new came along.

Whatever he was into, it was obvious he had a hold on the town. Even Vernon was in his back pocket. I wondered when he'd set it up to have the old couple murdered. Question was, had it been because of me? Or had they opened their mouths, perhaps to Vernon, about the things Darrow was up to? After listening to the way Vernon spoke of Ingrid, I had no doubt the woman trusted him. If she or her husband had come across something, anything, and brought it to Vernon, he could have turned right around and told Darrow.

I sat up and leaned against the cool concrete wall. It was all speculation. I needed to talk to Reese, find out the truth about Darrow. And I needed some time in the interrogation room with Vernon. Turn the tables on him a bit.

I'd get my chance with one of them soon enough.

33

"Jack? You still with me?"

The voice lifted me out of my slumber. I turned my head, blinked a couple times, saw Reese six feet away, leaning into the iron bars. Her slender arms slipped through the gaps, and she clasped her hands together.

"What the hell is going on?" she said. "I wake up, you're gone, and I hear from you once. Then you disappear. Now you're in jail?"

"I guess they couldn't figure anything out," I said, leaving out a ton of detail. "So they're pinning the murder on me."

"We were together. We told Vernon we were together. If you're in here, I should be, too."

I jutted my chin toward the ceiling, shook my head at her. They monitored the room by video, and likely audio. There's no way Vernon would allow Reese to enter the room alone to talk to me if they didn't have a way of listening in. I pulled myself out of bed, shuffled across the concrete floor and leaned into the bars so we were cheek-to-cheek.

"I just don't understand why they'd arrest you and not even bring me down for more questioning."

"Yeah, I don't know either. Sorry about leaving you in the morning, too. I had to—"

"It's OK." She wrapped her hand around mine. "I know you, Jack. I know how your mind works. You had unanswered questions that you needed to resolve. Lying there waiting for me to wake up wasn't getting you anywhere. I really wasn't offended."

"All right. I'll leave it at that, then."

"Tell me what happened."

I detailed what happened after leaving her apartment, up to the point where they rushed me on the sidewalk.

"I don't think I can go into detail on the rest in here," I said. "Obviously my journey ended when they arrested me."

"Just tell me," she said.

I gestured toward the cameras again. "At some point, I'm going to have a lawyer, and we'll be able to meet someplace that allows some confidentiality. Once we're there, I'll fill you in on what happened. There's a few things I'm going to need for you to do for me at that point."

"Like what?"

I paused. What I was about to ask her would require her to divulge her identity. Not long after, the FBI would get involved and move her again.

"There's a few people you'll need to reach out to."

She nodded. "Sure, anything."

I took her hands in mine. "Reese, doing so is going to blow your cover."

Her expression remained the same. She already knew, and was willing to assume that risk.

"I need you to level with me on something," I said.

"Sure," she said. "What?"

"Darrow."

She looked up at the stained ceiling. "Not much I can really say about that."

"Part of what I haven't told you has to do with him. Reese, look, I know he knows who you are."

She started to respond, stopped with her mouth stuck open a half-inch. Her grip tightened against mine. "That isn't something we can talk about in here. When do you think you'll have that lawyer?"

I shrugged. "No one's said anything to me. I'm sure there's some time requirement, though."

"What about an arraignment?"

"They do those here?"

"I don't think they've ever had to deal with a case like this. People aren't murdered here. They just straight up disappear if they cross the wrong person."

I lowered my chin to my chest. "Darrow."

She offered a terse nod.

"You should go," I said. "It's not safe for you here."

"Here in the police station?" she said. "Or this town?"

"Both."

"Why?"

I wanted to expand on my conversation with Darrow. Tell her about how he knew our history, and it wouldn't be long before he notified one of his contacts. Christ, I hadn't considered that he might have done it already. It wasn't necessarily the government she had to be concerned about. It was the terrorists her ex-husband had been involved with. And her part in bringing him down. If her identity were revealed, they'd have an assassin here in no time.

"Get ahold of your contact," I said. "Do whatever you have to in order to convince them to move you ASAP. Christ, you've been compromised. You should have done this a long time ago."

Her eyes glossed over. "It's not that easy sometimes. And I was told as long as I kept out of the way, he'd never divulge my secret."

The door banged open. Vernon stepped into the room. "Time's up, Billie. You can visit him again tomorrow."

She pulled away from the cell, taking my hands with her until they could stretch no further.

"I'll dig around, Jack. You'll be out of here in no time."

Perhaps I would. I didn't count on it.

Vernon left the door open behind him as he escorted Reese to the rear exit. They stopped and spoke for a minute in a tone too low for me to understand what was being said. The door cracked open and I saw a sliver of her pass through. A breeze whipped through the room. Smelled like a bacon cheeseburger. When Vernon returned, I asked if he could run over to the grill and grab me one.

"You got some gumption, man," he said. He stood about six feet from the cell, arms crossed, staring at me. "You two get anything worked out?"

"Not sure what you mean," I said.

He glanced over his shoulder at the camera on the wall. It remained steady. I don't think I'd seen it move a single time. Vernon came over to the cell, gestured me forward. I was leery of accepting his invitation, but met him at the bars anyway.

"I know you didn't do it," he whispered.

"Then what am I doing in here?"

He shook his head. "Can't help there, man. Just sit tight a day or two, and maybe it'll get sorted out."

"Maybe? You want me to sit on my hands for a couple days over a maybe?"

"Gotta trust me on this one, Jack."

I glanced around, leaned in closer. "Are you closing the investigation? Or are you still looking into it, asking around? Someone murdered those folks, and it wasn't me. You got a problem, man. There's a killer on the loose still."

He nodded. To what, I wasn't sure. Did he agree with me? Was he appeasing me?

"It's ongoing," he said. "Low-key is all. I mean, half the people in this town don't work, and most of them sit at home. I'm sure someone saw something. But so far, nobody's come forward."

I said nothing. I couldn't help from a jail cell. If he wanted input, he'd have to release me.

"All right," he said after a few moments of silence between us. "You just sit tight, like I said, and we'll get this figured out." He stopped by the door, looked back. "Coffee?"

"Not right now. How about a lawyer instead?"

He drew his lips tight, nodded once, then exited the room.

34

I FELL BACK INTO THE COT, NOT CARING THE LEAST BIT THAT it was as comfortable as lying on a rock. Exhaustion from the events of the past couple days had caught up with me. Within a few minutes, I dozed off. I wasn't sure what time I fell asleep. But the sun was out when I woke up again.

I fought through the pain of bruised muscles and stood up. Taking a deep breath felt like inhaling nails. Sons of bitches might've managed to crack a rib or two. I pulled off my shirt and checked out the paint by number they'd done on my torso. The primary colors used were black and blue.

Someone had slipped a tray of food into the cell. It consisted of a bowl of what might pass as oatmeal, some raisins that probably were large bugs, a juice box, and a mug of coffee. I grabbed the mug and pushed the tray out of the cell. I knew the coffee was cold, but took a large swig anyway. About as disgusting as java could taste. And I drank it all. Caffeine was a necessity.

All I could do from that point was play the waiting game. I lay back down on the cot, staring at the fluorescent-washed ceiling.

A few hours passed before the door opened again. My hopes of it being Reese or an attorney were quickly dashed. The fact that it was lunch didn't make matters better. I ate a white bread ham sandwich with no condiments. Couldn't even leave a dab of mayo or mustard on the side for me. It was like eating over-salted cardboard. At least I got a fresh cup of coffee out of it. Too bad it wasn't much better than the cold brew. I tried to lodge a complaint, but the officer left the room before I put the mug down.

Another hour or so passed with no visitors. And another after that. I began to think that it'd be a wasted day. How many more were to come? Were they content to let me rot in the cell?

I managed to doze off again, but sleep wasn't meant to be. Vernon entered the room, cleared his throat. I got to my feet and went to the edge of the cell. He only took a few steps into the room, held the door open, and shot me a quick nod and a smile.

Then Reese entered. She glanced at Vernon, then rushed to the cell.

"What's going on?" I asked.

"There's a lead," she said.

"Now don't get too excited," Vernon said. "And don't think you're off the hook just yet."

"What happened?" I said.

"A couple witnesses came forward," he said. "They saw a man enter the house about an hour prior to when you and Reese stated you found the bodies. Then they saw you guys, too, and the time they gave coincides with your call to me. The description they gave of the first man was vague, but they did say there seemed to be a difference between him and you."

"You get the guy yet?" I asked.

"No," he said. "But we think we'll have him by nightfall."

"So what's this mean for me?"

"I'm not going to keep you here. But don't go far, Jack. If this other suspect checks out with a super tight alibi, or our witness recants, I might have to bring you back in."

"How long would you say I have?"

"Forty-eight hours," he said. "Lay low and stay out of trouble. Don't go barking up any trees. Know what I mean? This town's troubles aren't yours. You need to forget everything that happened. Stay away from Darrow and his guys. I can't help or protect you if you go down that road."

He unlocked the cell, then handed me a folder with my wallet and cell phone.

Reese and I didn't wait around for any more advice. We left through the back door. Adrenaline shot through me so fast I barely noticed the smell of the grilled meat nearby. We hopped in Reese's car, drove straight to her apartment. I had concerns about going back, but she insisted. Once there, I showered and changed. Reese had a fresh cup of coffee waiting for me on the table. Not the best I ever had, but nowhere near as horrible as the stuff at the police station. She'd gone out for food while I was cleaning up and had brought back a couple burgers from the bar. I scarfed down all of mine and half of hers.

"Good?" she asked, smiling.

"Best I've had in a while," I said.

"It's my recipe, you know."

"No, I didn't know that. Don't recall you ever making me a burger before."

"Yeah, well, I guess we didn't get much time to hang out in my kitchen back in New York."

"No, we didn't."

"It's a shame." She leaned back and stared out the window. "I really think we could have changed each other's lives."

I glanced out the window in an attempt to see what she was focused on.

"Don't you think?" she asked.

"I'm pretty sure we changed each other's lives. If things hadn't gone down the way they did, you wouldn't have ended up in the program. I probably wouldn't have turned the corner I did, either."

The events of those two weeks set me on a path of darkness. It took years, and the grace of a young child named Mandy, to set me right again.

Reese leaned forward in her chair, elbows wide on the table, one hand supporting her head. "Tell me about what you've been doing."

"Not much worth talking about. Working for the highest bidder. Tons of collateral damage. Far too many friends lost and gone."

"They died?"

"Some." I wiped the plate with the tip of my finger, scraping off the remaining cheese. "Others are out of my life either by choice or necessity."

She held my gaze for a long second. "I miss my life back home. The sights and smells and action of the city."

I said nothing. There were times I missed it, too. Rather, I missed certain people who'd I always associate with my time in New York. Coincidentally, Reese was one of them, even though I'd known her for a few short weeks.

"Where will you go after here?" she said.

I shrugged, not sure if I wanted to talk about it. There was too much left to do in Texline.

"Just gonna drift some more?" she asked. "Solve the problems of one little town after another?"

I wiped my face with a napkin, smiled at her. "You make me sound like some hero in a book series. I'm not that good of a guy, Reese. If I've got nothing invested in a place, I couldn't care less what happens there."

"You don't have anything invested here." She bit her bottom lip.

"I've got you. I've got Herbie and Ingrid, and they're dead because of me."

"You don't know that to be true."

"You don't know that to be false."

"So...you still haven't said what's next."

"Mia," I said. "I'm gonna track down my brother and find my daughter and we're gonna leave and sail until we're on a nearly-deserted island tourists rarely visit. We'll create a life there. One that not a damn soul knows of. I won't be tracked down and coerced into a job. I won't be found by anyone. We'll just live."

"That sounds kinda nice," she said. "Maybe a little boring, but the right kind of boring."

"Then leave the program and come with me."

"Right now?"

"Why not?"

"We'd have trouble getting out of the country, don't you think?"

I laughed. "That's the least difficult part of all this."

"What's the most difficult part?"

"Getting used to the fact that you make a better burger than I do."

She stood, walked around the table, stopped in front of me. Her knees pressed into my thighs. She ran her hands through my hair, over my shoulders, down my back.

"Come on, Jack. Let's take care of those wounds."

35

CRYSTAL RIVER, FLORIDA, 1988

JACK CLUTCHED THE COMFORTER ON HIS BED IN AN ATTEMPT to pull himself up off the floor. His legs were wobbly, weak. He looked back and saw the guy unbuttoning his pants. The man looked down at him and laughed.

Jack summoned his focus and lunged up and forward onto the bed. He clawed his way toward the headboard.

"Saving me time," the guy said. "Appreciate that. But don't think it's gonna earn you any favors. The ending ain't gonna change. You're nothing more than one of those whores or kids from over there."

Jack faked a sob, forced his body to convulse. The performance earned a laugh from the man. Perhaps it eased the guy into false sense of dominance, thinking this would go easier than he could have imagined.

The bed near Jack's feet dipped. The guy kneeled at the edge. He felt the guy's hand on his leg, gripping and digging into his flesh. He forced another fake sob, all while sliding his hand underneath the mattress. The hilt felt cold at first touch. Jack worked his hand in further, cutting his finger on the blade and grunting in pain as he did so. The guy punched him in the back. Jack grunted again.

He had the knife in his grasp and pulled his hand free from the mattress as the guy pulled him toward the middle of the bed. Jack resisted the urge to swing frantically. No, if the man knocked the knife free, it'd be over. There wouldn't be a second chance. So Jack waited.

The guy grabbed and tugged on Jack's shirt, lifting his torso off the bed until the shirt gave way and ripped. He wasn't sure how much more he could take. Those tinges of panic surfaced. The voices of his family battled it, keeping it at bay. The man wrapped his hand around Jack's shoulder. He felt the guy's weight lift.

It was time.

Jack inhaled quickly and deeply. He pushed himself down into the mattress, then exploded up and around, swinging his arm in a controlled arc. The knife cut through the man as if he were made of butter. It penetrated his abdomen to the hilt. Jack twisted and turned and spun the knife clockwise, counterclockwise. Blood sprayed from the wound, warm across Jack's bare torso.

The guy stared down, eyes wide, mouth hanging open. A hollow scream turned into a high pitched grunt.

Jack pulled the knife free and struck again, this time aiming for center mass. It plunged in deep. And again Jack twisted and pulled the handle side to side. The man swung weakly at Jack's head. Jack returned the blows, landing a right cross on the man's chin, causing him to collapse forward.

The full weight of the guy smothered Jack. Unconscious, the man was like a massive paperweight. Jack squirmed underneath, working toward the edge of the bed. He managed to dump the guy over the side. The guy groaned after hitting the floor. He wasn't dead, but it couldn't be long judging by the amount of blood that covered Jack and the bed.

He hopped over the man, then spun and delivered a running kick to the guy's temple. He had to make it to his father's room. His dad kept a pistol in there, although the hiding spot changed every so often. But it would be in there somewhere. And it would be loaded.

36

THE SUN HAD SET, CASTING REESE'S BEDROOM INTO SHADOWS. She had countered by lighting an oil lamp. The sheets rose and fell with her relaxed breathing. It felt good to be at rest, and it might be my last chance for a while. Unless Vernon showed up with an arrest warrant and locked me up again. The chances of that seemed slim at the moment. Several hours had passed, and we hadn't heard from him. My mind slipped into overdrive, and I wondered where they were in the investigation. Had they caught the guy?

Perhaps sensing my shift toward anxiety, Reese rolled over and placed her hand on my chest. She smiled at me as her fingers worked up and down my sternum.

"What?" I said.

"Let's do it," she said.

"Again?"

She smiled. "Not that. Let's go to that island."

"All right. Gotta find Mia first, though."

It had been a while since I'd reached out to Sean. It might not be a bad idea to do so in light of recent events. The plan had been for me to disappear for a while, let things settle down. But now that Darrow had opened up an agency backdoor channel, and brought my name to light, someone was bound to start digging. And if that someone was Frank Skinner, I might never make it home again.

Wherever home was.

"Reese?"

"Yeah?"

"Tell me about Darrow."

She propped up on one elbow. "What do you want to know?"

I rolled to my side and mirrored her. "Why did he blow your cover?"

"He didn't."

"But he knows who you are, what you did, and that you're in the program."

"Yes, and that's because he vets every person that comes into this town."

"He's got some solid contacts. Figured out who I was."

She didn't look surprised. "I don't doubt it."

"What's he into?"

"He's got his hands in everything, really."

"Any legit stuff?"

"Some housing developments, though those aren't around here. Closer to Dallas. He owns a couple restaurants there, too. And a specialty grocery store, of all things."

"So why doesn't he live there if that's where his legal operations are located?"

"Because this small town offers him no opposition. He couldn't go someplace like Dallas and operate like that. Think about it. The police, FBI, CIA, DEA, who knows what other acronyms, they'd be all over him there."

"So not everything is above water then."

She exhaled and closed her eyes. "You already know that."

"I do, obviously. But I haven't been able to pinpoint exactly what it is."

She rolled over onto her back, letting her chin fall toward me. "Take a guess, Jack."

"Drugs."

"Of course."

"Illegal immigrants."

"Yup."

"Guns."

Reese started to answer, but hesitated. Her eyes narrowed as her gaze traveled toward the ceiling.

"Is that a yes?" I asked.

"It's a not quite," she replied.

"Not quite guns. Simple enough, I guess."

"Right."

"Knives?"

She laughed. "Come on, Jack."

"Arms in general, then. He's moving heavy stuff through here. Well, not quite here, but close. Got a nice private location where buyers can come to purchase automatic weapons, heavy artillery, explosives, and the like."

"You didn't hear it from me."

"So he figures out you're a cop, someone who could disrupt his operations, and he just lets you live?"

"Well, there's a reason he figured out I was a cop. See, the file the FBI put together was solid. His first go around, all he knew was what they said about me."

"OK. So, what's the reason?"

"I started snooping around. I knew his guys—Linus and the others—were bad dudes. They had crap jobs, and no prospects, yet they all had nice stuff. Their wives and kids didn't dress like they were poor. These guys walked around like they owned the town.

And the locals were scared of them. Well, most, anyway. A few, like Ingrid and Herbie, stood up to them. Anyway, it didn't take long to track them to Darrow. I started watching him. All it took was one anonymous phone call on my part, and he nailed me. His contact scratched below the surface and uncovered my life history."

"And yet he let you live."

"He did," she said. "He's not a total asshole, I guess."

"In all these years, why haven't you ever gone to anyone? Notified the FBI?"

"Darrow has clients around the world. He doesn't care who they are, or what they do. These people aren't boy scouts. You've fought people like this for years."

"The terrorists," I said.

She nodded. "Yeah, he knows them. And he told me he'd give me up to them if I crossed him. The line was already cast. That's what he told me. If something happened to him, the hook would be set."

That explained the secrecy, and why Reese had been reluctant to do anything. Of all places, the program had set her up in a town where everything could be unraveled.

"He had me brought out to some deserted area," I said. "They beat me, dragged me out there. Had me walk a half-mile to a little cabin to meet with him. And when I got back to town, I was arrested. Linus drove me right up to the cops. They were waiting in the middle of town. Guess they figured I'd bail out of the truck if we went to the police station."

Reese nodded, said nothing.

"Darrow had me arrested. I mean, you saw how happy Vernon was to cut me loose, right?"

She continued nodding.

"Darrow's not gonna like the fact that I'm free," I said. "He knows who I am, and what I've done, and what I can do. Once he learns I'm on the outside, all bets will be off. He'll come after me with everything he's got."

"He probably will."

"You've got to get ahold of your bureau contact, Reese. Get them to move you."

"Why?"

"You're life's in danger."

"So's yours."

"I can handle it."

"So can I." She rolled over and stood, wrapping the sheet around her chest and waist. "Let's just go, Jack."

I was tempted by the thought of leaving right that moment. What was the point of staying? I owed no living soul in the town a damn thing.

But I couldn't go. Not yet.

"I have to know," I said.

"Know what?" she said.

"Who did it. Who killed Ingrid and Herbie. And I have to hear *why* they did it. Maybe we can trace it back to Darrow."

"And if we can? Then what, Jack? You want to take him down?"

"Yes, I do. And if not me, then I'll get the right people here who can do it."

"You know it's not that simple. You won't just bring this man down, not as heavily connected as he is. And there's a good chance that whoever you contact, they'll just pick up a phone and call him. Then what are you gonna do? We might be in some small town in Texas, but Darrow has a far reach. Now, if we just go, he probably won't care. And even if he did, is he going to spend resources to track us down? Hell, he'll likely be glad we're out of his hair. But if something were to happen to him any time soon, even if we're gone, he'll know who to pin it on. Look at how easily he got your name. How many people can do that?"

"Not many."

"Exactly. Yet he had it within a day or two. Don't you get it, Jack? Doesn't matter where we go. He'll find us if he wants to. So it's best that we don't give him a reason to track us down. And think about this for a moment, too. He might not decide to go after you, but rather someone you love."

I knew she was right. I had to swallow my anger and pride on this one. Only a week ago it would have been simple to do. Darrow who?

But the bastard had made it personal.

"So why don't you call your brother, find out about your little girl, and make a plan," she said.

"You can bet your ass I'm making a plan," I said.

She stood in the doorway, silhouetted by the kitchen light. "Why don't I like the sound of that?"

37

WE LAY LOW THE NEXT MORNING. I DROVE ALONE ACROSS THE state border to New Mexico, stopping at the first town with a drugstore. Reese stayed behind. I was surprised she let me use her car again, considering last time I drove it I abandoned it in town. Not totally my fault.

The phone I'd been using was compromised. It'd been out of my possession at the police station and couldn't be trusted. The store had two options. I went with the cheapest. It was a burner, anyway. Outside, I tossed the old phone in the trash before hopping back in the car.

I found a residential street a few blocks away. Drove down a quarter-mile, then pulled to the curb at an intersection. A couple kids sat on the front stoop of their house playing with toy cars and figures. Their voices rose and fell with the action in their game. Their mother was busy pruning a tree in the front yard. She stopped to stack the branches on the ground. Her gaze settled on the car for a second, then moved on.

Seemed a safe enough spot. I pulled out the phone, placed a

call to Sean's forwarding number. He answered after a couple rings.

"Jack?"

"Yeah, it's me."

"Was wondering when I'd hear from you. How're things?"

"About like you'd expect."

"In trouble again?"

"Pretty much. How's Mia?"

"She's doing well. Deb is great with her. Been keeping up with her studies so she doesn't fall too far behind."

"That's great. You guys stateside?"

"Nah, we're pretty well-hidden, like you wanted."

"Good. Probably smart to stay there for a while."

"That doesn't sound promising, Jack. I mean, at some point I have to return to my firm. Deb, the kids, we all have to return to our lives."

"I know, I know. Problem is I crossed paths with someone who knew Dad at one point, and he's got a thing for me now. He managed to get my name and history, all from a photo."

"Get the hell outta here. What's his name?"

"Darrow," I said. "At least that's what he goes by here. Ring a bell with you?"

"Can't say that it does. I'll check with Dad and see if he recalls anyone by that name."

"Good deal. I'm not holding my breath on it, but let me know how it goes next time I check in."

"Will do. You want me to get Mia?"

I paused for a moment. We hadn't spoken since I'd left her with Sean. And even though she hadn't been in my life long, I missed hearing that little voice. I even missed the fits she threw. From what Sean said, she seemed happy, and hearing from me might throw her off. Soon enough we'd be together. I had to rest on that.

"Not now," I said. "Give her a kiss for me, though."

"You got it, little brother."

"I'll check back in with you soon. Let you know how this turns out."

I remained parked at the corner for a few minutes after hanging up. As I watched the two boys on the stoop, I conjured up memories of myself and Sean when we were little playing like that. Back during the years when Molly was still with us, and before hormones and girls dominated our teenage lives.

The woman carried her shears up a ladder, but stopped half-way. She'd spotted me watching her kids. Probably pegged me for a deviant or something. It only took a few seconds for her to cross the yard.

"Can I help you?" she called out from the corner of her lot.

I shifted the car in gear and turned right, waving my phone as I drove by her. In the rearview I watched her pull out her cell and make a call. Cops, presumably. I wondered if she hadn't managed to get the license plate number. Wouldn't matter. Reese hadn't done anything wrong.

I continued through the next intersection, and then navigated to the main road. Five minutes later I had cleared town with nothing but open highway between me and Texline.

Or so I thought.

38

THE TRUCK APPEARED OUT OF NOWHERE. NO SQUEALING brakes. No blaring horn. Only the sickening crunch of metal on metal as they T-boned me on the passenger side. The car whipped clockwise into a spin. I turned into it and punched the gas. The maneuver allowed me to regain control, but the car was in no shape to go far.

The truck slammed into me again, head-on this time, ensuring that Reese's car wasn't getting out of there.

Linus glared at me from behind the wheel. Blood seeped from a wound on his forehead. He wiped it away with his sleeve. The guy in the passenger seat hopped out and disappeared from sight. I tried to locate him, but couldn't. Was he armed? Linus slammed his shoulder against his door, but it wouldn't open. He slid across the seat and went out the passenger side, dropping from my field of view.

Instincts took over and I ran. I darted out of Reese's car and hurdled the guardrail. Pain shot up my leg as I landed. I didn't stop. There was a rare group of trees dotting the landscape not too far off. That became my first goal. I had no idea what I'd do from there, though.

I glanced back, saw Linus holding a rifle. He peered through the scope, panning left to right, looking for me. Where was the other guy? Had he been injured? I looked around, still didn't see him.

I stopped there for a moment, dropping to the ground in a spot where the land dipped. Not the best cover, but it'd do.

An eighteen-wheeler sounded its horn as it drove past. Taillights burned red and tires squealed. The semi careened onto the shoulder, coming to a stop a couple hundred feet down the road. The man who stepped out looked to be mid-forties and in decent shape. He had his cell phone to his ear, presumably reporting an accident to the highway patrol.

Perfect.

Linus took note of the guy. He backtracked to the pickup truck and tucked away his rifle. No one was watching me now. I jumped up and made a break for the woods. They were only a couple hundred feet away. My ankle ached with every stride. As I reached the trees, I looked back and saw Linus occupied with the truck driver. His friend had reappeared, however, and was lumbering across the landscape toward me. It looked like he was injured.

The woods consisted of a group of trees that were perfectly lined up in rows. Someone's pet project, I supposed. I cleared the first row, and took position behind a thick trunk in the second row. It did a horrible job of hiding me, so I crept back, deeper into the shade. By the time the other guy reached the area, he was bent over, heaving, out of breath. He looked up, gaze darting east to west. He glossed over my position without noticing I was there.

The guy straightened up, looked back toward Linus. The truck driver had his hand on Linus's shoulder. He gestured with his hand to the guardrail. Perhaps Linus had taken more of a beating from the accident than he realized. I know I had. Or I'd at least re-aggravated the injuries from the beating I'd taken from Linus and his guys. Pain tore through my right shoulder, down to my knee. The longer I remained still, the more intense the feeling grew.

I dashed six feet to another tree, one with a thicker trunk. I stopped there and checked in on the other guy. He leaned against a tree with his back to me. He was still watching Linus's interaction with the trucker. I needed him to take a step back, out of the open. I couldn't risk being spotted by Linus or the truck driver. Or someone else. There were bound to be more coming. And judging by the barren landscape behind me, I had nowhere else to hide.

I had to get ahold of Reese. I reached into my pocket, but my cell phone was gone. I traced my path through the woods. I wasn't even sure that I'd brought it with me. It might still be sitting in the console. Or maybe it'd been tossed around during the accident.

Dammit.

I had no way of reaching out. That meant I had to move.

There was another option. The guy who'd followed me out had his phone clipped to his waistband. It'd do in a pinch. I picked a stick up and tossed it to the left. I quickly ducked behind the tree and waited.

I heard the guy shuffle backward. He took each step slowly and deliberately. His labored breathing grew closer, louder, raspier. He grabbed the tree where I hid. His fingers wrapped around to my side. I stepped right as he went left, matching each step in tune with his so we rustled the ground at the same time until I'd come up behind him. I stood in a wake of foul body odor. Had the guy bothered to shower this week? Temperatures in the low nineties didn't help his cause.

He stopped and straightened up. I stood no more than three feet from him. I could make a move, but I wasn't in the best position. There'd be a chance he would be able to fight back. In this environment, that would be bad. All he had to do was knock me

down and then run out of the woods yelling. They'd have me
pinned in. Or I'd have to resort to running out in the open on a
wide expanse where they'd never lose sight of me.

He turned his head to the right a few inches. Soon he'd detect
me in his peripheral vision. I had no time left to wait.

I landed a near-perfect strike. A punch to the soft flesh underneath the rear corner of the jaw was enough drop most men. From
there I could finish him off.

He moved before my fist landed. I caught his earlobe and
grazed off his cheekbone and nose. Enough to make him grunt, but
not take him down.

Worse, I had braced myself for the impact and my recovery.
Problem now was the momentum carried me forward, and I stumbled over his right leg.

The guy jumped on me. Instinct, I guess.

I managed to get my knee up before he hit. His gut landed
square on it. His mouth twisted open, gasping with a sound like air
escaping from a balloon. I grabbed his shirt near the neck with my
left hand. Threw a cross with my right. Then I landed a second
and a third punch. Blood dripped onto me from his mouth and
nose, but he didn't budge. I tried rolling out from under him. He
countered by shifting his weight. He landed a couple rabbit
punches to my right side. Pain rippled through my abdomen.

He lifted his head and called out. Four of his teeth were gone.
I guess he tried to say Linus, but the words were more of a mashup of moaning and gargling.

I shoved both hands into his face, thumbs against his eyes,
palms pressing hard against his mouth and nose. His muffled
scream sent a stream of blood spilling out of his mouth. The sky
darkened as his hand covered my face. Nails dug into my flesh. He
worked his mitt down to my neck. I pressed harder into his orbital
sockets, felt one eye start to give. He tightened his grip on my
throat.

I forced a hollow yell.

He screamed.

I managed to slide my body enough to shift his weight off my core. Then I whipped my knee into his groin. He started to fall to the side, and his grip around my windpipe loosened. I released my right hand from his face, jabbed his throat, striking the area under his Adam's apple. He didn't budge. I struck again, then aimed for his solar plexus. Fire radiated from my wrist. Hell with it. A broken hand would heal. Death was permanent.

His arms went limp and his upper body fell. I pushed him off of me and rolled over. Shouts came from the highway. I scampered to my knees and used a tree to pull myself up. Linus and the truck driver were walking toward us. It didn't appear to be a mercy mission. The truck driver carried a shotgun.

"Son of a bitch," I muttered. He was one of them.

The guy on the ground stirred. I took a running start and kicked him in the gut. Wouldn't knock him out, but it'd keep him down for a few minutes while I took off. I reached for his cellphone, but at some point during the scuffle, it had become dislodged and was nowhere to be found.

I exited the woods in the back, scanned the terrain. It turned out to be less wide open than I'd thought. I had a chance here.

Straight ahead I saw nothing but dirt. To the right were a fence, some cattle, and a building beyond that. It appeared my best chance lay to the left. A cropping of buildings stood there. A house, maybe. Could've been two. And at least three garages or sheds. Maybe I'd find something there. If anything, the cover would buy me more time.

I sprinted toward the structures, hoping I was moving sight unseen.

Judging by the shotgun blast, I wasn't.

39

CRYSTAL RIVER, FLORIDA, 1988

JACK MADE HIS WAY DOWN THE DARKENED HALLWAY. THE
house was eerily quiet. What was going on outside? He felt pulled
toward the stairs as he thought of Sean and Molly. Had they found
his sister? If so, had they done to her what that asshole in the
bedroom attempted to do to him? Could they all be that crazy?

Stay calm, he told himself. He had a mission, and he had to
complete it before he could help his sister.

He entered his parents' dark room. Figured it was best to leave
it that way so he didn't draw any attention from outside. Jack
moved with his left hand on the wall. It smelled of a mix of his
father's cologne and his mother's perfume. He continued toward
the source, knowing that his father's nightstand was one of the
hiding places.

He opened the drawers one by one and searched, being careful
not to disturb the contents too much. Last thing he wanted at this
point was to be disciplined for going through their things. Being
the son of an Army officer made such things relevant no matter
what situation he faced. He made it to the last drawer, but didn't

find the pistol. Next he moved to the closet, feeling around in the dark for the shoeboxes where he'd seen his dad stash the handgun before. Again, no luck. Did that mean it wasn't in there, or had he just been unlucky and missed it?

A cool breeze coated him as he exited the closet. He stopped by the window to listen to silence. The air carried a hint of the Gulf. Salt and fish. He thought of their plans for the next day. A day of fishing that might never happen again. His gut tightened, and he forced the thoughts out of his head. Focus on the mission, he told himself.

Jack dropped to the floor and crawled under his parents' bed, sweeping his right arm across the carpet in search of anything. But the floor was barren. There was only one place left to search. He rolled out from under the bed, stopping in front of his father's nightstand. As he reached for the handle, he recalled that the man in the other room had held a pistol to his head at one point.

"Dammit," he muttered under his breath. Why hadn't he thought to pick that up? He made a note to retrieve it, so when he found Sean, they'd both be armed.

Jack pulled the nightstand door open. Musty air escaped. He reached in, felt along the top shelf, then the bottom. His hand collided with a box. Heard the sound of rattling ammunition. He skipped over the box and his hand came to rest on the butt of the pistol.

A sigh of relief slipped out and his body went limp for a moment as he recaptured his breath and steeled himself for the next step.

But that step would be delayed.

Perhaps permanently.

Hands dug into his calves and pulled him to the carpet.

And Jack lost his grip on the pistol.

40

I'd been shot multiple times. More than I liked to remember, in fact. There were scars on my body that looked like I'd been run through a cheese grater. On one of those attempts on my life, I had faced the business end of a shotgun in the humid Louisiana swamps. The assailant had been over a hundred yards out. Buckshot hit like molten hail on my lower back and right hip. If he had chambered a slug, I would have lost a kidney. I'd gone down, landing halfway in the water, attracting a nearby gator. The guy had advanced half the distance as I scrambled out of the mud. I saw him stop, raise his weapon, aim at me. I couldn't move fast enough. At less than fifty yards out, the buckshot could be lethal. Fortunately, my old partner Bear had arrived and ensured there would be no second shot.

Sprinting across an open expanse toward a cluster of buildings, the gunshot was the last thing I wanted to hear. The blast echoed throughout the area. How close were they? I anticipated the pain of the bullet tearing through me. It never came. A second shot did. A dozen fire ants dug into my right hamstring. I yelled out as I tripped over a shrub and toppled to the ground. I grabbed the back of my leg, then brought my hand around out of morbid curiosity, knowing that acknowledging the wound would triple the pain. But there were only traces of crimson on the tips of my fingers. I twisted to get a look at my leg. There were several small welts, and they were barely bleeding. Must've been birdshot.

Twenty-plus-year-old instincts kicked in and I planted my hand on the ground. My legs started grinding. I was seventeen again and nothing was stopping me from getting into the end zone.

The first building stood ten feet away.

Even though I had trouble regaining my balance, I managed to keep my feet churning. My right hand acted like a third leg, planting frequently to keep me from face planting. Those last thirty feet might as well have been thirty miles. Another volley of buckshot headed my way. It slammed into aluminum siding, leaving behind tiny holes.

"Just stay put, Jack," Linus called out.

Yeah, that's happening, I thought.

I leaned against the garage door for a moment to catch my breath. The men were closing in. There was no way I could remain stationary for long. Linus would be there soon. The trucker, too. Why the hell was the guy helping them? Perhaps he was sympathetic to Darrow's cause. Hell, maybe he was on his payroll. I wondered if the call to the cops had gone through. Didn't matter. They wouldn't be on my side either.

I scraped a couple years' worth of grime off the garage window with my palm and peered inside. Dim light left the identity of the contents in question. Nothing stood out as helpful, so I decided to move on.

I bent over, sucked in a deep, warm breath. Then I sprinted, ignoring the burning in my hamstring. The next two buildings were offset from one another. Made it a good place to hide. As I sprinted, I anticipated another shotgun blast. It never came. The buildings offered me a shield of sorts. I was out of sight. The men approached cautiously now. They might even be waiting for backup. Either way, their delay bought me time I desperately needed.

With the sun at my back, I had a better view of the second garage as I peered through a window that had considerably less dirt than the first. Aside from a few pieces of lawn equipment, which might prove helpful, a blue tarp covered everything else.

What did it cover? The contents appeared too small to be a car. Still, could it be some sort of transportation?

It could be, but considering the other items, I was more likely to find a lawn tractor than an old Corvette in there.

I turned and attempted to scope out the third garage. The lighting conditions were worse than the first. I noted a second window on the other side, and decided to go in and investigate since I had a means of egress if things got dicey. I took off my shirt, wrapped it around my elbow and drove it through the window. Glass shattered and splintered. If there was any doubt as to my position, the noise cleared it up.

"The hell was that?" someone said. I assumed it was the trucker since the voice wasn't as southern-sounding as Linus's.

"Something broke," Linus called back.

"No, stay back," the trucker said. "He can't hide in there forever. We got a better chance out in the open."

They sure as hell did. I wished one would try to take me in the narrow alley between the two garages. I had the advantage in a confined space.

I cleared out the rest of the jagged glass, and stuck my head through the hole. Dust danced in scattered rays of light. The garage smelled old, but dry. A thick layer of dirt coated some items. I climbed inside. A remaining shard of glass sliced my skin. I didn't bother to check how deep. The wound didn't inhibit my movement and that was all that mattered.

A set of wrenches lined with greasy fingerprints were spread out on a workbench. The largest was a touch shorter and lighter than a pipe wrench. I grabbed it. It'd do the trick if I met up with Linus or the truck driver. There wasn't much else left in the place. Some old containers full of used motor oil. A couple gas cans. A rusted chainsaw that looked as though the chain would disintegrate if I tried to use it. I found an axe hanging on the wall, but left it in favor of a dull machete. If anything it'd guarantee an infected wound for anyone standing in my way.

I glanced down at myself. My chest and stomach were coated in blood. Only some of it had seeped out of me. I held a large wrench in one hand, a machete in the other. I stood in a dusty old garage waiting for an attack. One thought ran through my head.

When the hell did I enter the zombie apocalypse?

I was prepared to do whatever it took to live through this situation. I had doubts I'd make it, though. The men were armed, carrying at least one shotgun. I knew there'd be more, too. They'd likely contacted Darrow, who would have a team headed out. I had two hopes. One, that the highway patrol would respond to the accident soon, before Darrow's men arrived.

The other was that I'd find some sort of transportation. Not happening in this garage, though.

I moved to the broken window and listened. Nothing. But that didn't mean someone wasn't around. I rose and peered through the opening. Nobody there. I stuck my head out. The alley was clear.

I climbed through the opening, machete in hand. Once out, I slammed the hilt into the window of the other garage.

"Come on, man," Linus said. "We gotta see what he's doing."

"Just wait," the truck driver called. "Reinforcements are gonna be here in less than ten minutes. We can see everything from here. He ain't going nowhere."

"Let's just end this!"

"God dammit," the guy said. "You told me who y'all think this guy is. You really want to take him on with just us two? Don't you think the odds of survival are greater if we've got more people here?"

"Pussy," Linus spat. "All right. We do this your way. But if he gets away, you answer to Darrow, not me."

The truck driver laughed. "He ain't getting away."

Keep thinking that.

I climbed through the window, landing hard on the blue tarp. I didn't have much choice in the matter. It covered the entire area under the window, and I figured with a riding mower underneath it was as solid a spot to fall on as I could get.

I was wrong.

Whatever was underneath toppled over and I went with it. My left arm caught and bent unnaturally at the elbow. I fought to keep in a pained scream. I glanced down, fearing I'd bent my arm backward. Everything looked normal. I tested the joint, flexed and tightened the muscles a couple times. Pain flared, but it didn't seem to hinder movement.

I got to my feet and peeled back the tarp.

"Son of a bitch."

I had a way out.

41

THE TWO DIRT BIKES LOOKED LIKE THEY WERE PROBABLY built back in the seventies. Didn't matter, though. Someone had taken care of them, at least for a while. Some of the parts were newer and didn't show a lot of wear. Other parts were rusted or broken. Nothing that would hinder performance, though. I pulled one bike off the other. The top one had an 80cc 2-cycle engine. I might get fifty miles per hour out of that. The bottom one had a 125cc 2-cycle engine, which, if I was lucky, would hit seventy miles per hour, maybe more. Considering the terrain behind the garages, it really didn't matter. I just had to get moving. Only problem was the door opened out to the center of the compound, where I figured Linus and the truck driver were waiting.

Soon there'd be even more men. Locked and loaded, they'd be ready to take me down. I had a feeling my chances of surviving an encounter alive were zero if Darrow had his way.

Knowing I had to make a move, I pulled the 125cc bike up and tried to start it.

Nothing.

"Come on, don't strand me here."

Tried again. Still nothing.

I set that one against the wall and picked up the smaller bike. It had a full tank of gas and what appeared to be fresh oil. Had someone taken it out recently? The engine turned, but didn't catch. I waited a few seconds, and holding my breath, tried again. It started. Now I had to get out.

If the men heard the small engine rev to life, they made no mention of it. Nor was there reason for them to. I pictured them positioned in front of the garage, shotguns aimed chest-high, ready to open fire the moment the door cleared the opening. I glanced back at the window and considered going out to scout the area. Perhaps the cops had showed up at the crash, and the men returned to straighten things out. The little I knew about Darrow told me he might have pull with the local state police, too. All Linus had to do was make things right by them.

Once again I leaned up against the wall by the window. I remained there for a few seconds, listening. Heard nothing. I poked my head out. Saw nothing. I climbed out, dropped to the ground, and then crawled forward until I had most of the clearing in view. The men weren't in sight. Didn't mean they weren't there, though. Linus had dealt with me enough to know his best option was to take cover and attack from there. I got up and backtracked, went to the rear of the garage, eased around the corner so I could see the highway.

Strobe lights flashed and uniformed personnel wandered the crash site. It wasn't the cops, though. An ambulance and fire truck had arrived.

I still hadn't located Linus and the truck driver. Were they up on the highway, out of sight? Had they gone to get help for Linus's partner? He'd probably managed to stumble out of the woods by this point. Unfortunately, the cropping of trees blocked a stretch of the highway, so I couldn't be sure. But if that's where Linus and the truck driver were, I had a solid chance of getting away.

I returned to the window, started to climb back in, but a thought gave me pause. I needed a distraction. I recalled the gas tanks and oil containers in the other garage. I went into the shed, gathered some supplies, then returned to the bike.

Every second that passed was either a second closer to my escape or death. I had to get out now.

A couple latches on each side secured the garage door. They gave with a bit of resistance, grinding against the metal railing. I stopped, stood back against the wall, listening for movement outside. There was none.

The men weren't inclined to do anything with emergency services on the highway. They weren't the kind of men to give up, either. I was sure they were monitoring the area and were ready to move. Hell, for all I knew, the reinforcements were already there and had surrounded the compound.

I started the bike, then lifted the door a foot and dropped to the ground. The area in front remained deserted. All I needed to do was pass the corner of the building. After that I would be out of range in less than ten seconds, perhaps more if I had to use some evasive maneuvering.

I got to my feet and lifted the door high enough to squeeze through. The bike rolled forward with ease. I had one hand on the handlebar. The other carried my planned distraction, a mix of gas and oil in a container. Some fertilizer thrown in for good measure. I'd dipped a rag in oil to use as a wick. Now I just needed a spark to set it off.

I used an axe on the concrete. It took a couple swings, but the rag caught a spark and slowly burned down. I placed the concoction in the garage and piled anything flammable around it.

"Over there," someone shouted.

A round ricocheted off the siding. A second hit the wall behind me. Sunlight beamed through the newly formed hole.

Dammit.

I'd spent too long setting up my distraction when I should have just gotten the hell out of there.

I shifted the bike in gear and took off. The voices called out from the right, my planned route. Going left would put me in full view of the highway where everyone could spot me. It was a chance I had to take. Emergency personnel had taken cover at the sounds of gunshots. They'd go into full lockdown mode until the police arrived.

Linus emerged from the woods unarmed, a cell phone pressed to his face. On the line with Darrow, I presumed. The truck driver was close behind, running with his shotgun across his body. He halted, lifted the shotgun and aimed at me. Linus called out to him to hold his fire.

An old Toyota pickup truck the color of Georgia clay bounded across the expanse coming around the right of the woods. It stopped to let Linus and the trucker climb into the bed. Stacks of dirt and dust rose as the truck peeled away, headed toward me.

42

I DUG IN AND SPUN THE BIKE TOWARD THE EXPANSE AWAY from the highway. I figured if I travelled out five to ten miles using the landscape to my advantage I was bound to come across a road at some point. The bike outmaneuvered the Toyota. They'd have to account for the terrain. Might break an axle if they took on a hill or dip too aggressively. I had to create as much distance as possible, because once we were on asphalt, they could easily top one hundred miles per hour, while I was capped at about fifty.

I pushed full throttle, resisting the urge to look back for the first minute. When I finally tossed a glance over my shoulder, I saw tall piles of dirt heading the same direction. The pickup lingered at the bottom, too far back to make out shapes in the cab.

The explosion rocked the area. The thunderous roar nearly threw me off the bike. A massive fireball rose at least fifty feet in the air, and a plume of black smoke higher than that. What the hell had been in that shed? It was sheer luck that the Toyota was about even with the compound when it blew. They turned hard to the right, sped away from the fire, and from me. For all they knew, there might be a string of explosives set to go off one by one. It bought me time, and I needed every second I could get.

I pushed the bike hard for several minutes, frequently checking behind me. The truck had started toward me again. It appeared they were traveling faster than I had expected. They risked a breakdown. Guess the reward of running me over was worth it. I continued to monitor their location. Every time I looked back, they had gained on me. I had to adjust my strategy.

The terrain looked dodgier a half-mile ahead to the northwest. I changed course in that direction. The welcomed dunes rose and fell like a motionless sea. They would provide the obstacle I needed. And just in time, too. The truck had pulled within a thousand feet of me.

I wove over and through the mounds of dirt, maintaining about forty miles an hour. One misstep and I was done. The truck had tried to follow, but the terrain was packed too tight. They'd breach if they attempted to cross. So they raced along the perimeter, due west. They lost ground with each passing second. Every so often, a shotgun blast rang out, but they were too far away.

Eventually the Toyota's engine faded. I slowed to a stop and scanned the horizon. They were nowhere to be seen. Had they gone back? Would they split up into two or three groups? These guys knew the area well enough that they'd have a good idea of where I'd end up, and could potentially beat me there.

I reconsidered my plan. I had to warn Reese. Linus had come after me while I was driving Reese's car. She could have been with me and they wouldn't have cared. My chances of getting to her back in town were slim. Darrow surely had her under surveillance by now. She was in the same position as me, unable to trust anyone, not even the folks she believed in.

With no phone, my best option was to reach the highway on

the other side of the New Mexico town. I could enter from the west, find a phone, and call Reese.

I pushed forward on an altered path. Things would end badly if I was wrong and the truck had maintained its westward trajectory instead of heading back to the crash site like I presumed. Did they care about taking me down? Or running me off? Did Darrow have any idea of how far I'd go? Exactly what I was capable of? How much was he able to learn about me?

The town rose into view. A thick haze surrounded the perimeter. I slowed down to about twenty miles per hour and circled behind, watching the streets as best I could, on the lookout for the Toyota.

I caught a whiff from a BBQ restaurant. My stomach knotted at the smell of smoked brisket. The sensation of hunger gave way to pain. My muscles ached. Ribs were on fire. I looked up at the chalk-ridden sky. Long thin clouds spanned east to west. I thought about following them clear through New Mexico. Escaping from everything. As long as I was gone, Darrow wouldn't care about me, and he'd leave Reese alone.

But that was a lie.

Plain and simple.

My clothes were covered in blood, and I looked every bit like a man who had been beaten and involved in an accident. It was best to lie low until sunset. I located a spot not too far from town to hide the bike. I wanted to have it available for my return to Texline. It was perfect for navigating the narrow alleys and unfenced yards.

I waited in a thicket of brush. Minutes and hours passed. The sky went from blue to orange to red to purple. Finally, the sun dipped below the town. Its final rays knifed through the creases between buildings.

I covered a quarter-mile on foot. The first residential street I came upon was deserted. Dim streetlights cast shadows of swaying tree branches. The evening air had cooled off considerably, stinging my wounds. I stuck to the sidewalk, headed to the center of town.

At the end of the street was a convenience store and gas station. Walter's. Not a name I'd ever heard. The pumps were empty. One parking spot was occupied by an early eighties blue Datsun with gold wheels. Hadn't seen one of those in years. Probably belonged to the kid behind the register. He didn't glance up when I entered. Probably for the better.

I ducked down an aisle, grabbing a box of bandages, a hat and an 'I heart TX' shirt, where the heart was actually a cutout of the state of Texas colored red. The bathrooms were tucked in between two beer coolers. I resisted the urge to snag a six-pack. Not like the kid would've noticed. I glanced back and saw him hovering over the counter, thumbs bouncing off a handheld gaming system.

The bathroom was dim and dirty and smelled like urine. But the door locked and the sink worked. I took off my shirt, tossed it in the trash. Cold water saturated a bundle of paper towels. I wiped my face, chest and arms down with them, peeling off layers of blood and dirt. Then I stuck my head in the sink, careful not to touch the stained porcelain, and rinsed out my hair. Pinkish water circled the drain, leaving behind a think residue of blood on the sink.

When I was done, I almost looked clean. A few of my wounds seeped fresh blood. I dabbed at them with fresh paper towels, then applied the bandages. Afterward I pulled on the shirt and jammed the hat on my head. Both were on the small side, but they'd do for now.

The kid hadn't moved the entire time. I walked up to him, asked if he had a phone I could use. He pointed over his shoulder at an old yellow phone mounted to the wall.

"Cost anything?"

He shook his head without looking up. "Just go ahead and use it, man."

I placed the cradle on my shoulder and dialed Reese's number.

And waited there while it rang a dozen times, unanswered.

43

CRYSTAL RIVER, FLORIDA, 1988

THE MAN SWUNG SEVERAL TIMES AT JACK'S HEAD. THE FIRST few blows landed before Jack managed to roll over and start deflecting the punches. The guy was weakened, that was obvious. The wounds hadn't killed him, yet.

Jack stared at the shadow in the darkness and estimated where he'd stabbed the guy a few minutes earlier. He threw a punch at the man's midsection. The blow was followed by a howl. Jack struck again. And again. Finally the man fell over, releasing enough of his weight that Jack was able to scoot back out from under the guy.

Jack kept calm and felt along the floor until he located the pistol.

The man stopped groaning and let out a yell.

"I'm gonna kill you, boy."

Jack grasped the pistol around the barrel. It would have been easier to shoot the guy, but that would draw everyone inside. He wouldn't stand a chance against four or five armed men. He could take one down, maybe two if they attacked separately, but his luck would eventually run out. So he held the pistol like he had held the rocks earlier, ready to strike.

The man let out another loud grunt. Jack pushed up to his knees, spun around. The guy weakly threw his arms up. Was he going to strike? Go for Jack's neck? Jack didn't know, didn't care, didn't focus on it. He dropped his right arm and then whipped it up and around. The pistol collided with the guy's nose with a heavy thud.

The man rocked back on his shins. As he rolled forward, Jack struck again, this time landing a blow to the man's cheek and eye. He pulled back and delivered another strike, landing it on the guy's temple. The man collapsed to the side.

Jack had left the guy for dead once. He wouldn't make that mistake again. He shoved the guy forward until the man was on his stomach. Jack positioned himself behind and threaded his left arm around the guy's neck. He hooked his left hand into the crook of his right elbow and squeezed it all inward. The unconscious man put up no resistance. After a few seconds, the guy's body convulsed, and eventually shut down. The weight of the moment pressed hard on Jack as he stared at the fresh corpse.

It didn't last long.

Jack felt no remorse.

44

REESE PACED THE SMALL AREA BETWEEN THE KITCHEN TABLE and the couch. Three steps there, four back. Alternating, over and over. She'd wear a hole in the carpet by the time this was over. She knew it.

It'd been all day. Where the hell had he gone? Had they got to him? Had he taken her car and split? It'd been years since she'd first met Jack. She was sure he'd changed over time, but she couldn't imagine him stealing her car and running out on her.

"Where are you?" she muttered while searching through her fridge for the twentieth time as though someone had come in and snuck something new in there.

Her bladder ached. It always did when she was nervous. She didn't want to miss a call because she had answered nature's call, so she held out as long as she could.

She occupied herself in any way possible. A magazine. The weather on TV. But nothing held her interest for more than a minute or two. She stood in front of the window, straining to see approaching headlights that never appeared amid the fading sunset.

There weren't many people left in Texline she could trust. At this point, even those few remaining had given her reason for pause. So she decided against reaching out to Vernon just yet. Sure, he'd released Jack from jail, but he had also arranged to detain him. On Darrow's orders, nonetheless. Certainly wasn't because they had cause to believe Jack was involved in the murder of Ingrid and Herbie.

The heavy rap on the door nearly caused Reese to drop the glass in her hand. She patted her hand over her racing heart, set the drink down and descended the stairs, pausing in front of the door. A brown hat was all she could make out through the small window. She pulled the door open and stared at the state trooper. In her heart she knew he was there to deliver bad news.

"Roberta Weddle?" he said.

She bit her lip, nodded, said nothing.

"Ma'am, do you own a seventies Dodge Challenger?"

"Yessir," she said. Her bottom lip ached where her top teeth had dug into it.

"Your vehicle was involved in a hit and run collision. We know you weren't at the scene. Did you loan your car to anyone?"

She shook her head.

"Are you aware that your car was taken out today? Do you have any idea who might've been driving it?"

"Who was in the other car?" she asked.

He was taken aback, likely wondering why she asked about the other driver. "I'm afraid I can't give that information out."

Nodding, Reese said, "I know who was driving. My cousin. Is he hurt?"

"He's the party that ran. Both ran, actually."

Reese said nothing. There was no point in telling the man that Jack ran because someone was trying to kill him.

"Do you have a way of getting ahold of your cousin?" the trooper asked.

"What about witnesses?" Reese asked, ignoring the question.

"Ma'am?"

"Someone had to have witnessed the accident, right? I mean, maybe the other car hit my cousin on purpose."

"Why would they do that?"

She'd screwed up by inviting a new line of questioning from the trooper.

"How bad is the damage?"

"Totaled, most likely."

"Christ."

"Back to your cousin, ma'am. We need to find him. It seems he just disappeared." He paused, narrowed his eyes, placed a hand on the door frame. "Your cousin, uh, he's not, uh, mentally challenged in any way, is he?"

Reese forced a smile. "That's debatable."

The trooper reached into his shirt pocket and pulled out a business card. "OK, well you call me the moment you hear from him. OK? And if you have any questions, don't hesitate to call."

She waited in the open doorway for the trooper to leave. He sat in his cruiser for a few minutes, door open, eyes cast downward. Entering something into his computer.

After the trooper pulled away, Reese went upstairs and placed a call.

"Vernon, it's Billie."

"What's going on?" he said. "You sound scared. Plus, you never call me."

"I need to talk." She paced between the table and couch. "Can you come over?"

45

I TRIED CALLING REESE SEVERAL TIMES, BUT NEVER GOT through. Did I have the number wrong? I'd written it down, but left it with the car. There was little chance of retrieving it any time soon.

"You gonna buy something, man?" the kid at the counter said. Apparently he'd grown tired of his game and wanted to harass me. "Hey, isn't that shirt and hat from here?"

"I haven't left yet. Gonna pay on my way out."

"Yeah, well, you better, man. Don't make me come over this counter for your ass."

I choked back a smile and burned through him with my stare. The steeled look on his face cracked. He backed off and turned away.

It was dark out now. That didn't stop me from pouring a stale cup of coffee. I grabbed a couple hot dogs, and two bottles of water. I scarfed down the dogs and chugged a bottle of water at the counter.

"Hat, shirt, 2 dogs, waters, and a cup of coffee," I said to the kid.

He rang it up. "$32.29."

"You gotta be kidding me."

He tossed his hands up in defense. "Hey, I don't set the prices, man."

I rolled my eyes, handed over two twenties. "You sell phones here?"

He nodded while counting my change.

"I'm gonna take one of those, too."

I grabbed my new phone and headed out of the store, moving into the shadows before anyone spotted me. The little town was sleepier than Texline.

How could it be the two towns existed ten miles or so apart with such small populations? Why didn't the original settlers of the area combine resources and build a town together? Wouldn't that have increased their chances of survival? I thought back to Herbie and his family. They had built the place with a couple other families. That's how it started, with families that had close ties and were reliant upon one another. They didn't want to grow too big, invite too many others into their group. That's when you lost control of things. Hell, I'd seen it with my own dealings. Things always went to hell when you added one person too many. They tipped the scales. You could only watch out for so many backs at once.

My muscles continued to stiffen. I wasn't sure I wanted to take another ride on the dirt bike, so I scanned the street for a car. I had considered that Darrow might have his men cruising the stretch between the towns, looking for me. Though I wanted to stick to asphalt, heading off-road was the better plan.

I spotted a motorcycle a couple blocks away. It was a custom piece, with neon green anywhere that wasn't chrome. Too flashy for my needs. A helmet with a six-inch faux-mohawk was set on the backseat. Since it was there, I figured the owner didn't mind if someone borrowed the helmet.

I cut through an alley that led to the outskirts of town and made my way back to the dirt bike. Each step cast me further into darkness. It got to the point I couldn't see a foot in front of me. I tapped a button on the side of the phone, cut the screen on, illuminated the path.

Ten minutes later I reached the bike. I swallowed a mouthful of lukewarm coffee, then tossed the rest. No big loss. The brew tasted like the grounds had been soaked in water along with two-week old gym socks.

I hopped on the bike, depressed the clutch and went to start it. Nothing happened. Tried again. Nothing.

"Come on, baby," I said. "Start for me."

Still nothing. Guess I'd lost my touch.

I'd checked the gas when I stopped. What was going on? Using the phone as a flashlight, I fiddled with the bike, but nothing helped.

"Son of a bitch."

In one direction I saw the town. The other three directions didn't provide a damn thing but darkness. I gave the bike one last chance. When it failed, I headed back to the store. Somewhere in that little town a car waited for me. I just had to find it.

I had to get back to Texline.

Back to Reese.

Before someone else beat me to her.

46

REESE STOOD IN FRONT OF HER BEDROOM WINDOW, STARING at the light-washed street beyond the edge of her driveway. Passersby were infrequent, and tonight was no different. Any vehicle that passed by would be suspect. There were none tonight from the time she hung up the phone to the moment Vernon's cruiser pulled into the driveway.

He emerged from the car, a bag in one hand, leash in the other. His Malamute, Dodge, stood at his side. Reese always found it odd that someone would sell the breed used for racing in the Alaskan Iditarod in such a hot climate. The poor thing seemed to be in the middle of heatstroke every time she saw him.

Reese hurried down the stairs, opened the door and waited for Vernon and Dodge. Vernon waved at her, and then glanced back over each shoulder in turn. Perhaps her tone during their brief conversation had left him worried. That had partly been her intention. She wanted to spur him into action.

"Mind if Dodge joins us inside?" he asked, smiling and extending the leash toward her.

She minded only because the dog shed uncontrollably and her vacuum cleaner would choke on the hair. But the assistance Vernon could provide outweighed the cleanup she'd have to perform later. Later no longer mattered if there was no Jack Noble to share it with.

Upstairs, Vernon seated himself at the table. Dodge bounded into her room, came back out with a bra.

"Dodge," Vernon said, laughing. "Go put that back."

Dodge disappeared again, returning this time with an empty mouth. He wormed his way between two chairs and lay down at Vernon's feet.

"Thanks for coming so quickly," Reese said.

"Sure thing," Vernon said. "What's this all about, Billie?"

She filled two glasses with tap water, set both on the table and took a seat next to him.

"A state trooper came by a while ago," she said.

"OK," he said.

"My car was involved in a supposed accident."

He rose quickly, knocking his chair back. "Are you OK? Let me look at you. Anything hurt?"

Reese leaned back and put her arms up. "I wasn't in the car, Vernon."

"It was stolen?"

She shook her head.

"Jack," he said dryly.

"Yes, he used it."

"Is he OK?"

"I don't know. I haven't heard from him. The trooper said it was a hit and run. Literally. Like, Jack ran and someone followed him."

"That's odd." Vernon returned to his seat, scratched the short stubble on his jaw. "Would he have a reason to run? Is he in trouble with the law?"

Reese shook her head. "Come on, Vernon. Everything that's happened here. Darrow. Jail. This was intentional."

"I suppose that's possible," he said slowly, obviously choosing his words to avoid saying too much.

Reese studied him for a moment. "I need you to look into it."

"I can try."

"No, don't just try. Reach out to your contacts and get me some damn answers. Christ, call Darrow himself and ask if he had anything to do with it."

Vernon leaned forward, large arms spread across the table. "Billie, I'm sure you can understand that Darrow isn't the kind of guy you just—"

She slapped the table with both palms, missing his forearm by an inch. It was close enough he pulled his hand back. The sound echoed around the small apartment. Dodge popped out of his hiding spot, ears perked, head cocked. He didn't know whether to play or attack. Vernon reached down and scratched him between the ears, settling the dog.

"Vernon," she said. "Please do something. Anything. Call whoever you can. If someone is after Jack, I need you to buy him time. Please. As a friend, do this for me."

He nodded without making eye contact, gaze fixed on the middle of the table. His face seemed to have paled, though it was hard to tell in the lighting. Was he holding back on her? Did he already know about the situation? Had she made things worse by bringing him over?

"Is everything OK with you?" she asked.

He took a deep breath, raised his head. His gaze swept past her and continued up to the ceiling. He opened his mouth to speak, but before he could get a word out, Reese's door banged opened.

"The hell?" she said, rising.

Vernon held out his hand and whispered, "Let me."

He secured Dodge's leash to the table, then stood. His raised shirt revealed a pistol. He reached for it, but it was too late.

A man Reese had never seen stood at the top of the stairs wielding an automatic rifle. He gestured with the barrel for Vernon to step to the side. Reese hoisted her hands over her head and closed her eyes.

47

CRYSTAL RIVER, FLORIDA, 1988

JACK HAD FOUND THE MAN'S PISTOL IN HIS BEDROOM A FOOT underneath his bed. He'd pocketed it and made his way downstairs, pausing at the backdoor to listen and gather his bearings.

"Got you surrounded," he heard a man with a deep southern accent call out. It was different than what he had heard in Florida and Alabama. "We're closing in on you."

No one responded.

"Just come on out," he continued. "Nothing bad will happen."

"Like hell it won't," Jack muttered. They weren't here for nothing. Chances were since Molly had seen them, they wanted her dead. No way that was gonna happen.

Jack thought about exiting the house through the front door, but then considered there were probably guards posted outside. Best to head right into the wolves' den. He crouched low and slipped out back.

"Got one," a guy shouted.

The other guy yelled back, "The girl?"

"Nah, just a boy."

"Hold your position and keep him there."

48

THERE WAS SOMETHING ABOUT THE OLDER MEN IN THESE parts. Every single one I encountered went out of their way to help. I hadn't noticed a trend like that anywhere else I'd been. If anything, my past had taught me I couldn't trust anyone, regardless of age. A seventy-five year old man wasn't a physical threat, and that was precisely the reason I had to watch my back around him. It was as easy for him to put a bullet in my head as it was for a younger person.

So when an old black man named Marcus offered to give me a ride since it appeared my motorbike had failed me, I tossed the faux-mohawk helmet into the dirt and jumped in his late-seventies Lincoln. The thing looked like a boat. Cruised along the highway like one as well.

He didn't speak the entire ride, just hummed tunes from a radio that probably hadn't worked in a decade. I peeled down my window, leaned back, and closed my eyes while the cool evening air worked its way over my wounds.

"We're there, man," he said.

I opened my eyes. We'd reached the western outskirts of Texline. The drive had passed by too quickly.

"Anywhere in particular?" he asked.

I had him take me to a dead end a couple blocks from Reese's place. He made a three point turn, repositioning the vehicle so I could hop out under the shade of a tree.

"Thanks again, friend," I said.

"No problem, man." He dropped the transmission into drive and pulled away, leaving me in a cloud of gas fumes. The oversized V-8 engine rumbled on even after he disappeared from sight.

The streets weren't safe, so I cut through yards, hopping fences where necessary, and sprinting across roads. My legs burned. My stomach ached. My chest felt as though it had split at the sternum and my lungs were falling out.

When I finally reached Reese's place, I collapsed against the back wall, using the hose caddy mounted to the siding to keep myself upright. I caught my breath and tuned into the surroundings. A cat prowled the backyard, waiting to pounce. A possum stood watch on top of the fence, doing something only another possum could understand. Leaves rustled in the stiff breeze. The remains of a barbecue cookout lingered in the air, flooding my mouth and sending waves through my stomach.

Soft light filtered through the back windows of Reese's apartment. I repositioned myself at the back fence and stood watch. No movement. There was no guarantee I'd spot any either. She could've been in her room, sitting on the couch, anywhere.

After ten minutes I made my move. I stuck close to the house, using the shadows to disguise my presence. The front porch light was out, leaving only the faded street light to illuminate the area a couple shades brighter than dark.

I turned the knob slowly, cringed when the latch clicked past the frame. The door creaked open. I climbed the stairs, stopping for a moment on each. Halfway up, something scurried across the floor. I resisted the urge to call out Reese's name. Before I reached the top, something crashed, followed by someone running to the back of the apartment.

I took the remaining steps two at a time and whipped around the corner, catching sight of the source of the noise. My heart pounded against my chest wall like it was trying to escape. My breath caught in my throat.

I dropped to one knee, extended my hand.

"Hey, fella."

The large dog sauntered over, ears back, tail down.

"It's OK, buddy."

His demeanor changed after he sniffed my hand. I stroked his head a couple times, turned his collar and held his tag to the light. "Dodge."

He cocked his head at the sound of his name, then resumed panting.

His owner was none other than Vernon.

"Son of a bitch."

I rose, glanced around the apartment. It looked exactly as I had left it, nothing out of place other than the broken glass on the floor. And that had happened moments ago.

"What the hell happened here, Dodge?"

I took a look at Dodge's tag again and punched the number into my cell phone. Was I calling in the cavalry? Or signing my and Reese's death certificate? The phone rang five times, then diverted to Vernon's voicemail.

My stomach turned, sank. The hotdogs I'd devoured were close to coming back up. I couldn't shake the feeling that both Reese and Vernon were in major trouble. I was no longer in a safe place. I flipped the mattress in Reese's bedroom. Underneath I found a .22. Not ideal, but it was easy to conceal and would prove lethal if I got close enough to a target.

I left some food and water for Dodge, then set out on foot to my next stop.

49

REESE STARED AT THE MOON THROUGH THE DIRTY WINDOW. IT hovered low and wide in the sky. Moonlight filtered in and cast a faded white hue across the wide wooden floorboards. The walls stood barren and worn. An old wood burning stove was covered in a layer of dust. The cabin was devoid of furniture aside from the chair they had tied her to. She strained against the rope that secured her ankles to the chair legs. It seemed every movement she made resulted in the knots tightening. Her wrists were bound with thick plastic zip ties, the kind they used to secure HVAC ducts. The hard plastic dug into her skin.

She'd seen no one other than the man who abducted her and Vernon at gunpoint. The guy was a mystery to her. In all her time in Texline, she'd never seen his face. At the base of the stairs, he'd placed a hood over her head. Vernon too, she supposed. There had been multiple vehicles idling outside. As she was led to one, she heard Vernon cursing his handler. His words had grown more distant by the second.

They had started off on the highway, but after a few miles had gone off-road. The car dipped and bounced and swayed for several minutes before coming to a stop. From there, she was led inside and tied up. They had removed her hood and disappeared through the doorway before she managed to catch a glimpse of them.

And now she waited in a dim room. Alone. Unable to move. Unwilling to yell out for help. There was no point. It was better to save her strength for when she needed it.

Darrow had everything to do with this. He knew her secret, but she'd upheld her end of the deal and kept quiet. So why go through with this? The obvious answer was Jack. But he wasn't at the apartment. Why not wait for him to return?

Perhaps they had planned on waiting, but she had triggered an acceleration clause by calling Vernon. And perhaps they brought Reese and Vernon out here to keep them away. At least she assumed Vernon was out there. She hadn't seen or heard him since the truck pulled out of her driveway. Had someone remained behind, lying in wait for Jack to return?

She thought about what he had endured that day, and tried to think like him. At the first opportunity, he would have called her. And when he received no answer, he'd grow suspicious. The man had a sense for when danger waited around the corner. That was the only explanation for how he'd survived for so long. Where others used stealth and cunning, Jack preferred brute force. He took what he wanted. Survived through sheer force of will.

The door behind her scraped the floor as it opened. Two sets of boots hit the floorboards. One stopped behind her. Large hands wrapped around her shoulders, gently massaging up toward her neck, then back down to her arms. It made her want to throw up. The man said nothing. His heavy breathing was the only noise he made.

Darrow walked past, giving her a wide berth. She was bound, but he'd take no chances. That was how he had survived so long.

That and having an army of idiots to do his bidding while buying off everyone he could in order to keep himself out of trouble.

Fucking weasel.

"Hello, Reese."

She said nothing.

"I suppose you're wondering why I've taken all these precautions."

"No, I think I figured that out on my own."

"Oh, yeah?"

"Yeah," she said. "You're a low-life pussy who can't face a woman alone without restraining her."

Darrow leaned back against the wall, arms folded. He jammed his right foot into the wall, pointing his knee toward her. He laughed for a good ten seconds. Reese expected him to follow it up with a smack across her face, or some other threat. Didn't happen, though. Darrow appeared relaxed and in control of his emotions. And the situation.

"You know you're not just any woman," he said. "I mean, we've got NYPD's finest sitting here. Right? The files I reviewed back that up. One of their best detectives, until you passed away tragically when your car went careening over a railing into the river. The body was never found."

"That's a nice story," she said. "But I'm not that woman anymore. I run a bar now."

"Oh, I think you're more that woman today than you're willing to admit."

"No, because if I was, I wouldn't be sitting here right now. Vernon and I would have made it out of that apartment and shattered your world."

"That wouldn't happen."

"It would. And you know what? Maybe you're right. As I sit here, I find myself rediscovering Reese McSweeney all over. I'm tired of turning a blind eye for you and your band of idiots. I don't care if a damn terrorist learns my location. I'd rather take my chances with them than watch you defecate all over this town and this country."

"I don't doubt that, Reese. I'm just saying you and Vernon never would have banded together against me. After all, he's one of the reasons you're sitting here right now."

"What are you saying? You had him followed to my apartment? He's the one you wanted, I'm just collateral damage?"

Darrow smiled, nodded, and lifted his gaze to the man behind her. The guy's hands slipped off her shoulder. He stepped to the side, looked down at her.

"Son of a bitch," Reese said while trying to elbow him in the thigh. The restraints dug in deeper, causing her to grimace against the flash of pain. "Vernon? What the hell?"

Vernon continued to the opposite side of the room, took position next to Darrow against the wall.

"I thought you were on my side," she said. "Hell, you even let Jack out of jail."

"Appearances, Reese," he said. "We knew we were more likely to get information out of you if you believed I was on your side. Mind you, I knew Jack wouldn't ever be, but you're just so damn trusting, Detective McSweeney."

"How long have you known my name?"

He glanced at Darrow. "Since about the time he told me, which I guess was—"

"The same day I found out," Darrow said, spreading his arms wide.

"This whole time," she said. "So why now? What's changed?"

"You're friend, Mr. Noble," Darrow said. "He has the potential to be a major pain in our asses. We figure this is the only way to throw him off his game. Apparently, he takes chances he normally wouldn't when someone he loves is in danger."

Vernon's eyes darkened. He smiled. "And we know how much he loves you."

"Asshole," she muttered under her breath.

"What's that?" Vernon said, walking toward her, rubbing his palms together.

She said nothing.

He grabbed her jaw with his meaty hand and lifted her head toward him. She fought to look away. "Watch your tongue around here."

How had the man who'd been like a father to her turned on her like this? What was there to gain? She knew the obvious answer, but still couldn't understand how he could treat her this way after showing so much empathy all those years.

"Jack's only passing through," Reese said. "He doesn't want to be involved in anything you guys are up to. Christ, even after what you did the first couple days, he wanted nothing to do with it. He doesn't care."

"Why'd he stay around then?" Vernon said.

She avoided looking at Vernon. Though he'd been a father figure to her, his feelings were the opposite. She'd known for a while that the man had felt something more for her. She'd done nothing to encourage those feelings, and did her best to avoid responding to anything he said that potentially had a dual meaning.

"What do you think is going to happen now?" Reese said. "You've pushed him. He's going to respond. You don't know him and what he's capable of."

"Oh, I know him all right," Darrow said. "And I'm counting on him responding. Because that'll make it easier to kill him."

50

I'D MANAGED TO REMAIN OUT OF SIGHT FOR NINE OF THE TEN minutes it took to get to Linus's house. The sketchiest part had been crossing Main Street. It was lit up, but empty. Someone could've been watching, though. Didn't matter, I had to take the chance.

When I reached the house, only the minivan was parked out front. The GMC was busted up enough to be out of commission after smashing into Reese's car. The house windows were lit up, offering a view inside. I saw the two boys and the woman seated at the kitchen table. Had Linus made it home? Was he still out looking for me?

I climbed the wobbly privacy fence, waited there for a few breaths, then continued to the back. Each window offered a view of a different part of the house. The bedrooms were empty. No sign of Linus.

I pulled the .22 from my pocket as I neared the sliding glass door. There were three rounds in the magazine. I had to make each one count.

Spread out on the table between the blonde woman and the two boys was a board game. Couldn't make out which one. The older boy looked happy, the younger one pissed. Looked about right. Sean and I had gone to war over Monopoly I don't know how many times. Never could I remember both of us happy at the same time playing that or any other game. My misfortune was perpetually his gain, and vice versa.

I remained outside the door for a few minutes, standing far enough back that it wouldn't be obvious I was there. Finally, I made my move. The unlocked door slid open without resistance. I moved inside quickly and decisively, pistol aimed at the family.

Both boys looked up. Fear drowned their expressions. The woman pushed back from the table, sending the board game over the edge. She leapt up wielding a knife. Not your garden variety weapon either. After a quick glance I pegged it as a survival knife commonly carried by Air Force pilots. Nice piece. I figured she knew her husband was an asshole and always had it in the back of her mind that she might end up in a situation like this. Good to be prepared.

"Who are you?" she said, her voice trembling.

"Where's your husband?"

"Dead."

"What?"

"He died two years ago. I moved in with my brother a couple months ago."

Looking at the woman, it made sense. She was beautiful. Linus looked as though someone had taken a tree branch to his face when he was young.

"Linus," I said.

"My brother," she said.

"Where is he?"

"What the hell did he do now?"

"He tried to kill me."

"Too bad he failed." She placed herself between me and her sons, clutching the knife to her chest. "Boys, go to your room."

I remained by the back door, ready to duck out should Linus pop out with an automatic rifle.

Down the hall a door closed. Kids' bedroom, presumably. The woman licked her lips, held out an empty hand. "What's my brother into?"

"You don't know?"

She shook her head, said nothing.

"You and I must be the only people in town who have no idea then. Everyone else seems to know what's going on around here."

"I mean, I had an idea," she said. "But, you know, not like I could talk it up with him. If he kicked me out, I don't know what I'd do. My husband took care of everything. We had a great life in Dallas. At least, I thought we did. When he passed unexpectedly, I learned that we had almost two hundred thousand in credit card debt, and the house was in arrears. I lost the house, my credit, had no job, and we were forced to move into a ghetto apartment. Soon after, I couldn't even afford that. I got married so young. Never finished school or built a career."

She reached back for a glass of water, took a sip, then continued. "And my brother is a son of a bitch. He's actually my stepbrother. Unfortunately, the only family I have left. Treats us like garbage. Beats my boys. Hits me."

"What if I could help you?" I said.

"How?" she said.

"There's an old weathered cabin in the middle of nowhere. Maybe thirty minutes from here. Cattle all around. Nothing else. He took me there. Any chance you know where it is?"

She narrowed her eyes. Was she thinking or plotting? The woman could lead me right into a trap. I'd already fallen for her story. Was it just that? A story? My read on her was sketchy and I couldn't get a good feel for her true intentions.

"I don't know," she said.

"All right," I said. "Is there anything—"

"But I did find this map one day when I was snooping around." She turned and walked to a desk, leaving her knife on the table. The writing desk looked like it was at least sixty years old. She started to lift the rolling top.

"Hold on," I said. "I'll take it from there."

She gave way to me. I pulled out the weathered map, unfolded it. The creases were worn so thin I feared the paper would split if I moved it too quickly. It covered a few hundred square miles, showing Texline, a few other towns, and the major roads in between. Handwritten in pencil was the word 'ranch.' I traced the route east out of town, then a couple small roads. Then off-road. I closed my eyes and recalled the journey there and back. What I saw on the map fit. Once I left pavement, it could be as simple as picking a line and riding it. That potentially posed problems, though. I could run into trouble with ditches, streams, hills, and possibly small cliffs in the way. None of that mattered until I had a vehicle.

"One more favor," I said.

"What?" she said.

"Got a car I can take? One that can get through the mud?"

She shook her head. "Linus has the truck. My van won't make it."

"If Linus shows up," I said. "I can trust—"

"He'd have no reason to even think I saw you, so it shouldn't be a problem. I promise not to bring it up."

"What about the boys? They're not used to an armed man entering the house. They might talk."

"Happens more than you think. They'll be in their room the rest of the night. He's not going in to see them. And you know what, they probably trust you right now more than that son of a bitch. I'll tell them you were here to punish him for the way he's acted."

I liked the woman. She was tough. Just needed a helping hand to pull her out of the pit she'd fallen into.

"I'm gonna take care of you when this is all over. Get that debt paid off, get you back on your feet. OK?"

She nodded. "Thank you, I think."

I left through the back door, hopped the fence into the rear neighbor's yard, and cut across two more properties to distance myself another block further. Now I had to find a car suitable for the terrain.

And I knew where to find one.

51

REESE SAT ALONE IN THE MOONLIT ROOM, COUNTING THE seconds in an effort to stay awake. The occasional rustle of cattle was the only sound aside from her breathing.

Darrow and Vernon had left without giving any indication what they planned on doing with her. She knew she wasn't leaving the room alive. There was no reason for them to let her go. She'd known about Darrow for some time. His secrets. The things he was into. Yet he did nothing to her. He knew her secrets as well. And he kept them safe in return for Reese doing the same. She found herself at war over the decision at first. She'd spent her entire adult life fighting criminals. Now she had to pretend to respect one so he wouldn't turn her in to a group of terrorists who would have been more than happy to know her location. They'd kidnap her. Rape her. Torture her. And eventually kill her. The last part she could handle. Bring it on. The rest, no thanks. She could do without ever encountering those bastards. As could most, she presumed.

The stakes had been raised tonight. All along, she believed

Vernon was on her side. Knowing the truth about the man changed everything and increased the likelihood she would be dead soon. He had too much to lose by letting her go. At this point, she was bait to draw Jack out of wherever he was hiding.

Did anyone else know she was there? She thought through interactions with people she had believed were working for Darrow. None had ever shown signs that they knew Vernon was on the inside. In fact, they typically clammed up with him around, if they didn't leave outright when he made his presence felt.

A secret of this magnitude could only be carried to the grave.

A solitary tear slipped from her left eye, catching the groove between her nostril and cheek, sliding across her top lip and settling in at the corner of her mouth. She touched it with her tongue and savored the salty flavor in her mouth for several seconds. She licked her lips, trying to generate saliva to wet her dry mouth.

She fought back against additional tears. Why let those assholes know they had gotten to her?

The door banged open. One set of boots hit the floorboards. He paced behind her, remaining out of her peripheral vision. Heavy steps, left to right, back again.

"What?" she yelled after two minutes of silent pacing.

The man came to rest behind her. Thin, bony fingers wrapped around her jaw, pulling her head back and to the right. She looked up into Linus's gaunt face. His deep-set eyes focused on her. A slight smile played on his mouth.

"What the hell do you want?" she said through gritted teeth, straining against his grip.

"Figured since you have a little time left, I'd come and make sure it was good for you."

She filled her mouth with saliva and spat. Half hit him, the rest sprinkled down on her face.

Linus jumped back, wiped his chin off with the back of his hand. "Bitch."

Her chair lurched forward. He kicked it again, sending Reese tipping over. She came down hard on her right elbow and cried out in pain.

"That's what you get," Linus said. He stood over her. His hands were balled into tight fists. He glared down, moonlight reflecting off his eyes. Anger faded as a smile took its place. "You think you can piss me off enough that I'd just leave, huh?"

Reese said nothing. She fought back another scream, one that would have been filled with violence and rage. Pain radiated from her elbow. She couldn't move her arm. Had she broken it? Dislocated it? She couldn't see her arm, and didn't dare try to reposition herself.

Linus reached down, grabbed the chair and righted it. The pain intensified as her arm hung limp.

"I think it's broken," she said.

Linus grabbed her left arm. "This one?"

Reese said nothing.

"No, guess not." He walked around to the front of the chair. Stopped. Placed his thumbs inside his pants waistband. "Open your mouth."

Reese stared up at him. Gritted her teeth tight. Pursed her lips even tighter.

Linus punched her right elbow.

Reese screamed in pain, doubled over. Tears flooded her eyes.

"That'll do it, huh," he said.

"Go to hell," she said. "I'll die before I touch you."

Linus stepped closer. His legs touched the inside of her knees. He pushed outward, spreading her legs a few inches. "It's not that bad."

Reese closed her eyes, rolled her head back, groaned from the pain in her arm. It had intensified and centralized. She glanced up, saw Linus smiling, head back slightly, not looking at her. She took a deep breath and focused on the fire in her elbow, drawing it into her center. Then she whipped her head forward as far and as fast as she could, striking Linus in his crotch.

The high pitched scream that left his mouth was followed by hollow nothingness. He dropped where he stood. Reese battled the pain in her arm and managed to lean forward, teetering on the tips of her toes. She aligned herself just right and dropped the chair rail onto Linus's neck, driving every ounce of her weight downward. The man weakly attempted to fight her off. The blow to his testicles had sapped him of his strength, and now he could do nothing but suffocate.

"God dammit." Vernon's voice boomed as he lumbered into the room. He lifted Reese off the floor, grabbing hold of her damaged arm. She screamed and Vernon leapt back a foot. "What? Did he hurt you?"

Feeling faint from the throbbing in her arm, she managed a nod before slumping to the side.

Vernon grabbed the writhing man off the floor like he was a tackling dummy, then threw him headfirst into the wall. Linus collapsed onto the floor, slimping into a limp pile.

"I said no one touches her," Vernon said. "Didn't you hear me say that?"

Linus said nothing. He lifted his arm a couple inches in an effort to shield his face.

Vernon ran three paces, delivered a kick to Linus's midsection. The guy raised up, then bowed forward, face first to the floor. Vernon brought his foot back again and struck Linus's face like he was taking a penalty kick. Linus's head snapped back. Dark splatters of blood arced in the moonlight.

"Stop," Reese said.

Vernon ignored her. He dropped down to a knee and wrapped both hands around Linus's throat. The sounds of the slim man choking filled the room. The hoarse pleading, gagging, and eventual silence and subsequent stink of human waste twisted Reese's stomach.

Vernon rose, breathing heavily. He placed a hand on the wall and leaned forward. Was he going to throw up? He stood there for a few moments, but nothing happened. Then he reached down and lifted Linus's corpse off the floor.

"I'm sorry, Billie, I mean, Reese. This won't happen again."

Vernon slipped through the opening with the draped body over his shoulder, fluids splashing against the floorboards with every step.

The door banged shut.

And Reese began to cry.

52

CRYSTAL RIVER, FLORIDA, 1988

THE CICADAS' SHRILL SCREAMS HAD NEVER RUNG THIS LOUD. It felt as though a hundred were perched on Jack's shoulders. He'd isolated the direction where his brother was being held. The long stretch of grass appeared desolate. Was anyone watching it? He had to assume they were. Deciding not to chance it, Jack stuck close to the house, crouching low, then darted the twenty feet into the woods on a diagonal line. Once behind the tree line, he dropped flat and caught his breath, listening for anyone close by who might've spotted him.

Several seconds passed. There wasn't a hint of anyone.

He rose to his knees and stared into the woods. Faint traces of light remained, enough to see outlines of shapes, but little else. Jack adjusted his position and crept toward where he believed his brother was being held. Every step seemed to disrupt dead leaves or snap a fallen branch. He glanced over his shoulder every few seconds, verifying no one followed.

"Y'all are gonna die," Sean said. "You don't know what my dad is capable of."

Someone laughed, told him to shut up.

Jack hadn't veered far off track. His brother was close. Step by step he inched closer until he had them in view. He retrieved the pistol, aimed it at the back of the guy's head.

"Freeze, asshole," he said.

The man turned around, took a step forward.

There would be no second warning. He'd given a directive, and the guy failed to follow it. His blood would not be on Jack's hand.

He squeezed the trigger.

Click.

Nothing.

What the hell? It's always loaded.

Whatever light remained glinted off the guy's teeth as he smiled.

"Oh, I'm gonna have fun with this."

Frozen in time. That's how Jack felt watching the guy attack his brother. Sean lay on the ground, his hands clutching his stomach. The man towered over him, standing just a few feet away. Jack stood there with the defunct pistol, unsure what to do next.

"I'm gonna rip your damn spine outta your mouth," the guy said.

"Jack, run," Sean said.

He heard the words. Visualized turning and sprinting through the woods, into the neighbor's yard, to their backdoor. Banging and screaming for help. Maybe he'd be in time to save Sean and Molly.

Or maybe with one on the loose, the men would cut their losses, execute whichever of Jack's siblings they held, and be on their way. Point made. Your move.

"Go!" Sean said.

Jack went. But backward was not an option.

He charged the large man that stood between him and his brother.

53

The lights inside the garage were on, casting long yellowish-white rectangles through the windows along the parking lot. I picked a shaded lane and moved to one of the bay doors to get a look inside. The Jeep was still there. Maybe they'd done some work on it. Maybe they'd rigged it to blow up. In the middle of the room sat the big guy I'd fought with outside the garage. Two other men I didn't recognize were there, too. They were seated around a table, playing cards. I didn't spot any weapons. Only alcohol. I'd hoped that the place would be empty. This was a close second.

The best option for entering was a door along the side. It appeared to open into the garage's walled office, which at that moment was darkened and presumably deserted.

I stuck to the shadows as I made my way to the side of the building and tested the door. Found it unlocked. I cracked it an inch, then waited. No alarm. No apparent movement inside. Pushing it open further, I eased inside with the pistol drawn and aimed in front of me. As expected, the office was empty. Through a large bay window I saw the men. Not a one of them could see me.

The room had two desks, each adorned with a computer monitor and stacks of paper. I opened the center drawer of the front desk, found pens, sticky pads, and some paperclips. Nothing useful. The side drawers were locked. I moved to the next desk and checked. In there I found a six-inch hunting knife and tucked it in my waistband. The side drawers were unlocked. As I opened the first, the room lit up.

I spun on my heel, pistol aimed at the door separating the office from the rest of the garage. It remained closed. The light came from beside where I stood. A computer monitor had come to life. The three guys at the table paid no attention. Maybe they'd seen it and ignored it. Common occurrence, perhaps.

I killed the power to the monitor, then resumed my desk search, turning up nothing else. I'd have to proceed with the .22 and a knife. Bad odds.

For them.

I waited by the door a few moments, trusting that the right opportunity to enter the garage would come soon. And it did.

The three men broke out in a fit of drunken laughter. They slammed their cards, covered their faces. One guy fell out of his chair.

Within a couple seconds I was through the door and halfway to the table, pistol drawn. The first guy who spotted me went silent. The guy with his back to me must've noticed his buddy's face go slack because he looked over his shoulder and then held out his hands.

The third guy didn't fall in line with his buddies. It was the same big guy I'd beaten down the other day. He scrambled to his feet and sprinted toward me.

I didn't hesitate. I squeezed the trigger, praying that a gun I'd never fired wouldn't fail me.

It didn't.

The bullet hit him center mass ten feet out. The big guy went down clutching his heart.

"Who's next?" I said.

Both men at the table hoisted their hands high in the air. I gestured for them to stand.

"Over there. Face opposite directions and get on the ground feet-to-feet, fingers interlaced behind your head."

The men complied as the big guy choked while he bled out on the floor.

"Ain't you going to help him?" one of the guys said.

"Depends," I said. "Is my Jeep ready?"

"That thing's dead, man," the guy said.

"You got something I can use then? It's gotta be four-wheel drive."

"Take mine," the guy said. "Bronco parked out front. Keys are on the table."

I found the skull keychain on the table with a Ford key attached. Shoved it in my pocket. Then I grabbed a spool of electrical wire and bound the men at their wrists and ankles. The big guy had stopped writhing around in the crimson pool surrounding him. Maybe he was dead. I didn't care.

"One more thing," I said. "You know where they took her?"

"Who?" the guy said.

I stepped on the back of his head, smashing his cheek into the concrete floor.

"Do you know where they took her?" I repeated.

"Who?" he shouted. "Jesus, man, you're crushing my face. I don't know who you're talking about."

At that same moment a door whipped open and smacked against the metal wall. The sound echoed throughout the room for the next few seconds.

"The hell is going on in here?" said a guy I'd never seen before. He held a rifle and aimed it in my direction.

I fired a wild shot at him and ducked behind the Jeep. There was nothing else between me and the back corner of the garage.

A shot erupted, tearing through the windshield and soft top. It ricocheted off the wall. The guy cycled the action of his the rifle again. Fired. The front passenger tire hissed as air spewed out.

I shuffled to the rear of the vehicle. Peeked over the spare tire. The guy spun on his heel and fired. The round knocked the spare off its mount. Son of a bitch was a decent shot. Years of hunting, I presumed. Too bad for him I wasn't a deer. He readied his weapon again. I pulled the cover off the tire and tossed it to the side of the Jeep.

BOOM.

Wasted shot.

I powered off the floor, pistol ready. Located the man. He was facing away from me. I pulled the trigger.

The shot missed.

He chambered another round, fired at me. It tore through my right shoulder. My arm went limp. He sent another round in my direction. I dropped to the ground, reached over with my other hand and felt the wound. The pain had subsided. The bullet had only grazed me.

But he didn't know that.

His boots echoed off the concrete floor as he slowly and deliberately approached me. He must've mistaken me for wounded prey.

"Free us," one of the guys said. "We can help."

"Shut up," the guy said. "Worthless." He spat on the ground, continued toward me.

I realized then that I had dropped the pistol after being shot. It lay on the floor in plain sight. I planned an escape. All I had to do was wait for him to get to the Jeep, then I'd take a few steps past.

Run as fast as I could to the door he came in through. There were two vans at the front I could take cover behind, if I didn't reach the Bronco first.

I peered under the vehicle and knew then that the plan would fail. I'd never make it to the door. Too much open space. My only hope was that he'd get close enough I could engage and disarm him.

He kicked the .22, sending it skating away across the floor. The handgun banged against the wall and spun in a tight circle before coming to rest twenty or so feet from me. I saw the rifle barrel first, pointed loosely at the floor. The man stepped out from behind the vehicle. He had on grey suit pants and a silk shirt. Gold rimmed sunglasses were perched atop his head. He looked Mexican, though taller than most I'd seen.

I kept my free hand pressed tight to my shoulder, against the wound, letting the blood seep out through my fingers. In my other hand I gripped the knife, holding the blade against my forearm, out of sight. I labored my breathing, playing it up that I was hurt.

He smiled as he looked down at me. "Estas listo para morir, puta?"

"Vete a la verga culero."

This drew a belly laugh out of the guy. He took his eyes off of me. Only for a second, but that was all I needed.

With everything I had in me, I hopped up, slicing forward with the knife.

The man's reflexes were like nothing I'd ever seen. He leaned back as I drew the knife across where his throat had been. I followed through with an elbow that caught him on the jaw. The rifle fell to the floor. He twisted his body and lunged after it. I dove on top of him, driving all of my weight down. He continued toward the weapon, carrying me with him. I crawled over him, gouging his eyes. I swung my other arm out, catching the butt of the gun with my fingertips, sending it sliding another fifteen feet.

The guy managed to worm out from under me. As he pulled himself up to his feet, I lunged at his knee, taking it on from the side. His leg buckled and he went down hard. His head smacked the concrete with a thud. Blood pooled around his face. He groaned, brought his arms in so his fists were by his neck and his elbows at his midsection.

"Stay down," I said between breaths.

He didn't. The guy thrust himself to his hands and knees. Blood spilled from the gash on his forehead. He looked at me, then the gun.

I pushed off the floor, bringing my feet under and hopping up. We both went for the rifle. He dove for it. I let him. A long stretch of pegboard was mounted to the wall. I grabbed a steel ratchet that was damn near a foot long.

The man scooped the rifle up, got to his knees.

I drew my arm back, letting the tool dangle ready to bring it forward with every ounce of torque I could muster.

He spun on one knee, hands adjusting on the rifle in an attempt to get his shot off.

I planted my left foot forward, thrust my right hip toward him, whipped my arm around in a side arc. The overhead lights glinted off the ratchet.

The guy cursed in Spanish. He held the rifle out and looked down at it. Had it jammed? Had he been in such a hurry he hadn't chambered a round?

He glanced up, his face twisting in surprised anticipation as the tool sailed toward his face. I thought for sure his reflexes would kick in and he'd move. He started to, but the hunk of metal hit first. The guy rocked back on his heels. I rushed forward, kicked him in the chest. He toppled over, dropping the rifle along the way. I grabbed it, shot him in the chest point blank.

Never cry mercy.

Never again.

54

"I'm coming back, and if you two so much as move I'm gonna do you like I did him."

The two men lay face down on the floor, hands tied behind them, feet bound at the ankles. They groaned through the duct tape I'd wrapped around their heads.

"And so help me, if this Bronco doesn't start, I'm gonna burn this building down with you two in it. Anyone tries to put out the fire, I'll kill them, too."

The Bronco was parked off to the side. It was painted black. Wheels were black. Windows were tinted. I couldn't have found a more perfect vehicle for what I was about to do. I climbed into the driver's seat, ignoring the wounds I'd accumulated the past two days. Tried to, at least. It was a state of mind more than anything. A warm trickle of blood down my arm made it difficult to block it out entirely.

The route I'd highlighted on the map had me leaving on Main Street, which became the highway. I sped along until I reached the first turnoff. I figured Darrow had lookouts somewhere along the way. No doubt he would tonight. They were waiting for me. I felt it. I cruised along the road for five minutes, then cut my headlights. The moon shone brightly overhead, refusing to allow me to proceed covertly if I passed a lookout too close. But if someone was a hundred feet off the road, they might not spot me. They'd hear the big ol' V-8, though.

Without the benefit of headlights, I almost missed the next turn. The drive wouldn't get any easier from this point. I switched the lights back on and drove a few miles, looking for a landmark. The map had a picture of a snake head with the tongue sticking out.

I wasn't sure what I was looking for until I found it. The head rose out of the dirt like an Egyptian pyramid. The mouth stood wide open, and fangs as tall as me were poised to latch onto its prey. The tongue stuck out like a large ribbon whipping in the wind.

I slowed down and peered into the mouth. A single glass door set in the middle led inside. What the hell was it? A museum? Snake World? If I made it through the night alive, I planned on returning to find out.

The turn off was located on the other side of the building. Nothing more than a dirt patch with two red reflectors on poles to mark it. I put the Bronco in four-wheel-drive and went off-road. From this point I had no idea what to expect. On a line, I'd reach the small little cabin in fifteen miles. What stood in my way?

The vehicle handled the terrain without a problem. As I bounced along, I thought through the possible scenarios of what I'd find at the cabin. It couldn't accommodate many people, so I didn't expect to run into more than one or two armed men inside. The property outside, well, that was a different story. I never saw any other structures there, but at night, there was plenty of room for them to hide out in the open. I had a .22 with two shots left, and a rifle with a handful of shells I'd taken off the guy at the garage. If there were more than a couple armed men out there, tonight would not go my way.

The moon rose higher. Seemed to glow brighter the smaller and tighter it appeared in the sky. That worked for and against me. It all depended on my approach, and how far out they were watching. With two miles remaining, I stopped the Bronco and cut the ignition. The engine ticked. The air smelled like antifreeze.

I performed a quick sweep of the vehicle. In back I found a Glock 19. The magazine was full, and the pistol smelled of fresh oil. Presumably the guy had taken care of it. Bad luck for him that he didn't have it in the garage.

Two miles of moonlit dirt stretched out in front of me. Twenty to thirty minutes to reach my destination.

I started the last leg of my journey on foot.

But I wouldn't finish it that way.

The men approaching in the truck behind me would make sure of that.

55

Reese heard the men talking outside on the porch. They spoke in hushed tones, too quiet for her to pick up on what they were saying. Her mind raced at the possibilities. They could have decided she was too much of a hassle to keep around. Better to end it now and deal with Jack later. He'd turn up.

Or would he?

She knew Jack was the kind of guy who'd be there for her no matter what. She only hoped that he'd arrive before time ran out.

The door flew open, grating against the floor. For a minute, Reese heard nothing but the sounds of the cicadas serenading them with their shrill voices. After a few moments, Darrow entered. He dragged a chair into the room and set it across from Reese. He didn't sit down, though. Instead, he leaned over the back and stared at Reese for thirty seconds without saying a word.

"What?" she said finally, breaking the first rule in negotiations. She'd given up on being able to compromise with him.

"This'll all be over soon," he said.

She bit down hard, trying to keep from spilling more tears.

"Your friend Jack is close. Once he's here, we'll give him a proper welcome. Then I've got a few things to tell him."

"Like what?" she said. "Gonna offer him a job?"

Darrow laughed. "I tell you, that thought crossed my mind. He would make an excellent member of my organization if circumstances were different. And I don't mean a thug like Linus and the rest of those idiots in town. They're my dogs, basically. I feed them scraps and they dig in my trash. Keeps the locals in fear and away from my fence and off my lawn. Got me?"

Reese didn't answer.

"Anyway, if I could have a guy like Noble, he would be part of my inner circle. The guys who I trust. The ones I know won't screw me over. And, you see, the problem is that once Jack learns a few things about me, there's no way he'd want to be a part of that group."

"Why not? What'd you do?"

Darrow shook his head. He straightened up and tipped the chair back so it stood on its rear two legs. "That's not something you really want to know." He paused, smiled. "Well, I guess you're gonna find out soon anyway."

Vernon stepped into the room carrying rope, duct tape, some heavy duty zip ties, and a brown leather briefcase. She was curious about its contents, but didn't ask.

Come on, Jack, she thought. Now is the perfect time to take these assholes out.

"How far out are they?" Darrow asked Vernon.

"They've got him in the truck and are interrogating him," Vernon said. "Should be here within ten minutes."

"Perfect," Darrow said, turning his attention to Reese, smiling. "This'll all be over in twenty."

This time she couldn't hold back the tears.

56

CRYSTAL RIVER, FLORIDA, 1988

HIT A BIG MAN LOW.

He'd heard it said a number of times. Had gone through it in slow motion with his father and uncle, both of whom stood over six-foot-four. Now it was time to put practice into action.

Jack feigned high, curled his arm back as though he were going to strike at the man's throat. As the guy reacted by throwing his arms up to block, Jack dropped his mass low and lunged at the guy's left knee, driving his shoulder through from the inside out with a satisfying snap and crack. As a linebacker on his junior high football team, Jack had perfected the art of tackling. The big guy toppled over, and not a second later, Sean threw his six-two frame on the man, locking him down in a choke-hold. The guy's hollow calls for help fell on no ears.

The man bucked against Sean, almost throwing him off. Jack stepped in with a kick to the ribs, and another to his shredded knee. The guy collapsed to the ground again. A few seconds later, he went limp, his eyes permanently opened.

The brothers stared at each other in the dim light. They shared a victorious smile.

But it didn't last long.

Molly's scream sliced through the humid night like a rusted butter knife.

57

HIGH BEAMS ILLUMINATED THE GROUND BEFORE ME. I SAW
nowhere to run. No place to hide. Two doors opened up. The
engine idled rough, like it might choke at any time.

"Hands up, turn around."

I complied and did a one-eighty into the light wash. It took a
few seconds for my eyes to adjust enough to make out shapes.

"Who else is with you?"

I could barely make out the guy's face. He wore his hat so the
bill covered his eyes. Every feature was shaded. Maybe I knew
him. If not from town, then somewhere else. He sure as hell acted
like someone I had known in the past. Definitely not like one of
the townies I'd been beating up on since arriving in Texline. I
figured Darrow employed at least a few people I'd crossed
paths with.

"I asked you a question," he said. "I expect an answer."

"Only my father had permission to talk to me like that."

He rewarded my noncompliance with a sap to the gut. I saw it
coming. Tightened my abdominal muscles. It didn't make a differ-

ence. It never did with that weapon. I fell to the side and was subsequently pushed back over by another man. Dirt filled my nose, mouth, and throat, and caked my lips as I desperately tried to refill my lungs with oxygen.

"I'll give you a minute," the guy said.

They all cleared away from the side of the truck, leaving me alone with my thoughts. Why'd I have to get so greedy? Any other time, I'd have huffed it the last four or five miles. I went in closer than I was comfortable and paid for it. I ended up driving right past these guys without knowing. They followed then ambushed me when I began my final trek.

The only positive to the situation was they would bring me to Reese, and I wouldn't have to walk.

Unless I was wrong, in which case, I was pretty screwed at that moment.

I leaned back, sucking in whatever air I could squeeze into my lungs. Oxygen slowly made its way through my body. Before I'd recovered enough to talk, the guy squatted next to me, jabbing the end of the sap into my gut.

"Well?" he said. "Who else is with you?"

"No one," I tried to say. It came out as a gravely whisper.

Shaking his head, he whipped the sap up, then back down.

I rolled to the side, mouth agape, hands grasping at the air in front of my stomach as though they could restore the oxygen to my lungs. A minute passed. Everything went dark. I felt like I was passing out. Someone came up and yanked me off the ground. My legs hadn't the strength to hold me up and I started to fall. Another man appeared on the other side of me. They grabbed my arms and dragged me to the truck. My feet couldn't keep up. They slammed me over the tailgate. My head ricocheted off the bed liner. Thank God the plastic was there to absorb the impact. I might've been knocked out otherwise. Come to think of it, that would have been preferable.

The guy with the sap hopped up in the bed with me. I rolled onto my back and scooted until my head touched the cab. The guy remained at the tailgate.

"I guess it's safe to assume that your dumbass came out here alone," he said.

I said nothing, because fuck him, that's why.

He nodded, took a step toward me. I didn't react. He lifted the sap over his head, threw a practice pitch. The sap whistled as it passed a foot or so in front of my face. There'd be no way to make it through an actual blow to the head with the weapon. I'd be knocked out cold. Possibly worse. But if that's what they wanted, he'd have done it already. He threw another practice pitch, bringing the weapon closer to my head. Fear tactic, that was all. Darrow wanted me awake and alive. No fun for him otherwise.

I closed my eyes and leaned my head back against the glass. Heard the guy laugh.

"Regular badass over here, huh?" He gave it a few seconds before continuing. "Well, enjoy the next couple minutes. They'll be some of the last of your life."

No, I thought. They'll be the last of yours.

58

THE SILENCE WAS BOTH WELCOME AND AGONIZING. Permanent silence was within reach. Reese had no idea when it would happen, though. She opened her eyes and saw nothing more than the faint glow and flicker of the oil lamp they'd brought into the cabin. It illuminated the walls, highlighting the shadowy corners. The cabin must've been a hundred and fifty years old. It was worn and scarred. Who had lived here? She imagined a family of nine eking it out, surviving on the land, all stuffed into the small space. Their days would have consisted of work and sleep. Nothing more. Maybe one or two of the kids got out and made something of their lives. Perhaps they were some of the original founders of Texline, or one of the other small towns. And one or two never made it out at all with mortality rates as high as they were back then.

Would she make it out alive?

Dealing with the criminal element as long as she had, Reese had long ago accepted that she could succumb to an untimely death. It wasn't a pleasant realization, but she knew it, accepted it, and continued on with her work. You couldn't live in fear as a detective. She took the stance that being cautious, prepared, and educated were the traits that would help her through her career. False bravado was as bad as walking around afraid. Both would get you killed.

But tonight she felt fear in a way that was primal and unlike anything she'd ever been through. Every howl of the wind sent shivers down her spine. Every rustle of the trees filled her with anxiety. Panic laced every breath she took.

And now the silence she'd grown accustomed to had dissipated and given way to the low rumble of a vehicle approaching. Soon it would be close enough to hear the ground crunching beneath the tires. After that, Jack would be brought in. At least, she hoped so. If she had to die, she wanted to see the man one last time. Tell him her feelings. The feelings she'd held on to for the past eight years, since the day they'd first crossed paths in New York.

But what if she never saw him again? What if they killed him just outside the door and she had to listen to it? All along, she believed it was her suffering Jack would be forced to witness. She had not considered that it might be the other way around.

"Screw what ifs," she muttered under her breath.

"What?" Vernon said.

She didn't respond to the man. He was dead to her. Hell, she hoped he had to be the one to pull the trigger and end her life. The ultimate betrayal of a friend. What a joke of a word. She hadn't had a true friend since, well, since she met Jack the first time.

"Sounds like the truck is near," Vernon said.

Darrow agreed. "We shouldn't both be on the porch."

"Why?"

"Do you have any idea how dangerous this man is?"

Vernon said nothing.

"I wouldn't be surprised if he's the one driving that truck right now."

"Thought your guys were good," Vernon said.

"Jack Noble is better."

59

CRYSTAL RIVER, FLORIDA, 1988

"JACK, GO," SEAN SAID.

But he didn't need to be told. He scampered in the direction of the scream, tripping over a stump. He sliced his hands on briars as he regained his footing. He seemed to encounter a new obstacle with every step. It didn't matter that he'd run through every square foot of the woods over the course of his childhood.

It felt as though hours had passed, though in reality it had only been a few seconds when he finally saw their outlines. Molly knelt on the ground, her sobs growing louder. A man stood behind her. He extended his arm. The pistol glinted against the beam of his flashlight.

Molly glanced in Jack's direction. Could she see him? Nothing in her blank stare told him she could. She didn't look scared, though. No, the steeled look on her face told Jack she was about to act. And act she did.

The girl dipped forward and drove her foot back, catching the man in the crotch. He stumbled back, then bowed forward, losing control of his pistol. Molly got to her feet and started running.

The guy was too winded to say anything. He just pointed frantically, trying to spur others into action.

Jack flipped the pistol in his hand and charged, letting his right arm drop to his side, gaining momentum, using every ounce of torque he could muster as he swung his arm and the pistol toward the guy's head. The man glanced over, brought his arm up. The flashlight beam nailed Jack in the eyes, temporarily blinding him. The light fell to the ground as Jack smashed the pistol into the guy's face. When the man finally fell, he landed on the flashlight, darkening it. Jack kicked him off it and cut it off as he scooped it up.

Molly screamed out again. Had she encountered someone else? Jack strained to hear anything other than the cicadas at that moment, but they drowned out every sound other than her cries. As he neared the sound, Jack reached behind and pulled out the pistol he'd taken from the man who'd assaulted him in the house. He had no choice but to trust that it worked.

He reached one of the clearings amid the woods. Molly stood there facing another man.

"Please, don't," she said, her hands shaking in front of her, sobs trying to choke her words. "Please..."

Jack extended the pistol. His finger hovered over the trigger.

Stay calm. You've got one shot.

They weren't his words. And they steeled his nerves. His finger brushed the cold steel.

Squeeze it!

Thunder rang out.

Jack waited for the recoil that never happened.

Molly's body jerked, then fell back.

Jack dropped to his knees, relinquishing his grip on the pistol on the way down.

60

"I WANNA ASK YOU ONE MORE QUESTION."

I looked up at the guy. The moon hovered behind him. He had a twisted smile on his face. One that said no matter how I handled this situation, he planned on delivering a beating.

"What?" I said.

"Damn, you can still speak," he said. "I was certain we'd knocked the voice outta you."

I rolled my eyes and looked past him. We were close, but still far enough out that he could do this and they wouldn't hear us at the cabin.

"This is how you get off?" I said. "What happened to good, old-fashioned mercenary work? Go in. Do the job. Get paid. Move on. You must have some kind of little man complex if you're getting your rocks off on this."

He lunged forward, feigning a blow with the sap. I didn't budge. He didn't move far enough to make the threat credible.

"I mean, seriously. By all accounts, I'm about to meet my

maker. You're just piling on at this point. And with me outnumbered four-to-one out here. I'd like to see you try and pull this off when it's just the two of us."

He laughed.

"Yeah," I said. "That's what I thought."

"What?"

"You wouldn't try it. You *know* I'm better. Anyone can tell you aren't the kind of guy who can take a beating. One asskicking and you're out. Hell the thought of it is enough for you to turn tail."

"Oh yeah?" He took a step toward me, balancing as the truck bounced through a rough patch of terrain. "Well, it's just the two of us right now. What do you say? Wanna go at it?"

He didn't wait for me to respond. He lunged forward with that sap up high, ready to strike. I'd been waiting for this moment. I dove at him, driving my shoulder into the front of his knee. He grunted as he swung the sap down on my leg. It burned like hell, but it wasn't enough to stop me. This was my kind of match. A six foot by five foot truck bed. No chance to move away. Grappling at its finest.

I drove an uppercut into his groin. He dropped to his good knee. The other buckled backward as he collapsed. He held tight to that sap, swinging it at my head. I ducked to the side and brought my left arm up. The weapon hit my triceps square on. Felt like he snapped the humerus with the blow. I managed to lift the arm and thread it around his, neutralizing the sap from further use.

He found my face with his free hand. His fingers clawed in search of my eyes. I grabbed hold of his Adam's apple and squeezed with every ounce of hand strength I had left, only letting up to dig in deeper. He jammed his thumb into my nose and pushed up. I released his throat and punished his stomach with three quick strikes. One must've hit just right because he let go of my face. I brought my arm up and wedged his neck between my forearm and bicep. Using my other arm, I secured the choke hold.

With the sap now free from my arm bar, he tried to hit me with it, but his strength was severely reduced. His arm flailed weakly. I pulled him back, allowing myself to fall back to the truck bed. He was suspended on top of me, which meant he had no means of using the sides or lift gate to take pressure off of his throat.

I whipped his head left, then right. His thrashing diminished. With my right arm around his neck, I repositioned my left to the side of his head and in a single counter-motion, I snapped his neck. I shoved his limp body to the side and found the sap.

How the men in the truck hadn't noticed what was going on was beyond me. I was sure I'd hop up and have to fight both of them. But the truck rolled on, the small house nearly in sight now.

I had two choices. Jump off the bed and stealth to the cabin, or take out the driver and see what happened next.

Jumping seemed the safest route.

I chose the driver.

It'd take two taps. One to break the glass, the other to smash his head in. I could guarantee the first. The second was trickier. Chances were he wouldn't remain in perfect position for me to turn his forehead into a crater. It was a matter of how he reacted. Some men would push inside, away from the attack. Others would be so startled they'd simply turn toward the danger.

I had to take into account the passenger, too. No doubt he was armed and could take me out before I ever got that second swing in. I considered attacking him first, but realized that wouldn't work. The driver could simply start evasive maneuvers with the truck. I'd have to drop or ditch. Either way, they'd know and be ready for me at the house.

I closed my eyes and took a deep breath. Steady mind, steady hand. I knew how I had to do this.

With my back to the cab, I held the sap in my right hand. It wouldn't take much to break the glass. I brought my arm across my chest, toward the passenger side. The sap tapped lightly against my ribs. Then I whipped my arm around, following with my torso, twisting at the waist. The sap hit the window, shattering it. I flicked my wrist back towards myself and let go of the weapon. I continued twisting and turning toward the front of the cab. Time slowed and everything happened in slow motion. The sap hung in midair as the truck pushed forward. I saw the guy turn his head toward the window. Fragments of glass spun in the air. My left hand found the weapon's handle mid-arc. I grasped it loosely, my arm continuing on its path. Jagged glass lined the window frame, sliced my flesh near the elbow. Warm arterial spray hit me in the face. I flinched against it, but never lost track of my target. The heavy weapon hit the guy dead on in the middle of the face, crushing his nose, splitting his lips, shattering his teeth or straight up knocking them out.

The truck veered off path, bouncing up and slamming down hard as it cleared a deep rut. Nearly tossed me out. I dropped to my knees. Inside the cab the other guy pulled the driver to the middle and worked his way over to the driver's seat. He held the wheel with one hand, his pistol with the other. He looked back, in search of me. He brought the pistol up and aimed it at the glass.

I didn't give him a chance to shoot. I whipped the sap around the cab and caught him on the side of the head. He slumped face-first into the steering wheel, slowly falling to the right and sending the truck in the same direction. I reached for the door handle. Pulled it open. Stepped my left leg over the side of the bed and found a foothold along the frame. I grabbed hold of the driver's shirt and yanked him out of the cab. The truck bucked as it rolled over the man. I kicked the other guy to the floor of the passenger seat, and then slid in behind the wheel.

The cabin was close. Maybe half a mile away. The windows

were dimly lit. I spotted a dark shadow on the porch. How many lay in wait, ready to pounce?

It wouldn't be enough. The dumbasses who detained me kept my weapon cache in the truck up front. And I'd managed to pick up another Glock. I had plenty.

There would be no survivors.

61

"THE HELL IS GOING ON OUT THERE?" DARROW SAID.

"What's wrong?" Vernon said.

Reese attempted to get a look at the land beyond the front porch, but the narrow door opening limited her view, as did the trouble her eyes had adjusting against the lighting inside the room.

"The truck," Darrow said. "Looked like it went off track for a second there."

"Hell, your guy coulda dropped his cigarette," Vernon said. "He was slapping his crotch to put out the cherry and lost control."

"The simple approach," Darrow said. "You know that's why I dropped you almost thirty years ago. You never considered the worst could've happened."

Vernon waved him off. "It'll just make you a miserable old son of a bitch."

Darrow turned toward him. "A living son of a bitch."

Reese strained to see anything past the men. Headlights swept across the space between them. Her heart dropped into her stomach, leaving her feeling like the contents of her stomach would soon surface. The end was close, and her questions would soon be answered. Would she get a chance to see Jack one more time? Was he OK? Was he going to help her get out? She couldn't do it alone, and neither could he. They had to work together on this one.

"Maybe we both shouldn't be standing here together," Vernon said.

"Now you're thinking," Darrow said. "Take that rifle and go thirty yards east."

Vernon hopped off the porch and lumbered away. The truck drew closer. The headlights grew into large orbs, washing over the porch. It was time. She took a deep breath, tightened every muscle in her body and did what she'd been working up to for the past hour. Years of gymnastics had left certain joints loose. Her thumb regularly popped out of place. Newbies to the station in New York were routinely fleeced by her on a bet that she could escape from their handcuffs in less than thirty seconds.

It hurt like a bastard, though.

She brought her hands together, pressed her right thumb into the bottom joint, and her right index finger across the left thumb pad. A quick counter movement was all it took. The thumb put up little resistance and slipped out of place with a faint pop. Reese bit down on her bottom lip to keep from calling out in pain.

The truck slowed to a stop. The engine rumbled. The headlights brightened as the driver flipped on the high beams. Darrow brought his arm up to shield his eyes against the barrage of light.

Jack.

"Where is he?" Darrow called out.

No one replied.

Reese slipped her left hand through the heavy zip-tie that bound her wrists together. With a quick tug, she popped her thumb back in place. It hung useless now, but that wouldn't last long. She glanced around the room for the hundredth time. No weapons had magically appeared. She didn't need them. She might be out of practice, but she could handle herself.

62

CRYSTAL RIVER, FLORIDA, 1988

THE MOON CAST A HALO OF LIGHT IN THE CLEARING. MOLLY lay on the ground, motionless. Two men faced each other

"Dammit," the man with the deep southern voice called out. "What the hell just happened?"

"I got her," the guy said, walking toward the other man. He had a noticeable limp on his right side,

"Not here," the other man said. He passed within ten feet of Jack, but the boy was unable to muster the ability to do anything. Standing over Molly, the man continued, "This is bad. We gotta get out of here."

Jack started to come to. He felt along the ground for the handgun.

"You all hear that," the man shouted. "We're out of here. You know the drill."

The guy with the limp rushed past. The other man stopped in front of Jack. His teeth glinted in the moonlight as his mouth broadened into a smile.

"Two for one tonight, I suppose. That old bastard Colonel father of yours had this coming. Understand?"

Jack shook his head, trying to conceal his movements as he searched the grass for the pistol.

"Most men die at the age of twenty-five, even if they go on to live to a hundred." He leaned over, placed his pistol to Jack's forehead. "At least you won't have to suffer that fate, kid."

63

I waited behind the wheel, high beams directed at the house. The surrounding area was lit up like daytime. Darrow stood alone on the porch, straining to see inside the truck. I scanned the area for any others. Through the door opening I spotted Reese secured to a chair. She stared at the truck. I breathed a sigh of relief knowing she was still alive.

Darrow raised his rifle and aimed it toward the truck. He wasn't going to fire. Not until he was sure who was inside. I had to attack first. The thought of killing the man before he could get a word out didn't bother me.

I opened the door and let it rest against the frame. I held a pistol in each hand, and secured the .22 in my pocket. I hadn't formed a plan beyond get out of the truck, take cover behind the door, and start shooting. But then it got murky. For one, I could miss, which would result in Darrow and his men firing on my position. I could hit Reese accidentally. Darrow could take cover in the room, holding Reese hostage. Then I'd have no choice but to enter on his terms. I'd be good as dead, then.

Of course, my aim could be true and I'd kill him with one shot. And then I'd face an unseen army.

"Come on," I muttered. "Show yourselves."

No one did. Not like I expected them to anyway.

I kicked the door open and slid out, placing one foot on the ground.

"We got him," I called out.

Darrow lifted the rifle like he was going to shoot. He was a military man. Maybe an agency man. He followed and created rules. Presumably they had a code word to use for this very moment. I had to act panicked, create a reason and belief as to why his man wouldn't follow protocol.

"He took two of our guys out," I said. "I had to subdue—"

"Shut up, Jack."

Vernon appeared in my peripheral.

"Drop those pistols, get outta the truck, and take three steps back."

I stood there for a moment, debating. I didn't doubt Vernon could shoot. It didn't matter how fast I attacked, he'd get me. And at a close distance, I wouldn't get back up.

"Come on, Jack. Don't do it like this. Drop the pistols and let's head up to the porch."

I remained still, said nothing.

"It doesn't have to end this way. Darrow's not the devil you think he is. He wants to work with you. Yeah, see, Jack? There's a way out of this that doesn't involve us burying you in that grave we had dug out about a hundred yards from where we stand."

I didn't buy that for a minute. I was a dead man. Only matter of who I took with me now. I relaxed my grip on the pistols and let them slide off my fingers with my hands held outside the vehicle. They hit the ground with a thud.

"All right," Vernon said, stepping back. His limp was more

noticeable tonight. "Now slide out, hands up, and step back three paces."

I did as instructed, keeping my gaze fixed on Reese inside the cabin. She strained to see what was going on. Darrow had moved off the porch, toward the truck. He stepped through the high beams and into the darkness. He reached inside the truck, grabbed the keys and killed the lights.

Everything went dark while my eyes adjusted to the moonlight.

"He secure?" Darrow asked.

"Yeah," Vernon said.

"I can trust you on this?"

"I'm a cop, for Pete's sake. If I say he's secure, he's secure."

Darrow turned, crouched in front of me so we were eye to eye. "Maybe you've truly lived all of your years past twenty-five, but I'll be damned if you'll make it one day closer to a hundred."

Lightning shot through my nerves. Those words, at that moment, in the dark. A chord deep within me rang out like a madman smashing every key on a church organ. Pain knifed through my soul, rocking me to my core, radiating through my entire body. It debilitated me.

I'd heard that voice before. I'd heard those words spoken. It happened the night Molly was murdered.

Was it possible? Had some force carried me here to this town only to face down the man who haunted my dreams? I thought it had been Reese who drew me here. It was Darrow instead.

"Follow," Darrow said.

The man turned his back on me, but it didn't matter. Even if I could reach him, I wouldn't have time to snap his neck. Vernon would be on top of me after my first step. He wouldn't fire, though. The bullet could pass right through me and take down Darrow too.

Hell, that was a reason enough to make a move now.

I'd have a chance before this was over. I had to take it at the right time. If I died, so be it. But I had to take him down with me and ensure Reese made it out alive.

Darrow stopped on the porch, turned toward me. I searched through memories, trying to match his face with the memories from that night. The men who haunted my darkest dreams. And it had been twenty-eight years since Molly's murder. How was I to compare a man in his thirties to Darrow now?

"Did I ever tell you how much I hated your father, Noble?"

I said nothing. I wouldn't give it to him. I closed my eyes, listened to him talk.

"All I wanted was to kill him."

I still said nothing. The voice matched. It was him.

"You'll be a close second, I guess." He smiled as he pulled a hunting knife from a sheath on his belt. "Or should I say a close third?"

64

I WAS FACE TO FACE WITH THE DEVIL HIMSELF. HIS SMIRK told me he knew I had realized who he was. Every damn detail about the night of Molly's death flashed through my mind at rapid speed. I relived every pained moment from the knock on the door to holding my sister's lifeless body.

My hands steeled into fists. The smoldering embers of revenge burst into flames enveloping every nerve and muscle fiber in my body. "Every ounce of pain she felt, all the fear her soul absorbed that night, I'm gonna deliver a hundred times over to you, you son of a bitch."

I dropped my right foot back, bent the other knee. A simple move, but one that would allow me to maximize the force I delivered as I plowed into him.

Pain flashed through my knee. I glanced down and saw the butt of Vernon's rifle inches from my leg. He drew it back to strike again. I lost my balance. His next swing drove the weapon into my side. I hit the ground. Scrambled to my knees, further aggravating the injury. Darrow rushed forward and delivered a kick that caught me on the side of the head. The rifle butt slammed down on my back. I writhed on the ground, out of breath, fighting the black swirl that threatened to take me into the land of the unconscious. Hell if the bottom of Darrow's boot was the last thing I wanted to see.

"This is going to be fun," Darrow said.

They each hooked a hand under my armpits and dragged me into the room. My shins banged against the stairs. I barely felt the impact.

"Jack," Reese said.

I glanced up, placed her in the center of my field of vision. Her face was twisted in a grimace.

Darrow and Vernon tossed me against the back wall. I managed to twist and hit it with my shoulder instead of my head. Fresh blood seeped from a flesh wound I'd sustained earlier. I slumped to the ground. Every inch of me ached. But I was far from done.

Vernon ran outside and returned a moment later carrying two rifles. He set one next to the doorway, turned the other toward me.

Darrow grabbed the back of Reese's chair and turned it so she faced me. Then he positioned himself behind her, placing his hands on her shoulders. His fingertips turned white, he gripped her so hard. She stared at me through tear-filled eyes. They slipped past her lower eyelids and streamed down her cheeks. She feared what they'd do to me, and her.

"Do you know about Jack's past?" Darrow asked her.

Reese said nothing.

"You never told her?" he said to me.

I said nothing.

"Well let me tell you," he said. "You see, Jack's father and I went way back. I served under him. At one point, the old man said I was the greatest soldier he'd ever commanded. You can imagine how elated I was to hear that. I mean, Noble never complimented anyone. And, you see, some other son of a bitch received my medal. What I'd done, for Jack's dad nonetheless, no one, not even him, could ever report. Not even to the man at the top of the chain. That wasn't uncommon, actually. But I'd potentially saved our country." He paused, smiled. "I'm not that same man. I'd just as soon let it die if faced with the decision again."

I glanced past him, past Vernon, and let my gaze fall on the truck. Soon, I told myself. Soon I'd get my chance.

Darrow continued. "Anyway, that praise and honor quickly faded when I learned that the Army was screwing me over. All those black ops, and someone else reaped the rewards of my missions plundering governments and taking over money- and power-rich strongholds. I never saw an ounce of it. So I took it. Then your damn father had to turn on me and my men. I waited until the time was right. Until I had the necessary resources. Until that moment when I could strike and move on and no one would ever know. I had the power then. And I have more of it now."

"Why Molly?" I said. My throat burned at the words that would lead to an explanation I didn't want to hear. I had to buy more time, though. The moment wasn't right yet.

"We went there to kill your father. Plain and simple. When it became clear he wasn't there, I made the decision to take your sister and hold her until the good Colonel exchanged himself for her. In fact, I would have preferred that. Then I could have taken him out to the gulf and tortured the bastard."

I looked down at the floor between my legs.

"That make you uncomfortable, Noble?"

I shook my head. "There were times I wanted to do the same to him."

Darrow laughed. "Even at this point, you've got minutes left, and you're cracking jokes. So much like that asshole father of yours." He took a few steps to the side, turned back and pointed at

Vernon. "And if it weren't for the good Sheriff here, Molly might still be alive."

I looked up at Vernon. His face went slack. His mouth dropped open as though he were going to say something. Instead, he turned away.

"You son of a bitch." I straightened up. "Both of you. I'm going to inflict all the pain I've felt for twenty-eight years on you. If you plan on killing me, do it now, otherwise you'll never get the chance."

Darrow nodded. "Oh, your time is coming. First we've got to take care of your girlfriend here. I want you to see this, Jack. I want to hear you beg for mercy for her. It's not going to happen yet. I'm gonna keep both of you around, just to give you a taste of what business is like for me. See, I have a big deal coming up. Gonna supply a group of people that aren't so friendly toward this great country. I bet you'd like to be a part of that, wouldn't you? I know Reese would. See, it turns out, these are the people she's been hiding from all this time."

Reese closed her eyes. Her face tightened. She was trying to keep from crying. I wouldn't have thought less of her if she had let it out. Most people would.

"I'll do that now," I said. "Let her go, and you can do whatever you want to me."

Darrow shuffled to the door, leaned in and said something to Vernon. The sheriff slipped out of sight. Patrol, I presumed. Had to make sure no one had followed me over. Dammit. I wanted both men in the room. The time was almost upon us.

And then, as Darrow shouldered a rifle and made his way back to the middle of the room, Reese attempted to screw everything up.

65

DARROW JUMPED BACK, STARTLED AT FIRST. THE OLD soldier's instincts took over and he readied himself to defend. Reese screamed as she whipped both arms to the front. An empty zip tie loop dangling from her right wrist. She leapt forward. An awkward move with the chair attached to her legs. It held her back, threw her off balance. Perhaps she thought it would break under the sudden movement. The chair looked as though it had been in the cabin for the past hundred years.

In the moment it took for Darrow to react, Reese had regained her balance and spun toward him. He swung the rifle in front of him, catching Reese in the chin. Fortunately, he hadn't had a chance to draw the weapon back. The strike was more like a half-bunt, half-swing. Reese raked her nails across his face from his forehead to his lips, leaving behind red marks that filled in with blood. The man pawed at his eyes, grunting in pain.

Reese's attack left her unbalanced, and she hit the ground hard, twisted at the waist. She rolled right and went for Darrow's legs. Her outstretched arms wrapped around each, and she attempted to crocodile roll the guy.

He attempted to draw aim on her, but could barely manage to open his eyes. So he flipped the rifle and drove the butt stock down.

I scrambled to my feet after accelerating the timer in my head to zero. There was no more waiting. I lunged toward Darrow. Vernon ran up the stairs with his weapon aimed forward.

Thunder rang out. I gritted my teeth against phantom pain. Splintered wood rained down throughout the room. Vernon stopped to reload, buying me a few precious seconds.

I reached into my back pocket and pulled out the sap. The dumb sons of bitches hadn't bothered to search me. They saw I had two pistols and must've figured that was it. Big mistake.

I whipped the sap around, aiming for Darrow's head. He ducked and somehow managed to position his body so I ran into him. My legs were already weakened. I lost my balance and tumbled to the floor. When I stopped sliding, I glanced up, greeted by the barrel of Vernon's rifle.

"Everyone chill the hell out," Vernon said, positioning himself so he was out of reach. He aimed the rifle at me. "So help me, Reese, I'll blow his goddamn brains out right here."

She stopped thrashing, but refused to relinquish her grip on Darrow's legs. Our gazes met, perhaps for the last time. She pursed her lips tight, shook her head. I nodded, closed my eyes, dropped my forehead to the wooden plank. She'd blown our chance.

Hell, I'd blown it.

The timer in my head reset back to its original countdown. Time was almost up.

Three.

Two.

One.

Nothing.

I'd stopped the truck just outside range of being spotted by anyone at the house. There, I took the shirt off the man in the passenger seat, wiped some oil on it, then stuffed it in the gas tank deep enough to hit fuel, and lit it. It should have exploded by now.

"I'm just going to put an end to this now, Noble," Darrow said. "Consider yourself lucky that you're not going to face the torture I had planned for your—"

BOOM.

66

CRYSTAL RIVER, FLORIDA, 1988

THE MAN WITH THE LIMP WHO'D SHOT MOLLY APPEARED. HE pushed the gun away from Jack, and dragged the other guy toward the woods. "We gotta get outta here, man. The cops are close. The other guys are cleaning up."

"Guess your fate's changed," the guy said before slipping into the cover of darkness.

By the time Jack found the pistol, the men were gone. He crawled through the high, damp grass toward his sister's body. "Molly," he said. "Please say something."

Her dark eyes stared up at him, the moon glinting off them. She said nothing. There was no way she could.

He cradled her head in his lap, feeling the warm flow from the hole in her head trickle over his fingers and onto his legs. Tears streamed down his face. He could have saved her. The man was in his sights. All he had to do was pull the trigger.

Sean appeared a few moments later, followed by the sound of sirens. His frame blocked out the faded moonlight.

"Christ, what happened, Jack?" he dropped to his knees and

grabbed Molly, pulling her toward him, shaking her. "Molly, come on, sweetie. Say something. Tell me I'm a crappy brother. Anything."

"She's gone," Jack said.

"Shut up." Sean drew one arm back like he was going to punch his brother. Tears streamed down his cheeks. Jack readied himself to be struck, but his brother backed down. He eased Molly to the ground. "No, no you can't be dead. Molly, come on, wake up."

Jack said nothing as he watched his older brother break down. As much as it hurt, he imagined the pain would be a hundred times worse when his parents learned of their only daughter's death.

Minutes passed as the brothers stood watch over their sister's body. Jack aimed the pistol at the darkness, swearing that if one of them showed their face, he'd shoot first.

Beams of light cut through the darkness. "Hello? Police. Anybody back here?"

Neither boy spoke. They stared down at their sister as the lights brightened the area.

"Is anyone back there?" an officer called out.

"Here," Sean said.

Jack glanced down at his brother, who gestured at the pistol. Jack tossed it into the grass and held his arms out as the light washed over him.

"OK, just stay put," an officer said. "You on the ground, stand up."

"I'm not leaving my sister," Sean said.

"I said stand up."

"Y'all can drag me to jail," Sean shouted. "I'm not leaving my sister."

There were at least three of them, all apparently ready for a gunfight with a twelve- and fourteen-year-old.

"Our sister was shot," Jack said. "She's...she's dead."

"Jesus Christ," one of the officers said. He stepped forward, and Jack recognized him as John Wiley, a friend of their father. "Oh, Christ. Jack, Sean, you boys all right? Are you hurt?"

Both shrugged. Their injuries were nothing to worry about at that moment.

The other officers eased up. They convinced the brothers to leave watch of their sister's body. They walked off into the darkness, allowing her soul time to leave.

67

THE CABIN ROCKED ON ITS FOUNDATION. PROBABLY SLID OFF it. The windows exploded inward. Fragments of glass and shrapnel from the truck sliced through the air. Something gouged my back. Reese screamed in pain.

Darrow fell backward, clinging to the rifle. A cloud of smoke enveloped him. I swept the area for Vernon, but he was nowhere to be found.

"Reese," I called out. "Are you OK?"

Seconds passed. I pushed up off the floor, ignoring the pain that ransacked my body. Smoke continued to blanket the room. Heat pushed down on me. I looked up and saw the ceiling ablaze. The weathered wooden structure would go up in a matter of seconds.

Reese lay motionless on the floor. I rose into the smoke, slid my feet across the ground, doing my damnedest to keep them from lifting up and letting glass underneath. Didn't matter how I proceeded. The shards found their way into the soles of my feet.

"Come on, sweetie," I said. "Show me you're OK."

She didn't.

Movement out of the corner of my eye caught my attention. Darrow sat up. He held his head in one hand. Blood seeped through his fingers. I followed his gaze to the floor. The rifle was halfway between us.

Without hesitation, I dove for it. Dozens of tiny glass fragments sliced through me, embedding themselves. I landed a couple feet from the weapon and had to crawl forward.

Darrow jumped after I had, yet managed to land a bit closer. He had a hand on the rifle.

"Not today." I pushed off the floor and dove forward. The side wall blazed orange. Smoke rushed out through the doorway. The structure creaked and groaned. It would collapse at any moment.

Darrow turned the rifle sideways. He had one hand under the barrel, and was bringing his other to the trigger. I lurched forward, grabbed the barrel, and twisted it around toward me. Not my best idea. All he had to do was squeeze the trigger and I was done for. I rolled to the right and aimed the weapon to the left. If it went off now the slug would come close to Reese.

"Don't move, Reese," I called out.

The blast deafened me. The discharge left me momentarily blinded. The barrel scorched my hand.

A second later the first part of the structure came down. A beam that ran the length of the cabin landed on Darrow's legs. The roof caved in, sending flaming joists and pieces of roof down. I lurched forward, twisted and yanked the rifle from his grasp.

He reached back in an attempt to free himself from the flaming wood. The flame wrapped around his hands and shot up his shirt.

"Help me!"

"I'll help you all right." I put the barrel to his head and pulled the trigger.

Another section of the roof came down, this time close to

Reese. She didn't budge. Had Darrow's shot hit her? Was she choking on the smoke? I scooped her up and carried her out of the cabin. Moments later, the structure came down in a fiery crash. A wave of heat blew past, knocking me to a knee. The flames rose high, and lit up an acre or two of the surrounding area. I swept the landscape. Didn't spot Vernon or anyone else. Maybe the coward had run. Only thing I saw was the burned out truck and a late model F-250.

"Reese?" I cradled her in my arms. Her face was close to mine. I placed my cheek on her mouth, leaving a gap under her nostrils. I felt hot, erratic breath. She showed no other signs of life. I was torn between performing a more thorough evaluation to make sure she was OK, and getting us away from the burning remains of the cabin. I stopped next to the F-250 and went over her as quickly as I could. There were no apparent major injuries, so I placed her in the cab, then climbed into the driver's seat. I reached for the ignition. The keys weren't there. Son of a bitch, they must've been on one of the men. No chance I was finding them now.

Before giving up hope, I checked the glove box. Nothing. Then the console. Nothing. Headlights appeared in the rear-view.

"Come on, not now."

My first thought was to get the pistols that I'd dropped by the other truck. The chances of them surviving the blast and remaining in working condition were minimal. Glancing over to the fire surrounding the other truck, I realized even getting to where they were on the ground would be impossible.

I climbed down from the cab. There were at least two sets of headlights on the way out. Vernon must have called in some reinforcements. The bastard was in hiding, waiting for them. I had a feeling he'd emerge once we were detained. Finish the job.

I ran my hands under the driver's front wheel well. Then the passenger's side. At the rear I found what I was looking for. A small magnetic box held a spare key. I jammed it in the ignition, closed my eyes, took a deep breath. The engine cranked, failed to turn over. I tried again. Same result. Not good. Two vehicles incoming. At least two men to a car. No way was I taking on four people in my current condition. We'd have to run. And we wouldn't get far. Out of desperation, I slammed my foot down on the gas pedal and turned the key. It cranked. I held the key in the same position, pumped the gas. The engine roared. I drove past the blaze, away from the incoming convoy, into the darkness without any idea what lay ahead or if there was a way off the property. All I knew was I had to get somewhere I could try and revive Reese.

And then find Vernon.

For the first few miles I kept the headlights off. The truck bounced over hills and through ditches. We made it across a stream and through a patch of thick mud. We did this all at under twenty-five miles an hour. The moon illuminated the ground enough that I could make out most obstacles before it was too late. The ones I didn't see weren't anything the truck couldn't handle.

Reese moaned, then called out in pain. She opened her eyes, flinched and struck out at the air.

"It's OK." I reached for her hand. She fought me off. "Reese, it's Jack. We're all right."

"Jack?" She forced herself up, staring at me as though she hadn't seen me in years. She grabbed her head. "God, it hurts. What happened?"

I told her how I had rigged the truck, and how she had attacked Darrow moments before the vehicle exploded. I explained that the house caught on fire, and that something had struck her, rendering her unconscious.

"Are they dead?" she asked.

"Darrow is." I glanced up at the rear view. It appeared they hadn't followed us. Not closely, at least. I still wasn't certain we were far enough from the house to turn on the lights.

"What about Vernon?" she asked.

"He got away. At least, I assume he did. There were two other trucks when I'd arrived. This was the only one left."

"We have to find him. He could turn everything around and pin it on us."

I had a feeling we'd find him in one of three places. But first, we had to get to town.

"Look around," I said. "Any of this look familiar to you?"

Her ensuing laughter was one of the best sounds I'd ever heard

"What?" I said.

"It all looks the same. Cut on the lights."

"I don't know if we're far enough away yet."

She closed her eyes and leaned back against the open window. The wind created a part in her hair on the left side. "Head northwest. That should bring us near town."

I'd been on a westward trajectory, so making the adjustment didn't require us to pass through harm's way.

"Just keep pushing forward," she said. "We'll be there soon."

And with that, she drifted off again.

68

We reached town a couple hours later. The moon expanded against the horizon. Streetlights lit up the perimeter of Texline. I searched the truck before ditching it a quarter mile from town. Came up with a tire iron and not much else. Reese said she had a Smith & Wesson M&P 40 at the house. That'd only do us good if we could reach it. I had a feeling the path would be littered with cops.

We hiked into town, made it there by dawn. We stuck to side streets and backyards. Reese had refused to remain behind with the truck. She'd recovered enough to keep moving, but required assistance over any unavoidable obstacles.

My hope was that Vernon waited at the police station. It was the only place he was safe anymore. Presumably he had surrounded himself with two or three of his best deputies. He would have concocted a story in his favor.

And against ours.

We reached the street behind Reese's place, found a spot to hide that allowed us to keep watch. I stared at darkened windows.

Saw nothing. I was partly relieved, and partly disappointed. I'd rather have a showdown and be done with this.

"Let's just go, Jack," Reese said. "What are the chances someone's in there?"

"Better than you think," I said.

"Darrow's gone. His guys aren't gonna bother with us. The townies are idiots, and the rest are recouping, trying to figure out how to pull off that deal. All we have to worry about is Vernon. He can't hide the truth forever. So if they're waiting for us, or they come for us, let them take us. I'll make whatever call I have to and get us moved. OK?"

I nodded. "OK, here's how we do this." I laid out a plan that had Reese staying behind and watch the front entrance after I went inside.

She reached out, pulled me close, kissed me. It hurt like hell, but neither of us stopped for several seconds.

"We don't have to find him," she said. "We can get in there, grab a few things and go, Jack. The two of us, we'll disappear."

I held her hand, gently tracing around the scratch the zip tie had left behind on her wrist. "Then we'll be running. Forever. I don't live like that. Hell, I can't live like that. It's not in my DNA. We have to end this. If you're uncomfortable, then stay behind and let me do it. I'll get you after it's done, then we can go."

She looked down. "I'm just tired. I hurt. And I can't believe all this is happening. I knew about Darrow, but Vernon was my friend, and he was willing to kill me to hide his secret."

"That's one of the deepest parts of men. Let them get away with something truly evil and they'll draw from the darkest part of their souls to protect that which no one else can ever know. You did nothing wrong. And now we have a chance to set everything right. We can put Vernon where he belongs, and stop anyone from profiting on this deal Darrow had set up."

She steeled her face. The tough-as-nails NYPD detective had

shown back up. "You're right. Finish this and then we'll leave." She smiled. "I hear Hawaii is beautiful this time of year."

I hopped the fence and sprinted to the corner of the house. The driveway was empty. I only saw half the street, but there was no one there. I leaned against the house, tuning out the chirping birds, the rumbling garbage truck and its squeaky brakes on the other street, and the faint sound of barking dogs.

I slowly made my way to the front. The fifteen feet from the corner of the building to the doorway felt as though they took forever. I was exposed in a way that left me feeling naked.

Someone rushed in from behind.

I turned, arms up ready to fight.

Reese threw her hands in front of her face to deflect the possible blow.

"Jesus," I said. "The hell are you doing?"

"I'm not going to let you face any of this alone, Jack."

"Fair enough, but next time warn me."

I led the way to the door. It was still unlocked, and opened without a problem. I peered around the corner. Dodge sat at the top, ears back, head down, his eyes focused on me. He lowered his head until it rested on his front paws.

"Anyone?" she asked.

"Vernon's dog."

"Dammit. I forgot he was there when we—" she hesitated "—when I was taken."

It was still easy for her to forget Vernon hadn't been on her side at that time.

"I'm going in," I said. "I want you to remain in the foyer, keep the door open a bit and watch outside for anyone coming at us."

I took the stairs one at a time, stepping on the edges to minimize noise. The wolf-like dog remained at the top of the stairs until I was eye level. I reached out to pet him. He stood and turned, disappearing behind the knee wall. I continued to the top, poked my head around the corner. Dodge stood in front of Reese's door now. He looked back at me, made eye contact, went in the room.

"We good down there?" I asked.

"Yeah," she said. "How about up there?"

"It's quiet. Just need to check out your room."

"What's the dog doing?"

"Don't know. He just went into your room."

"I'm coming up." She let the door fall closed and climbed the stairs.

I moved forward without her, stopping to check the bathroom. There was no need to go inside, I could see it all from outside the doorway. I whistled for Dodge. He didn't come. When I reached the edge of Reese's room, I saw why.

"Jesus."

"What is it?" she asked.

I stepped aside and let her look.

"Vernon," she whispered.

We stood at the side of the bed looking down at the man. He'd found her pistol, and put it to the same use I would have. A single shot through his head. A cloud of blood, skull and brain painted the wall.

I ushered Reese out of the room, then returned for Dodge, slipping a makeshift leash on him in order to get him out of the house. We weren't out there thirty seconds when a cruiser pulled up. Miles got out and raced toward the house. He looked over each of us, his face twisted with confusion. Shaking his head, he composed himself.

"We're too late?" he said.

I nodded. "He's upstairs, in Reese's room."

"Whose room?" Miles said.

"Sorry, Billie's."

"Oh." He reached into his pocket and pulled out a piece of yellow notebook paper. Handed it to me.

I read over a suicide note and confession of sorts. It started off outlining Darrow's final deal. The one he alluded to at the cabin. It was a massive deal, with three working parts consisting of Darrow, a drug cartel, and a terrorist cell. The meeting was to take place the next day.

"I can put you in touch with the right people, Miles. They'll take care of the rest of Darrow's crew, and whoever else shows up for this. I'm sure they'll want to *talk* to all of them."

He nodded as he walked past me, toward the door. "We'll head to the station in a few. I just want to verify the body and call it in."

Reese pressed against me and placed a hand on the notebook paper. Vernon's letter continued with a confession to the murders of Ingrid and Herbie. He admitted that he did it to pin the case on me in hopes that I'd be out of their hair after he'd locked me up. I had trouble accepting that, as Vernon was the one who freed me from the jail cell. There had to have been a reason why, but he didn't make note of it. Perhaps he had regretted what he had done to my sister all those years ago.

Finally, the note ended with him telling his wife and family he was sorry for his sins, and asked them to forgive him for taking his own life.

Miles came back down a few minutes later. Another cruiser pulled up and the female officer joined us.

"Billie," he said. "Would you mind waiting here with Jaimie for the coroner? He's on his way. I want to sit down with Jack and make sure we don't lose any time contacting his people."

"Sure, Miles. I'll wait." She turned to me. "Hurry back?"

"Of course."

She leaned in and kissed me, then whispered in my ear. "I'm not kidding about Hawaii."

I whispered back, "I might have a connection or two there."

69

CRYSTAL RIVER, FLORIDA, 1988

JACK AND SEAN SPENT THE NIGHT AT THE HOSPITAL IN THE same room. John Wiley remained outside their door, working frantically to reach their father. Jack was woken up every hour on the hour when some nurse or doctor poked or prodded or forced him to take a pill. Every time he rose, he remembered the events of the night. First, as a nightmare, but as the sleep faded away, he knew it had happened.

By the time the sun came up, he felt as though he were ready for another night of sleep.

His parents entered the room sometime after seven. Both broke into heavy sobs before reaching their boys. The family huddled together, crying, for several minutes. Wiley remained on the fringes, torn between his police duties, and his duties to his friend. He had to act, though. Every second they worked with no lead, the greater the chance of never finding Molly's killer.

"I'm sorry to do this," John Wiley said, "but we've got to interview your boys."

"Like hell," the elder Noble said. "This is no time for that."

"You understand how this works. I know you do. If we don't get some information now, we'll never know. Do you want Molly's death to go unavenged?"

At that moment it seemed their father was ready to avenge it himself. He lunged at his friend, pinning him to the wall with a hand around his throat.

"That's my daughter, you son of a bitch. You hear me? My daughter. You think I don't care about catching the bastards who did this? Do you?"

The brothers broke away from their mother's grasp and pulled their father off of Wiley.

"Dad," Sean said. "It's OK. It's fresh. Jack and I will talk to them. We'll do it for Molly."

Jack and Sean spoke to multiple detectives the rest of that morning and most of the afternoon, retelling the story start to finish. For some reason two FBI agents questioned them. The boys told them everything they could, descriptions of what they remembered from faces, accents, words and names they had heard.

Jack figured with that and the two bodies he'd left for them, they had enough to solve the case.

But it wasn't enough. He learned a little while later that no bodies had been found on the property. The men who had killed Molly had swept the house and property and gathered up their fallen.

The remaining evidence was collected from the home, but in 1988, forensic science was in its infancy. Blood, fabric, and other items were filed away. Despite the best efforts of the police department and FBI, Molly's death remained a mystery. Perhaps one day the case would be revisited, but the family couldn't push it.

The funeral had been the largest the town had ever seen. Molly was buried in the church cemetery in a ceremony only open to family and close friends. In less than twenty years, her mother would join her.

And Jack, Sean and his parents never spent another night in that house.

70

I spent an hour at the station with Miles, first detailing the events of the previous twenty-four hours, and then we contacted an old friend at Langley. He took down all the information and let us know he'd disperse it to the proper agencies, and that he'd have someone from his office at the police station within a few hours.

"You need a ride back?" Miles asked me after we'd finished.

I glanced up at the clock on the wall. It was just after seven am. "I'm fine walking. Not like it's that far."

"Sorry for everything that happened here, Jack. I know things haven't been perfect in this town. Hell, that's why I left a football scholarship at Baylor and came back. I wanted to help the folks here. People like Herbie and Ingrid, well, they were the lifeblood of this place. Now they're gone, and I can already see that lots of folks are considering moving on. At least the ones who can afford it. Shoot, lack of money's what keeps anyone young here anymore. Not everyone had the kind of opportunities I had. You should see the way some of my old classmates look at me. It's like they curse me for hanging around here."

"Did you know?"

"About Darrow?"

"Him, and that Vernon was mixed up with him."

"I knew some about Darrow, but I thought it was drugs. Little we can do there since he kept that part of his business out of town. I passed along whatever I found to Vernon and he assured me that it was going to the D.E.A. He said the Feds were building a case. Guess that was all a lie." Miles opened a drawer and pulled out a phone. "And Vernon, well, I knew nothing about him and Darrow working together. In fact, I knew little about his past. Only that he grew up here, left for the military, did some contracting afterward, then returned to Texline when he was in his thirties. He took over the department maybe ten or fifteen years ago. Always seemed like a nice enough fella. Everyone liked him. He helped folks out where he could."

I nodded, said nothing.

"Hard to believe he did that to Ingrid. She was like a second mother to him."

"I'm wondering if he had a choice in the matter."

"You think Darrow made him do it?"

I nodded. "The guy had a lot on him. Knew his past. Guess they both had that on each other, but Darrow was in a position to ruin more than just Vernon's life."

Miles leaned back, glanced at his watch, then peeked at the phone he'd pulled from his desk. "Shoot, Jack. I've kept you here long enough now. Get out of here. Let Billie know I'm here if she needs anything."

The walk back to Reese's didn't take much longer than the drive to the station. I was able to take a more direct route, one that didn't involve backyards, too.

I wanted to call Sean, let him know what had happened. Tell

him that Molly's soul could rest at ease now. He could break the news to my father, if he felt it was a good idea to do so. For some people, it was better to glance at a scar from time to time, rather than tear open an old wound.

I reached into my pockets. Both were empty. I'd have to wait until I got to Reese's to make the call.

I turned the corner to the narrow alley that led to her driveway.

"What the hell?"

I ran toward the house, passing two black sedans parked on the street. A third idled in the driveway. A man in a dark suit emerged from the doorway of Reese's place carrying a box full of her plants.

"What's going on?" I said.

He walked past me toward his car without acknowledging my presence.

"Hey, asshole," I said. "I'm talking to you."

He kept going.

I continued to the house. Another man came out with a suitcase.

"You," I said, finger aimed in his direction.

"One second." He nodded slightly as he passed. I got a good look at the cred pack attached to his belt.

FBI.

"Where is she?" I asked.

He turned, looked around, took a couple steps toward me. "Are you Jack Noble?"

I nodded, half-expecting him to arrest me.

"Reese McSweeney's identity was compromised. Word was out that she was here, and that word has reached the wrong people. We expect someone to show up here within the next few hours with the intention of executing a hit on her. There'll be a team that stays behind to handle that threat."

"Where is she now?"

"I can't tell you that, sir. She—"

I bumped into him. "Like hell you can't. Tell me now. Where is she?"

The agent glanced toward the house. "I think you should back up, Mr. Noble. You don't have the friends you used to have."

I didn't recognize the guy, and doubted he'd ever run into me before. But someone had briefed him on me, and what I was capable of.

"Sorry," he said. "But you know how this works. Nobody can know where she is. Neither friends nor family. Not with the people that are out after her."

"I can handle them."

"And they can handle you. And probably in ways you've never been subjected to. Sure, maybe you wouldn't talk. But maybe you would."

I stood there, staring at him, but past him. His face blurred. I heard his words and let them float by at the same time. All I thought about was Reese. We had a plan, one that I had intended to carry out. And now she was gone, and so was the possible life we could have had together. Maybe we wouldn't have made it long, but at least we could have tried. Now it was just a guessing game. Where would they take her? Would I ever see her again?

The agent continued. "That's a risk the FBI can't take while she is a part of our program."

She could have refused their help. Told them to screw off, go away, something. Looking at these guys, I could see that they hadn't come here to present an option to her. Darrow had tipped off the men who wanted Reese dead. Not just dead, but tortured until she decided it was no longer worth taking another breath.

I couldn't blame her for taking the FBI's help. It was simple, leave or die. I never factored into the equation.

The door to Reese's apartment slammed shut. Two agents walked past me, one on either side. They took position next to their partner, one pulling his coat back so I could see his holstered pistol.

"Now," the agent continued, "I think you should go get your things and get out of here."

"Got no car," I said.

"That's gonna be taken care of. You'll have one at the old couple's house in about twenty minutes. That's where your stuff is, right?"

I said nothing. How'd he know that? In light of everything that had happened, it didn't matter.

None of it did now.

I FELT THE WEIGHT OF EVERYTHING THAT HAD HAPPENED IN the small town since I'd arrived. Reese outted. The old couple murdered. Killing the man who had orchestrated Molly's death. Vernon's suicide. Every wound I'd suffered as a twelve-year-old and while in Texline tore open at once. I nearly collapsed on the street.

It was hotter than normal that morning. The sun beat down on my brow. Sweat formed and slipped down my cheek into beard stubble.

A group of kids played a block ahead. Some of the same ones I'd run into before. I didn't see the blond-haired boy. I wondered if the FBI had stopped by their house and offered them a deal to skip town. I hoped not. I had to make good on the promise I'd made the woman.

As I approached, the kids scattered. There'd be no showdown today. I still wondered what the hell they were hiding that day. Guess I had to let it go.

I slowed down as I approached Herbie and Ingrid's. Yellow

police tape surrounded the place. I'd have to break the law to gather my things.

No place would ever be safe with me around. I'd figured that out a while back. The events of the past couple days cemented the fact that I was toxic, especially to the normal folks. I'd move on while the residents of Texline had to recover from the mess I'd made.

No, it wasn't entirely my mess. I managed to get caught up in the middle of it. Like always. Hell, at least I helped sweep it up. History wouldn't look at it that way, but it was what it was.

It always is.

I grabbed the spare key from under the mailbox that hung next to the back door. Then I yanked the yellow police tape away. Stepping into the kitchen, I was reminded of Ingrid, her welcoming smile, the smell of whatever she was baking that day lingering in the air. I could still grab a hint of the bread she'd cooked on her final day.

There was a note on the fridge that I hadn't noticed the last time I was in the house. It was made out to me. I slid it out from under the magnet.

"Jack," it read. "Come find me the moment you get home. - Ingrid."

What would she have told me? She'd been crying earlier that day, the last time I saw her alive. Was she going to tell me about Darrow? Vernon? Had she uncovered his secret? That would have explained why she was so upset. And when she confronted him with it, he killed her and Herbie.

I thought back to how I found her. She hadn't expected to die at that moment.

I folded the paper into a small square and stuck it in my pocket. Walking through the house felt like stepping back in time. They hadn't updated for at least forty years, and in some cases, never. I climbed the stairs, stepping over the spot where Herbie had fallen into the next life.

The door to my room was closed. I turned the knob and pushed it open, waiting in the hall in case there was movement inside.

There wasn't.

I gathered the few things I owned, shoved them in my bag and threw it over my shoulder. Then I popped into the old couple's bedroom to say goodbye. Superstition, I guess. They weren't there, but maybe their spirits were hanging around for a few extra days.

"I survived, somehow," I said. "I don't know, maybe you had something to do with it. Thank you."

Back downstairs I stopped in the kitchen to get a glass of water and placed a call to Sean. The conversation was brief. I simply told him I was leaving town and would be in touch soon with instructions. I wanted to fill him in on all that had happened, but decided a two minute conversation was not the way to do it. We'd be face to face soon. After hanging up, I spotted a black sedan outside. It had been more than twenty minutes since my initial encounter with the FBI agents outside of Reese's apartment. I figured they were delivering the car for me to leave town in.

Then another sedan pulled up, followed by a third. Why the hell were they coming to see me here? Were they going to tell me where Reese was? Maybe they'd brought her along to say goodbye.

I watched as the men exited the vehicle. Studied their faces. Didn't recognize a single one of them. How many teams had they sent out here?

I exited through the kitchen door and came face to face with two of the men.

"You guys missed her," I said. "They found her at her place. They're already on the move."

"Jack Noble?" the guy on my left said.

I couldn't tell if it was my heart that sank, or if my stomach had risen.

I turned and was face-to-face with two more Feds. They had circled the house. I caught sight of others positioned so as to cut off my escape routes.

"Mr. Noble," the guy said. "It's best if you just stop right there."

I turned in a circle, looking for a way out. Another agent emerged from the kitchen door. And another stood across the alley. They had me boxed in. All of them trained their pistols on me.

"Arms up," the guy said.

I didn't move.

"Now." He raised his weapon. "We have orders to shoot if you don't comply."

"Who sent you?" I asked.

He said nothing.

"Dammit," I said. "Who sent you for me?"

A black windowless panel van pulled up, drove past the cars, and screeched to stop a few feet away. The door opened. A guy in tactical gear with a pistol strapped to his leg hopped out.

The Fed closest said, "Arms up."

I had no choice. I lifted my arms. The Fed holstered his weapon, patted me down.

"I'm clean," I said.

"Get in the van," he said.

I hesitated. He shoved me forward. I climbed in. It smelled like a hospital. Like they'd disinfected it recently. There were three rows of seats. The driver and passenger seats were occupied by men in jeans and t-shirts. They wore ball caps and cheap watches. I slid into the middle row. The agent who did most of the talking climbed in next to me. Two more took the back seat. The guy in tactical gear hopped in and crouched. The remaining Feds returned to the sedans and we pulled away convoy style.

"You gonna tell me what this is about?" I said.

He pulled out a cell phone and placed a call.

"Yeah, we got him."

I strained to listen to the voice on the other end, but I couldn't hear a damn thing.

"No, he has no clue." The guy glanced at me. "You sure about that? No telling how he's gonna react." He paused. "All right."

He shoved the phone against the side of my head.

"Yeah?" I said.

"Jack Noble."

It couldn't be. "You son of a bitch."

"That's how you treat your old pal?"

"You're not my pal, Frank. Your ass shouldn't even be alive right now."

Frank Skinner laughed. "Only have you to thank for that."

"The hell do you want?"

"You."

JACK NOBLE'S story continues in DEADLINE, links and an excerpt below.

WANT to be among the first to download the next Jack Noble book? Sign up for L.T. Ryan's newsletter, and you'll be notified the minute new releases are available - and often at a discount for the first 48 hours! As a thank you for signing up, you'll receive a complimentary copy of *The Recruit: A Jack Noble Short Story*.

Join here: http://ltryan.com/newsletter/

I enjoy hearing from readers. Feel free to drop me a line at ltryan70@gmail.com. I read and respond to every message.

If you enjoyed reading *Never Cry Mercy*, I would appreciate it if you would help others enjoy these books, too. How?

Lend it. This e-book is lending-enabled, so please, feel free to share it with a friend. All they need is an amazon account and a Kindle, or Kindle reading app on their smart phone or computer.

Recommend it. Please help other readers find this book by recommending it to friends, readers' groups and discussion boards.

Review it. Please tell other readers why you liked this book by reviewing it at Amazon, Barnes & Noble, Apple or Goodreads. Your opinion goes a long way in helping others decide if a book is for them. Also, a review doesn't have to be a big old book report. If you do write a review, please send me an email at ltryan70@gmail.com so I can thank you with a personal email.

Like Jack. Visit the Jack Noble Facebook page and give it a like: https://www.facebook.com/JackNobleBooks.

ALSO BY L.T. RYAN

The Jack Noble Series

The Recruit (free)

The First Deception (Prequel 1)

Noble Beginnings

A Deadly Distance

Ripple Effect (Bear Logan)

Thin Line

Noble Intentions

When Dead in Greece

Noble Retribution

Noble Betrayal

Never Go Home

Beyond Betrayal (Clarissa Abbot)

Noble Judgment

Never Cry Mercy

Deadline

End Game

Mitch Tanner Series

The Depth of Darkness

Into The Darkness

Deliver Us From Darkness - coming soon

Affliction Z Series

DEADLINE: CHAPTER 1

The sedative they injected into me prior to boarding the Gulf-stream G650 knocked me out cold before the flight from Texas to who the hell knew where departed from a private airfield some-where north of Dallas, Texas. I'd been there twice before. Both times while working for Frank Skinner and the SIS. It seemed fitting that we used it as the first step on a journey to see Frank, presumably for our final meeting.

Waking up hours later as the jet touched down, I felt the full hangover effect of the knockout drug. At least it made it easy to forget about everything that had happened over the past few days.

To forget them.

To forget her.

Especially her.

It was futile to dwell on it. The FBI had made Reese McSweeney vanish. She was out of my life. Again. Somehow I always figured we'd meet again. We had one shot. And we'd blown it.

Nothing new there.

We should've left Texline when we had the chance.

I sat in the rear seat of the sedan with an agent on either side. The windows were blacked out, and a divider separated us from the front. I couldn't see a damn thing. The Feds weren't much for conversation, either. They didn't even crack a smile at my recent bad dad joke repertoire. It made it difficult to ascertain where the hell we were. The end destination had been made evident by my brief conversation with Frank. Based on that, I figured we were somewhere in Northern Virginia.

Frank had been placed in charge of the CIA's Special Activities Division, Special Operations Group. Didn't take much of a stretch of the imagination to assume that my escorts were his men, and that we were en route to his office.

One of his offices, at least. The kind of place the rest of the world assumed was a farm, but underneath the barn or the house was a labyrinth of Agency offices and interrogation rooms. I, like others before me, would learn my fate there.

What did Frank have planned for me? We'd last seen each other a few months ago. Our farewell consisted of me holding a pistol to his head. The only thing that stopped me from pulling the trigger was that my daughter, Mia, stood thirty feet away. I saw the fear in her eyes. She hardly knew me as a father. I sure as hell didn't want her to remember me as a monster. So I let Frank live. I knew then that it was a mistake. Things weren't the same between us, and hadn't been for years. Tension escalated every time we were near each other. I could've ended it there. I should've ended it.

I assumed, since my identity had been exposed while in Texas, it had landed me on a watch list. One that Frank had access to due to his position in the CIA. He used resources to determine the credibility of the report, then acted on it. At least he'd left me enough time to clean up the mess in Texline.

I had to be prepared for other outcomes of our pending meeting. I'd pissed off plenty of people over the past decade, and performed enough shady deeds for even shadier individuals that any city, state, or federal agency would want to bring me in. Frank was the only one with a solid motive, though.

Instinctively, I glanced at the side window as the vehicle slowed to a stop for the first time in over an hour. The blacked out glass revealed nothing. One of the men, a bald guy with bushy eyebrows and a tattoo behind his right ear, glanced at his phone. He leaned forward, made eye contact with his partner. They both nodded.

We were close.

A wave of panic traveled through my body, numbing my fingers and toes. I took a deep breath, relaxed my arms, legs, chest and abdominal muscles. The feeling slipped away. I had no control over whatever was about to happen. My job moving forward was to react. Whether that was to an attack, or just information, was to be determined. I prepared for either.

The ceiling vents stopped spitting out cold air. In its place was a warm stream that smelled like gasoline and oil. The men squeezed in close to me. If I started to move, they'd know.

The vehicle turned left and right a few times. I pulled up a mental map of Langley, tried to match our changes of direction with streets, and the accompanying buildings, training facilities, housing. I recalled what was underground as best I could. And hoped that we wouldn't end up down there. It was an exercise in futility. We could have been back in Crystal River, Florida. The turns would line up the same. It was impossible to tell with any accuracy.

The guy with the tattoo lifted his phone to eye level and poked at it with his index finger. After a minute, he lowered it, grasped it with both hands, and typed out a message with his thumbs. He used his hands to block the screen from view. For a few moments the haptic feedback tone was the only sound inside the car. We'd come to another stop. The engine idled quietly.

I counted the seconds in my head. Thirty, fifty, ninety. Tattoo played on his phone, no longer hiding the screen. No need to. Angry Birds was hardly anything to conceal. At least if he was twelve it wouldn't be. His partner stared straight ahead. I didn't bother to ask what was going on. They weren't going to let me know.

The front passenger door opened. The vehicle dipped to the right, then rebounded, swayed side to side for a few seconds. I strained to hear footsteps, couldn't make out any. The inside of the vehicle must've been soundproofed. What else was the car used for? Transporting foreign dignitaries? High profile refugees and asylum seekers? Double crossing agents coming over to our side?

Our side.

Made me want to laugh and puke at the same time. I'd reached a level in intelligence where there were no sides. No good versus evil. Just a bunch of bad men doing bad things all in the name of an ideology that no one at the top believed in anymore.

And for a guy like me, one that worked on the inside, and outside, who sold himself to the highest bidder and was willing to do any job, none of it meant anything. Give me an order, pay me enough, and I'd execute any command, and any person.

But the truth was that used to be me. Now, I wanted nothing to do with any of it. I'd reached a point where my only goal was to drift and disappear with Mia. I realized we should have left together, rather than taking a few months to let things blow over.

It all led to me stuck in the back of a government sedan, parked outside of God knows where. Presumably I wouldn't have to wait much longer to figure that part out.

The rear passenger door opened, and I squinted in anticipation of sunlight flooding in. Didn't happen. Dim yellow fluorescent light was the flavor of the day.

Tattoo exited the vehicle first. He stepped out, turned, leaned in, then gestured with his pistol for me to follow him. His partner remained seated, hand hidden inside his jacket. I climbed out and glanced around the parking garage. There were two similar cars parked there, and a Mercedes in the corner. Couldn't fit much else in there. It was smaller than I expected, which meant we were near one of the less frequently used offices.

The kind of place few people like me walked into, but when they did, they were brought out in a body bag. If they left at all.

Four agents boxed me in and led me forward. It wasn't until we neared the steel doors set into concrete walls that I recognized where we were.

It wasn't Langley.

Hell, it wasn't in Northern Virginia, either.

They'd taken me to New Jersey. And I stood in the parking garage of the now-defunct SIS headquarters.

DEADLINE: CHAPTER 2

We walked through the hallway, and into a series of memories. Ones I'd fought to forget over the years. For all the good we did during my time in the SIS, there was no fooling anyone that we were a bunch of choir boys. We had been able to operate without restriction Stateside, and elsewhere. Rules rarely applied to us. I'm sure that made Frank Skinner an appealing candidate to head up the SAD-SOG. He'd run a similar operation with a much smaller budget, and much less backing from the politicians. He was unstoppable now.

The carpet in the corridor had been ripped up in favor of concrete. Chemical-laden air blew through the oversized vents in the ceiling. Overhead lights hummed and blinked on and off at irregular intervals. I figured they hadn't been on since the SIS was dissolved. Of course, I had to question whether it had been shut down after all.

Walking past my old office, I thought of specific missions we'd run. The faces of men, women and children we'd saved. Agents, and friends, we'd lost along the way. The six-by-nine room now stood empty, save for a vacuum cleaner in one corner. Judging by the floor, I doubted anyone had ever used the machine.

We stopped short of Frank's office, which was next to mine. Tattoo knocked on the door, waited a second, nodded, then entered. Two of the remaining agents left us. Coffee, maybe. Readying the interrogation room, perhaps. I hoped it didn't get to that point because it didn't appear Doc's office was occupied anymore. Who'd set their broken bones once I was through with them?

Tattoo emerged from the office, looked past me, nodded at his partner.

"Skinner will see you now." Tattoo took a step back, gestured at me like I was a plane making my way toward the runway. He guided me toward him, then into the office.

Frank remained seated behind his desk. He offered no greeting or handshake. One hand remained on the chair's armrest, the other hidden beneath the desktop, presumably gripping a pistol so tight his fingers turned white. His neutral expression gave nothing away. I might die in the next five minutes, or he could ask me to assassinate a politician in Colombia.

Despite the chair next to me I remained standing.

"Good to see you, Jack."

Was it? I responded with a slight nod. Nothing else.

He lifted his hand from the armrest and gestured toward my waist. "You mind?"

"They checked me out half a dozen times, Frank."

"I'm sure they did. How about you humor me. Please?"

I lifted my shirt a couple inches, turned around. "Good enough?"

"Sure." He scooped a pen off the desk, aimed it at me. "Have a seat."

I sat back in the chair, rested my head against the glass window. It was bulletproof, and when the light in the frame was switched on, no one from the lobby could see in. It'd saved Frank's life once. Unfortunately.

"Comfortable?" he asked.

I'd taken that posture in this very office a hundred times in the past. Don't know that I was ever comfortable in here. Still, I nodded at him.

"Little," Frank said, talking to his agent. "Close the door for me."

Tattoo reached in and pulled the door closed.

"Little?" I said. "Guy's built like a tank."

"Ironic, right?" Frank placed his other hand on top of the desk. He'd left the pistol mounted to the underside. I glanced down at the steel divider preventing me from accessing the weapon. Frank leaned over his forearm. "Jack, what the hell happened down in Texas?"

I waved my hand in front of my face to disperse the smell of his aftershave. "Don't wanna talk about it."

"Can't tell you the feeling in my stomach when your name flagged. I mean, there's only a handful of people in the world who would show up on that report. Damn, we hadn't had anything come up on it in three months. I'll tell you what, Jack, it scared the crap out of everyone around that table. It went all the way to the top. You were included in a daily briefing that usually ends up with someone dying."

"That's why I'm here? My time's up?"

He gnawed on the end of his pen, shook his head.

"Then why mention it?"

"The meeting? Just thought you should know."

"And Texas?"

"Curious is all. I've been getting texts keeping me in the loop about a massive weapons deal supposedly going down soon. There's four different agencies collaborating on this. The FBI, Homeland, DEA, one of those Texas groups. It's supposed to be huge. Hearing we'll take down one of the largest terrorist cells in the southwest."

I said nothing.

He twirled the pen between his fingers, index to pinky and back. "Earned yourself a lot of goodwill with this, Jack."

"That's great."

Thinking about Texas led my thoughts to Reese. Frank had always been perceptive to the inner workings of my mind. Today was no different.

"I understand witness protection had to get involved. Someone you knew, right?"

I held his gaze for a few seconds, wondering where he was headed with this. "Yeah, old friend of mine. Met her during the Brett Taylor mission. Remember that?"

"I do, and I know about Reese McSweeney. Maybe I can pull some strings."

"I figured I was here to die."

"That's up to you."

I straightened in the chair. "How so?"

"The past is the past," he said. "That's how I feel, at least. I understand why you acted the way you did. If the roles were reversed, I probably would have put a gun to my head, too. You had me dead to rights. But you let me live. And, Jack, I'm grateful that you didn't go through with it. Now, don't you think I've totally forgotten about it. I may understand why. I may thank you for not killing me. But I can still get pissed thinking about it. And remember, I could provide enough testimony to put you away for ten to twenty, at a minimum. And we both know you wouldn't last long in a cage."

"So that's it, huh? You don't care, but you do. You'll use everything you have against me, unless you won't." I placed my arms on the table, leaned forward. About a foot of air separated us. I could smell the ham sandwich he had for lunch, and the beer he washed it down with. "Listen up. I've got just as much on you, if not more. We can both go down, for all I care."

Frank leaned back, spread his arms with his palms facing me, smiled. "Sorry, that came off as a threat, didn't it? That's not how I meant it. I really am over the whole thing."

I was growing tired of the game. He was beating around the bush about whatever it was he wanted, making not so subtle threats toward me.

"OK," I said. "Then my answer's no."

Frank laughed. "No to what?"

"Whatever the hell you're about to ask me."

"Let's walk, Jack."

Given the confines of the SIS headquarters, taking a walk was never a good thing. I had little choice at the moment, though.

We left his office and headed down the hallway away from the entrance. All the other offices were dark and empty. Same with the interrogation rooms. Frank and I had spent a lot of time in them, sitting on the same side of the table.

Obviously Frank no longer operated out of this place anymore. No one did. Not regularly. Perhaps it had been left in place for situations like this. Or worse. With the building now being off the grid, it could be used to deal with hostiles in a certain way. One that the politicians generally frowned upon.

The lights in the stairwell barely functioned. They illuminated the area enough to make it down the stairs, but that was about it. There could've been someone hidden on the first landing, and I wouldn't have seen them.

The first sub-level smelled the same as it had five years ago. Which is to say it smelled like two week old squid nachos. We stopped in front of the meeting room where the team used to get together weekly and before any large missions. I expected to be greeted by some of Frank's SOG agents. He reached inside, flipped a switch and the lights cut on. The room was empty.

He took a seat at one end of the large conference table. I sat on the opposite side.

"Other than Texas, what've you been up to?" he asked after settling in.

"That's why we came down here?"

"Things were getting a bit intense upstairs. Figured a few minutes hanging out and catching up might help."

"I've been drifting. Nothing more, nothing less. Saw my family for a day, left without saying goodbye, and started driving."

"Poetic."

"Isn't it?"

"I lost track of you after you left Florida," he said.

He was about to bring up his next bargaining chip. I hadn't fallen for his threat to turn on me in court. Mia was his ace, though. I wanted nothing to happen to my daughter, especially because of me.

Frank continued. "I know you left without your daughter."

I clenched my jaw, shook my head.

"What?" he said.

"Don't say it, Frank. You can hold whatever you want against me, but so help me God, if you bring my daughter or family into this, I will unleash every ounce of my fury against you. Neither of us will leave this building alive today."

Frank rose, walked down the side of the table closest to the hallway. I countered on the opposite side. We stopped in the middle. Four feet of cheap particle board separated us.

"I've got nothing on her, or anyone else in your family, Jack. You know me. That's not how I operate."

"Things change." I could feel my blood pressure skyrocketing, my pulse pounding in my head, against my temples. My ears and cheeks burned.

"That they do." He held out his hand as though he wanted to shake mine. "But I have a few strands of moral decency left. Hell,

I'd help you protect them if your ass wasn't too proud to ask. I've got the best operatives in the world working for me. No one asks questions."

"Makes it that much easier, doesn't it?"

"Christ, Jack. I'm trying to help you."

"Think I would risk giving away their position to you?"

"You think I can't find that out anyway?"

"There you go again," I said. "You come across as saying you'll help, but then you have to make those threats."

"You are a paranoid son of a bitch, you know that, Noble?"

He was right. "Aren't we all? How else have you and I survived in this business so long?"

"By trusting the right people." He placed both hands flat on the table and leaned forward. It left him vulnerable. I could lay him out cold before he could move his jaw. And he knew it. "There was a time when you and I had each other's back. Every goddamned minute of the day, man. We didn't always get along, but we sure as hell made sure that we went home alive at night."

"Your point?"

"Trust me that nothing is going to happen to your family. Not even if word of this gets out."

"Word of what?"

He looked up at me with a grave expression I'd only seen twice before. "We should head back up to my office."

Click here to purchase Deadline now!

ABOUT THE AUTHOR

L.T. Ryan is a *USA Today* and international bestselling author. The new age of publishing offered L.T. the opportunity to blend his passions for creating, marketing, and technology to reach audiences with his popular Jack Noble series.

Living in central Virginia with his wife, the youngest of his three daughters, and their three dogs, L.T. enjoys staring out his window at the trees and mountains while he should be writing, as well as reading, hiking, running, and playing with gadgets. See what he's up to at http://ltryan.com.

Social Medial Links:

- Facebook (L.T. Ryan): https://www.facebook.com/LTRyanAuthor
- Facebook (Jack Noble Page): https://www.facebook.com/JackNobleBooks/
- Twitter: https://twitter.com/LTRyanWrites
- Goodreads: http://www.goodreads.com/author/show/6151659.L_T_Ryan

Made in the USA
Columbia, SC
13 March 2020

89147952R00192